Ants in My Dreadlocks

Cynthia Rowe

First published by Zeus Publications 2005
http://www.zeus-publications.com

ISBN: 978-0-9874554-2-0

ISBN 10:   0987455427

National Library of Australia Listing:
Rowe,C.

Ants In My Dreadlocks

By the same author:

Our Hollow Sofa

Stinger in a Sugar Jar

My French Barrette

Bad Grass

Couscous Threads

Driftwood – poetry collection

Author Biography

Cynthia Rowe has a degree from the University of Melbourne and has taught French and English for most of her working life. She has also spent time in France and the French Territories and was awarded a *Diplôme Approfondi de Langue Française* by the French Ministry of Education. She is a Writing Fellow of the Fellowship of Australian Writers NSW.

Cynthia's short stories have appeared in magazines and been broadcast on National Community Radio. Her poetry has won many awards and can be read in numerous literary journals internationally. She is Editor: Haiku Xpressions; President: Australian Haiku Society; Past President: Eastern Suburbs Branch (Bondi Writers) Fellowship of Australian Writers NSW.

ANTS IN MY DREADLOCKS is the second in a series of her books.

Dedication

For Mathieu and Christophe

Acknowledgments

I gratefully acknowledge Simon and Anne Françoise's input on the daily life of New Caledonians, and their help with the setting of the book.

For their assistance and support I particularly thank Belinda and her Publicis team, Scott Cuthbert and Essence Media, Anna Carmody, Catherine Hammond and Marilyn. I would like to thank Cathy Symonds and the Waverley Library staff for their ongoing interest and involvement.

A special thanks to Chris Headford, webmaster extraordinaire!

For his faith in me and marketing nous, I thank Bruce.

Chapter 1

My best friend's mother killed herself by peeing on a hair dryer.

Win—ice-blonde hair duller, skin less perfect than before—yacked about the death a lot. I guess she thought that by shocking people it took some of the hurt away. You know, laughing about your old lady having kangaroos loose in the top paddock, joking about the safety saucepans you used when you cooked the mush that you spooned into her mouth.

She was up-front about Alice's passing: "The Korsakoff's Syndrome did it. She wouldn't *normally* have peed upon a hair dryer." D'oh. It went without saying that *nobody* would've peed upon a hair dryer. I cringed when I heard Win—into New Age stuff now, meditating and catching the bus into nearby Kingston for Pilates classes—rave about her mum. It was the pits.

Rocked by Alice's death, too, I deferred my affy year and enrolled at South Central Community College. Which was where I met Clarence (pronounced Clahr-rohnce), my new French teacher. He offered me a work experience stint as English *assistante* (flash word for assistant) at the Oriel Lycée (flash word for high school) in Noumea, New Caledonia. Naturally, I grabbed the chance to see the place where I was born. And a sweetener came with it. Oriel Lycée English conversation assistants always holed up in this yummo mansion.

Sounded kind of cool.

So I was filling in time during the flight from Australia, jotting down a few things about myself. My long-term life plan was to return to Cairns when my French was up to speed. I'd head for the Northern Beaches, mosey on down to the Amédée Apartments and hang around Sandrine Bas Salaire de Lyon and her partner, Claude, see what I could pick up. I was almost certain Sandrine was my birth mother. (Even though Namilly, the only mum I'd ever known, refused to admit it.) And I knew Sandrine wouldn't be in Noumea while I was there. She and her father hadn't spoken in years.

Namilly still wasn't revealing much.

After my 'birth mother search' trip, I expected her to break down and spew out the truth about my origins. She didn't. Instead, she waffled on about our hollow sofa. She said she'd given me two cups of the 'local drink'—some voodoo thing, I suppose—to knock me out, during those terrible Events when violence reigned in New Caledonia, and blood was spilt in the quest for independence. She told me her heart fluttered in her mouth like crazy as she watched the sofa swing on board the ship and prayed.

When I decided to embark upon my work experience programme, Namilly told me to keep away from the country of my birth. "You won't like what you find!" she said.

Namilly and Win (fan of rock chick vintage clothes) had set up business together only last week: a recycle seconds outlet on the highway, just down from the Zabaglione Woollen Shop—50% of the proceeds to the consignor, 50% to the consignee. No overheads, bar forking out the rent for the shop, it was money for jam they reckoned.

Stefan Becker and I? Well, we were an item now. Lots more killer kisses, and not just in his mother's sunken garden. We'd gone all the way, too. Twice. Responsibly. In the Becker's bathing box, with rubbers and creams and lying on a fresh white towel. But it was over quickly, and unfulfilling. Had those lowlife bogans who jumped me in the ti-tree bushes affected me *that* way? But it was great to hear him say "Love ya, mate!" and lie in his arms listening to the waves break on the shore outside.

Stefan had lost his blizzard bubble look a bit. He still wore buckets of zinc cream on his face, but you didn't get such a nasty surprise when the protection wore off. Apart from a few pit marks, a mega number of freckles and a strange pink thickening of the skin on the tips of his elbows, his psoriasis was unusually clear.

A definite Kurt Cobain look-alike.

Of course, Win said she didn't know how I could stand to touch him. But Elizabeth Stubbs (real competition with her newly-acquired, rake thin, dudette body) continued to hang out everywhere my boy-friend went.

Stefan turned eighteen just the other day. His father's ticker still dicky, there'd been no party, just the promise of a car.

Lately, he'd been making a ginormous number of trips to Kingston—which could've been connected with his Nature Shop beside the lube bay of Vince Becker's service station (you chucked a right past the SWAP 'N' GO Cylinder Swap Program sign, then chucked a left past BEST BURNING FIREWOOD). He sold jars of blue ringers, bits of Palaeozoic rock in sealed cellophane packets, and marine spiders trapped in sea bubbles. Plus other tat for tourists. Like, crested spoons and stuff.

Since he'd saved Namilly from drowning (she told me she'd slipped on the rocks, but Stefan claimed otherwise), they'd become chummy. It was the first time I'd seen her take an interest in anyone of the opposite sex.

The guy in the seat beside me, wearing a gross wedding ring and an even grosser identity bracelet, stuffed the computer printout into his briefcase. The plane plunged from the sea of sooty cloud soup into clear air. He gulped as the cabin shuddered.

And I gulped, too, for I was about to come face-to-face with my French examiner. I went a hectic shade of red as I remembered the boo-boo I'd made when I stood before *monsieur* on that fateful day in Ravella Community Hall, and used the wrong word for 'to kiss'. (Fancy telling your examiner Emma Bovary'd gone all the way—which she had, but you didn't use *that* word with a total stranger.)

The oral exam wrecked my ENTER score, limiting the courses for which I could apply. So I accepted this offer.

The plane dropped its wheels for landing.

My stomach twisted as we jerked onto the runway.

Chapter 2

Rain chugged like mad onto my head. Struggling down the metal steps (no direct terminal entry in *this* place, they just wheeled up a bunch of steps), I hefted my backpack and laptop in its Cartoon Network carry bag. Trickles of water zigzagged through the logo squares along the side of the fabric, collecting and dripping into my right Reebok as I walked.

A swarthy-looking dude, wearing a red, gold and black Koori band around his neck, wrestled with his diving gear and surfboard, untangling them and re-untangling them from the railing of the stairway. Some optimist! This weather was a long way from beachie.

My French plait was turning into a rat's tail from the humidity. Frizzy bits nagged at the corners of my eyes as I dodged past the guy with the diving gear, and scurried through the puddles to the boxy airport building.

Standing in the queue, I admired the photo in my new passport (countersigned by Namilly with a Pooh! look on her face). Soon to turn eighteen, I still looked a kid.

I began to wonder what Pascal, my French oral examiner, would be wearing. His shiny grey suit? A bit over the top in this mugginess. Perhaps he'd be attired in a flapping floral number?

The guy with the diving gear and surfboard managed to muscle in in front of me. Voices were raised. A full-on drama in machinegun French was happening, and I couldn't understand a word. (Fortunately, I was only taking English conversation at Oriel Lycée.)

My mobile phone—a farewell gift from my boyfriend—was chucking a spazz in my jeans' pocket. I wriggled it out and pressed *Show*. A text message from Stefan sat there:

win said 2 tell u bill einstein in dire str8s

That was *all* I needed: a horse's bowel movements intruding on my trip. I had enough problems of my own trying to negotiate my way around a foreign country.

Clicking on *Reply*, I began to tap the words:

wood u say THE END 4 him or not gr8? didn't hose

"Mademoiselle?" The voice from behind the glass screen made me jump. I jammed the phone back into my pocket, planning to finish my SMS later.

The bored-looking immigration official peered at my photo, and then flicked through the empty pages of my passport. Stamped one with a thump.

"Fine," he said, nodding me on.

"Merci beaucoup," I replied, relieved I was able to spit out the words without my tongue becoming twisted, proud to be able to respond in his language. (Even though he'd spoken to me in mine—making me wonder if I'd lost my Caldoche appearance.)

Shuffling forward, I scanned the faces of the people in the terminal. I stood there wiggling my toes inside my Reeboks, my right foot going squelch, squelch. But no one resembling Pascal appeared. Not one person in a silky suit. Few in flapping floral numbers. Not a sign of his disapproving face, which I'd thought more French than French—a *z'oreille* as they called those from metropolitan France. How wrong I had been. The examiner came from New Caledonia. He was a Caldoche, like me.

And where was he?

The crowd began to dribble off past the car rental booths. Tourists tumbled into taxis. The brims of their holiday hats caught on doors as they gathered themselves inside.

I waited and waited.

Night fell. Soon I was feeling abandoned. Should I rush for a bus? A taxi? But I wasn't sure if I had enough dosh for the one-hour taxi ride to Noumea. I felt fidgety. Little worms crawled over my skin. Had I received another fake email from another fake person—like the emails the Internet stalker had sent while I was searching for my birth mother in chat rooms? Had the French examiner persuaded me to come to this steam-bath place for no good reason?

A bald eagle in pleated walk shorts, lugging a video camera, headed towards me. Leering, he said, "Can I 'elp you?"

Shoving my nose in the air, I turned my head away.

Bald Eagle made for the SORTIE sign. He disappeared into the bucketing rain.

Apart from two gendarmes in kepis chatting by the exit, and a couple of people arguing with customs officials in a screened-off area, I was the only one left from the incoming flight. My T-shirt was clinging to my sweaty chest as I continued to stand there like a derrbrain. Had Namilly been right? Had I been stupid to take up the offer? At that moment, I would've given anything to be home in Ravella, helping Win shove a hose down her horse's throat.

Where are you, monsieur?

I jiggled my toes even harder inside my trainers, gazing at the bumps rippling beneath the canvas.

From the corner of my eye, I spied a tall, shifty looking creep in a beanie. He circled. Eyed me. Circled again. Stood at a distance, his hands folded behind his back, as if thinking. What did *he* want? With headgear hauled down over his ears, he looked like a boxer.

Where *was* the French examiner?

My skin crawled with fear. My toes were cramping in my right shoe. The calves of both legs were turning into tight knots.

Lugging my things, I trudged off to the public loo. I emptied the water from my Reebok and counted the little seventies wall tiles—*un, deux, trois*—while I tried to work out a plan of action. I reached *cinquante-cinq* before I decided I was behaving like a wuss. I had enough cash for a bus. I would find my own way to the capital city of Noumea.

Heaving my backpack and carry bag from the floor, I marched from the toilet and made for the SORTIE sign.

Behind me a voice said, "*Mademoiselle* Geneviève Perrier?"

"Monsieur?" I whipped around. "Boy, am I glad to"—gulp!—"see you …"

It was the creep in the beanie.

Chapter 3

"My name is Genna," I quavered. "But my surname is Perrier."

"Then you're the one. Pascal asked me to pick you up. Sorry I'm late, it's the weather." He held out his hand. "Roch Colline. Spelled R-O-C-H, pronounced Rock."

We shook. His palm was rough, as if he did manual labour for a living.

"You can call me Rocky."

Nobody'd said anything about Rocky Colline coming to pick me up. And did he always spell out his name when he introduced himself? Did I want to go with him? I don't think so. But I had no choice. It was night-time, and I was in a strange country. I thought of asking him for ID, with photo. Perhaps he had a letter from someone? Something that'd explain he wasn't some weirdo trying to come on to me.

Then again, he had known my name. Sort of.

So I followed Rocky, past the box-like stalls where the car-hire operators waited for stragglers still struggling with customs officials, to the carpark. There I found myself staring at a Peugeot so old it must've been invented soon after the horse and cart.

My driver wiggled a key in the lock of the door—no high-tech extras like central locking, ABS breaking or dual air-bag protection. But I could see a radio.

"Roch's a groovy name. Is it a family handle?"

Not answering, he took my backpack and laptop from me. "I'll put your baggage in the boot." He seemed to have second thoughts. "No, back seat's better."

What's wrong with the boot? I wondered. *Too dirty?* He didn't look the kind of guy who'd be bothered by a bit of dirt. Strangely, his English had an Aussie twang.

"No worries." He bustled me into the car.

Rosary beads dangled from the rear-vision mirror.

No worries? "Are you from Australia?"

"No." He clambered behind the steering wheel. "I'm not a *poken.*" The ignition made grizzle noises. "And I'm sure the name Colline, 'hill' in English, was the inspiration for Roch." He gave a raspy laugh. "Either that, or the old lady had a thing for Rock Hudson. She used to catch a ride into town with the fish supplier from Yaté, go to the movies in the fleapit overlooking Place des Cocotiers … on her own." The motor turned over. "At least, that's what she told my *papa.*"

A wheeze, a cough and we jolted forward. "Pierrot's the name of my Peugeot, and the *bagnole* doesn't like this weather." He grinned. "Back to me. My mother's family was from *St. Roch Mayères* in the *Haute Savoie*, and my name reminds her of her origins. *St. Roch Mayères* sits at the foot of Four Heads."

"Four Heads? Doesn't sound very French."

"Quatre Têtes," he murmured.

Driving on the right-hand side of the road seemed strange, and my body kept veering left as we juddered from the airport. Pierrot the Peugeot swung around a bunch of road works, while the crucifix swayed and a paper bag slid across the dashboard. Rocky opened the bag. He offered me a croissant.

"You must be hungry. Airline food? Pouf!" The car pranced.

"No thanks. I only eat raw vegan."

"Raw vegan? What's that?"

By now, I was seriously sweating from the mugginess, tacky from the trip.

"No meat, fish or dairy. And, above all, no heat. Although, raw veganism"—and I brightened as I began to bang on about my favourite topic—"according to Namilly, my mother, means I've removed the *kill step* by not cooking. She says I need to watch out for salmonella, cryptosporidium, cyclospora." I wiggled my fingers. "All those nasties. But, when I tell her she's gladhanding with botulism, she's like, 'Well, at least I can *see* the bumps on the ends of *my* cans'."

I glanced at Rocky to see if he was interested, but his eyes had a glaze about them.

"I considered fruitarianism," I continued, "but too many problems, like excess sugar, highs and lows, tooth enamel, loo frequency. Then there's the vegetables-only gorilla diet, but humans are not folivores, so ..."

"You seem like a candidate for kava," he interrupted. His gums had a yellow tinge.

"What's kava? I do the odd bit of illegal loose tobacco. Is it like that?"

"No, it's perfectly legal. The root of the pepper tree makes you relaaax, baby. And it's healthy. You pound the root, mix it with water, strain through a cloth and drink. You'd like it." He pushed up the sleeve of his windbreaker and scratched at a rash—which made me think of Stefan, who I was missing already.

My eyelids began to droop from the heat. The radio belted out Bob Marley, and Pierrot the Peugeot did its own reggae dance. We swerved around another bunch of road works. Gears grated as Rocky changed to first.

I felt like chucking from the swaying.

The beat of the music changed. *Je t'aime ... moi non plus* ground through the airwaves. Rocky bopped. He flipped the steering wheel back and forth in time to the music.

Gulping back the chucks hovering in my throat, I said, "Namilly'd bury *you* beneath the Norfolk Island pine tree."

Rocky suddenly reverted to French. *"Comment?"* He sounded far away, as if thinking of something else.

"I used to pay a school friend fifty cents for pirated copies of that song, and Namilly kept burying 'em beneath the pine tree. Boy, did my friend make a packet!"

"You're funny."

Was I *that* amusing? Or was my driver blissed out? But surely the stitched-up French examiner didn't have junkies for friends? Doing a surreptitious sniff, I detected no alcohol, just an off-base earthy odour.

"Are you a friend of *monsieur*?" I asked.

"Of the Manet family."

"Manet family?"

Rocky nodded. "Of Pascal and Marcel, and their parents."

Was Marcel the French examiner's brother? I wondered.

"We go way back, as neighbours, and then university, skiing. But we disagree on the subject of independence. Pascal, particularly, believes no one's interested since the signing of the Matignon Accords."

"I'm not surprised. *Monsieur* … I didn't realise his surname was also Manet … looks *really* conservative. I, like, only met him once, during my oral exam. I know Marcel, though."

Marcel Manet's story still screwed around in my head. I found it hard to imagine my mum poncing about as a nanny, taking me to the rotunda in Place des Cocotiers, listening to reggae music while car bombs exploded during those terrible Events. None of what he'd told me squared with the mum I knew—dirt beneath her fingernails, knitting cardigans dripping with naff bobbles, listening to radio serials for the print handicapped when she saw just fine.

Rocky pushed the edge of his beanie up and scratched. "Did you do schoolies week when you finished your exams? I heard about schoolies week from friends of mine, holidaying in Surfers Paradise. They said it wrecked their vacation."

I shook my head. "Too far, too dear. And I don't do drugs."

My eyes latched onto the hair beneath his beanie. Rocky's locks were golden-red. And, up close, he was kind of spunky—teeth white and even, serious grey eyes, mouth sculpted as if he'd put lip liner around the edges.

I still felt like gromiting from the swaying, and wondered if I should ask Rocky to pull up. But it was dark out there, the rain was drumming, and I was beginning to pack polenta. I peered through the water streaming down the grimy windscreen, looking for lights. Everything was black. And here I was, sitting beside a bopping Kanak skier with an Aussie twang. A serial killer, for all I knew.

A high-pitched squeal rang through the car. Alarm bells rang through me.

They say to keep talking if you're afraid.

"My best friend, Win Winstone, a plonker I s'pose, used to drink perfume." I could hear myself babble. "Which is not the same as kava,

I know. And Namilly used to bury Win's used bottles beneath the canna patch to protect her reputation. Alice, Win's mum, was the root cause of the problem, a shingle short due to Korsakoff's Syndrome. And now she drinks hippie tea, ultraviolet raspberry and hawthorn berry to counter capillary fragility. Win I mean, not Namilly. And not Alice." Phew. "'Cos she's dead."

A second squeal rang through the car. I sucked in my breath. *Was someone trapped back there?* But Rocky didn't seem to notice. Skewing my head around, I saw only my backpack and laptop on the rear seat. I'd heard about black rats in New Caledonia. Was it a rat?

"Do you see *rats*, like, about much?"

"Rats?" Rocky raised an eyebrow. "Of course! We sheet girdle the coconut trees to prevent the rats from going up them. We have black rats in our crops as well."

"Crops?"

"I'm a peasant."

Shivers! I'd never met a peasant before.

"What do you actually do as a, um, peasant?"

"I grow kava, and bananas." His mouth went small. "But the bananas are a problem. We've got bunchy top, and that's serious. Didn't you see the signs back there, forbidding transportation of the plants? Carrying bananas about this island helps spread the bunchy top disease. So we concentrate on growing kava."

That agonised squeal—getting louder—was starting to freak me out. A scraping noise. Did Rocky have a person in the boot, trussed up with a rope? Possibly gagged? And was he, or she, trying to alert me of their plight? My heart began to thud. Would Rocky tie *me* up? Sling me in the boot, as well?

I cringed away from my driver, knowing the real reason he'd put my backpack and laptop on the back seat, rather than use the boot. It had nothing to do with dirt. A human being was in there!

Chapter 4

Surreptitiously jiggling out my mobile, I tapped *help!* and sent my message to Stefan.

"I think you need kava *bad*." Had Rocky noticed my slippery fingers? "If you like I'll take you to a nakamal."

"Um, I don't think so." No way did I want to go anywhere with this man.

"Les Monts Koghis," he shouted.

He raised his hand from the steering wheel, flapping it high and to the left.

A vast smudge loomed over the landscape. Peering through the windscreen smears again, I counted two peaks.

"Cool!" I was not feeling at all cool.

The squeaks and squeals in the rear of the car seemed to have stopped.

A few kilometres later—and no more agonised noise— I began to chill out. I'd heard about Mount Koghi, knew you could set up camp in the carpark of the inn. I planned to go there after I'd finished my work experience.

The aging bucket of bolts ground to a standstill. Rocky handed over a pile of CFP francs to the man in the tollbooth. I heard an exchange in machinegun French.

"Le cyclone arrive!" said the attendant. The striped boom lifted, and we pitter-pattered off along the highway.

I was bothered by the 'cyclone' word. I'd never considered cyclones when I took up the offer to come here. And the pilot of the plane had only said there was 'a lot of weather about'. Which probably meant this rain.

City lights in the distance.

"Mont Montravel!" Rocky pointed to an illuminated cross on a hill. He looked at me. "You seem tense, Genna. Would you like to go to a nakamal?"

I'd never heard the word 'nakamal' before. "What actually, um, is a nakamal?"

"A nakamal is a kava bar. You drink piper methysticum and you relaaax, baby." Rocky wiggled his eyebrows. "Come with me to a nakamal and you'll be calm when the wild winds arrive. You drink. You forget. Yet your senses are heightened."

Senses are heightened? Was this a come-on?

"I'd prefer not to go to a kava bar. I need to get to the place where I'm billeted. Like, there's stuff for me to prepare before I front up at Oriel Lycée on Monday morning."

A tickle against my leg. Was this a black rat? Reaching to fend off the vermin, my hand brushed against a card sticking from the side pocket of the door. I eased the card out to see a girl making a bungy jump. Her face was frozen with terror.

"You are holding the final communication." Rocky indicated the card.

"Final communication from whom?"

"Maman."

"Your mum? I thought she was French. Doesn't she live here?"

"I forget where she lives." Rocky's voice was harsh.

Squinting grimly, I was able to make out the word Kooracoondoo beneath the picture. The placename sounded Australian.

"Your mum lives in Australia?"

"She *is* Australian."

"But you told me …"

"I said her family *came* from France. I didn't say she was metropolitan French. Or Kanak. Or Caldoche, white and born in this place. I did not say any of these things. She's bloody Australian and my dad's a Kanak. A rare union. I'm a *métis*. And, since you're interested, my baby sister's a *métisse*. Satisfied?"

Rocky sounded stroppy, but I needed to know something. "Is that her in the photo?"

Then I realised I was holding a commercially manufactured post-card, and an old one at that. Rocky's sister would be grown up by now.

"She's hippie person, my *maman*." Rocky's English was deteriorat-ing. "Wis head covered in tiny braids, beads on ends. She sink freedom is a game, our country is a game, independence is game ..." His voice trailed off, and the smile disappeared. "She breaks my *papa*'s heart into pieces when she leaves." Rocky looked angry.

"And your sister?"

"Douce?" He spat the word out. "I wouldn't know her if I passed her in the street."

"Oh, that's awful." I was feeling bad vibes. My driver had seemed blissed out before; now I could feel an undercurrent of unresolved issues. I decided to change the subject, take his mind off his mother and his sister and his rash. "When's the cyclone due?"

"Liliane will come tonight. Or in two days. Or maybe more. Or perhaps she'll sneak away." The angst was gone, the josh tone back. "We are still on pre-alert. Get worried when Alert 2 is broadcast." His English was back, too.

"So you're suggesting I get wasted in a nakamal while I wait?"

"Look!" He pointed at a vast plume pouring from a smokestack. "Doniambo, the nickel smelter."

We zipped through the city in a flash. Bleached buildings whipped by through the pounding rain, and I discerned a sort of deadness. Was the deadness due to the cyclone? Or had Doniambo ripped the heart from the city?

As we swooped past blue-capped huts beside a bay, Rocky shouted, "Baie de la Moselle! You can see the Municipal Markets. That's where we buy our fresh food."

A new bay, brightly-lit and crammed with bobbing yachts, careered up. "Baie de l'Orphelinat!" A huge anchor leaned to one side.

"When will I get to meet *monsieur*? And why didn't he meet me at the airport?"

Rocky shrugged. "His brother, Marcel." He made a money sign with his fingers. "Business problems. They're close, but they disagree much of the time."

I now knew Pascal and Marcel Manet were brothers. But Marcel had never told me he had a brother, conducting examinations in Ravella while he was also there. And Pascal had seemed metropolitan, as I'd always imagined a Frenchman to be.

Pierrot the Peugeot groaned up a curved incline.

"The Manets were neighbours of yours?"

"They had a *station* in the Brousse, in the hills not far from Yaté." Rocky changed gears. "We all grew up together. Jean-Pierre Manet raised deer, not far from our farm. One night poachers turned up, and Madame Manet shot them. Her husband took the blame, but before he could stand trial …"

"He died of cancer, right there." I prodded my finger in my throat.

"How did you know that?" Rocky pointed through the sheeting wetness. Before I could answer, he said, "That's Baie des Citrons!" He gave me a brief glance. "Axelle Manet moved to Paris after Jean-Pierre's death. She now lives in the 16th arrondissement. Pascal shared her apartment, only returning here a short while ago."

"Which explains his, um, accent being different from Marcel's?"

Restaurants, clubs, palm trees and ferns jostled alongside domestic housing.

"And how do you explain *your* amazing English?"

"I never spoke anything but English with my *maman*."

"That makes sense, your mum being Australian."

People partied, apparently unconcerned by the cyclone hanging offshore. Grunge music filtered through the air. A guy in Rastafarian striped trousers waggled his hips in a doorway. Pooped from the travelling and the tension, I no longer felt tense. The squealing and scraping had stopped. I decided the noise was in my imagination.

I checked my Swatch. "Are we nearly there? We've been driving for almost an hour."

"Not long now. Nouméa is a small place."

I changed my opinion about Rocky Colline. Rocky was okay. Perhaps I *would* go with him to a nakamal, and investigate the local culture. Kava sounded like the ultimate in raw vegan drinks. Healthy, relaxing and totally natural.

The road was shiny from the wet as we swerved around a curve. Rocky rode the clutch and we rattled past Hippodrome Henri Milliard.

"Sewage runs from the middle of the racetrack, and out into the waters of Anse Vata." He rubbed his chin with his index finger.

I'd been planning on swimming. "So the beaches aren't terrific?"

"Not great, close to the city. Fantastic on the Loyalty Islands, though."

"Will the cyclone put an end to my plans for chilling out on the beach after a hard day taking conversation classes?"

"Depends."

Silence for a while.

"We're almost at Jacques Forestier's," he said.

My heart hurled itself from the high dive. Wasn't he the father of Sandrine Bas Salaire de Lyon—the chick who'd denied I was her natural daughter?

Nobody told me I'd be staying at Jacques Forestier's house.

Chapter 5

"Jacques Forestier?" I could feel my heart flitter.

"Didn't they tell you Jacques has a community awareness programme, promoting the French-speaking region of the South Pacific? He puts up students, here to do their work experience."

Aha, did this mean I could explore my origins?

"The house in Val Plaisance is a bit rundown, but Jacques is rarely there. He's mostly at Bouchon, his farm in Bourail."

I decided not to tell Rocky about my potential connection with Jacques.

"Six bedrooms meant the house was too big for the old man." Rocky wrinkled his brow. "So he decided to help people starting on their careers."

Rocky's words washed over me. I would be able to poke around now, see the place where Sandrine lived before she fell out with her father, discover a bit about her hopes and dreams. Would there be discarded stuffed toys in an attic? Boxed photos of Yves-Laurent, the man I believed to be my birth dad? Love letters tied with velvet ribbon?

I couldn't wait to find out.

My mobile vibrated against my hip. I yanked the phone from the pocket of my jeans and pressed *Show*. A text message from Stefan opened up:

hose no help bill einstein still in dire str8ts

Uh-oh. I'd tacked *help!* onto the end of my unfinished text message. No matter. The scary sounds had stopped—a faulty carburettor, or something—and I no longer felt in danger. In fact, I was starting to like my driver.

I decided to find out more.

"Which of the Manet brothers is the eldest?"

"Qui?" Rocky said in French. His mind was far away.

"Pascal, or Marcel, who is …?"

"Pascal," he murmured, reaching to wipe the condensation from the windows with the sleeve of his windbreaker. "And Marcel's a couple of years older than me."

"Monsieur Manet looks so stitched-up."

"Yeah." A grin split his face. "He's like that. Born old." His smile faded with the gnashing of the gears. "Pascal was stabbed in the stomach during the Events, you know. Those weeks and months in hospital force you to mature."

"Guess they do."

We lapsed into silence. Rain flung at the windscreen, hurled great blobs of heaven spit. The car shimmied. We ground our way around a zillion curves until we finally wheezed to a halt in front of a massive house surrounded by melaleucas.

Feathery leaves of cycad palms sprayed from rows of fat pots, casting shadows across the walls. Water spilled from a leaky piece of guttering hanging loose above the entrance, creating a fountain over the front door. I was about to become seriously wet.

"Are you coming inside?" I fiddled with my French plait.

"Uh-uh. I've got things to do." Rocky's words were accompanied by a screech from the back of the car. Frantic clawing.

My heart lurched. *Things to do*? Like murder and dispose of that person in the boot?

As I climbed from the car, my foot jammed against the hinge of the door. Rocky's postcard flew out, landing in a puddle. Uh-oh, his mother's final words would turn into a mucky, melted heap.

"Don't move. I'll get it." Rocky clambered out. He extricated my foot from the opening of the door, picked up his mother's card and wiped it on the leg of his jeans, before stuffing the card in his pocket.

A low growl echoed through the vehicle. Like a furious human being.

"Thanks, I mean *merci* for the ride." My voice shook in time with the jerking of my heart.

A howl.

I had to get away from this axe murderer. I snatched my belongings from him.

"Tais-toi!" Rocky banged his fist on the lid of the boot.

I gulped. How crass of this guy to yell at his captive, telling her to shut up in front of me.

"I'll sling her in the back seat. She dribbles, and I was worried about your things."

"Dribbles? Because she's tied up?" I frowned.

Rocky stared. "I never tie her up. She's not *that* strong."

Another screech from the boot.

"Are you sure you're not meant to accompany me inside?" I hoped he'd say no.

"I don't fit in."

No, I thought, *kidnappers don't, as a rule, 'fit in'*.

Rocky hauled the lid of the boot up with a grunt. I expected to be confronted by a desperate chick. Instead, I found myself gazing at a marmalade cat with a berko look on her face.

"Meet Belle!" He swung the cat by its scruff in my direction.

"Ooooh," I gooed. "Isn't she beautiful? I've never had a cat. My mother doesn't like cats." I became stern. "Do you *usually* carry your cat around in the boot of the car?"

"Not usually"—and he laughed—"but when a cyclone's due she goes berserk. I have a bird in a cage, a cagou." He locked eyeballs with me. "Protected, they're called 'ghosts of the forest'. They bark, like dogs, before the dawn, a haunting yelp." He adjusted his beanie with his free hand. "Belle stops the rats from attacking the cagou, or its chick. I was worried she'd panic, do something stupid. A female ..."

"Get lost!"

The grin on his face told me he was joking.

Right then, I decided Rocky was cute. And, despite his age, almost as cute as Stefan. He spoke the most amazing English, too. I hadn't been forced to speak French once.

"Would you like to come with me to a nakamal tomorrow night?" His eyes were thoughtful. "There's a meeting. I could introduce you to my, ah, friends."

"Meeting?"

"A breakaway independence group."

A shiver of excitement ran through me. "I'd *love* to go to a nakamal with you."

"Pick you up at five, then. Make sure you're very ready."

Very ready? Perhaps Monsieur Colline's English was not so perfect. I crunched my way along the gravel path to the front door.

"Wait!" he yelled. "I've got your key." He loped towards me, handing me a gross key like the ones you see in Dracula movies—more rust than shiny bits.

"Is Monsieur Manet inside?" I was beginning to wonder if I would ever get to meet the man who'd arranged my work experience.

"Don't know. The whole thing's pretty casual." He headed back to Pierrot the Peugeot. *"À demain!"* he shouted, as he climbed into the car.

"À demain!" I answered in my best French.

I found I *was* looking forward to seeing Rocky tomorrow.

The vehicle rolled off down the road, puttering and spluttering as it gathered speed. Rocky worked the clutch. Belle the cat gazed from the rear window, until they had disappeared around the bend.

I placed the key in the lock of Jacques Forestier's front door. Twisted. The key refused to turn.

Chapter 6

Water dumped on my head from the broken guttering. My T-shirt was detaching itself from my back. The wind had whipped up, and I shivered from the cold and a feeling of edginess. I'd gone from tropical hot to distinctly chilly.

Easing the key from the lock, I examined it. Was the rust the problem? Or had Rocky given me the wrong one? Was this the key for his farmhouse in the Brousse, near Yaté (wherever that was)? I knew *brousse* was the French word for 'bush'. And it sounded far away. The night was dark. What if no one was home? What if this trip had been an elaborate scam from the start?

Making a tunnel with my hands, I peered through the shutters of the window near the front door. The blades were narrow, and the light was off inside. I couldn't see a thing. I wedged the fingers of my right hand between the slit of the splintered blades in an effort to widen them. My nail bent back so far that I winced with the pain and jumped about swearing.

"Merde, merde, merde!" I yelled.

Sucking my finger, I headed for the window on the other side. A whoosh as I passed. A spew of water frisked my shoulder as it hurtled from the guttering. The cascade missed my laptop, copping my backpack where gaps were dotted through the canvas. All I needed was my new day-glo tube skirts to shrink, and I'd have zilch to wear to class on Monday morning.

I made my way back to the front door. I wiggled like mad and the key suddenly gripped. The door opened with a rush. My luggage jabbed the back of my knees and I was catapulted into a dim entrance hall.

With wobbly legs, and feeling as though I'd stepped into a time warp, I gazed around. A Persian carpet, held in place by brass rods, snaked up the staircase before me. The door to the room on the left was ajar. I peeked inside. A portrait in oils of a young man hung over a fake fireplace, looking arrogantly down over the mismatched chairs and magazines heaped on a coffee table. No one sat there.

I went back into the hall.

"Bonjour. Il y a quelqu'un?" I called out.

No answer. I pushed wisps of wet hair from my eyes, wondering what to do next. I could see a light beyond the stairwell, and hear muffled voices.

"Hello, anybody there?" I repeated in English.

Still no answer. The smell of French cigarettes floated down the staircase. Was Pascal Manet up there? Marcel had smoked Gauloises Blondes. Did his brother do the same? An odour of cigars, as well. Was Jacques Forestier with them? I resisted the urge to run upstairs and start banging on doors. I was tired and hungry, and this scene was creepy. Last time I had spoken to Marcel, I decided never to have anything to do with him again. Now I would've been stoked to bump into Marcel.

Making for the light beyond the stairwell, I took a breath and crept towards the voices. The moment had arrived when I'd be forced to speak French.

I entered the kitchen to find an ocean of stainless steel and downlighting. A scream of laughter greeted me. "Get outta here," a girl said in English. I found myself gazing at an angelic face, framed by fluffy fair hair.

"Sorry! I didn't mean you. I was talking to them." She pointed to her friends, seated around the table.

A spotlight lit up a new European stove, unused. A cold oven? *Then why could I smell cooking?* And that cooking smell was almost delicious enough to entice me into abandoning my raw vegan diet. But the aroma didn't come from this kitchen.

"I'm Cluny Belpomme." The chick with the fluffy locks pushed back her chair and held out her hand.

We shook. (I'd been warned about the French custom of shaking hands, even when arriving at work in the morning.)

"I'm Genna Perrier."

"And this is Spud Underwood." Cluny pointed to a guy with slicked back hair, a beard and a joint between his fingers. He kept his eyes lowered, and continued staring at the table. A freaky feeling ran through me. Didn't I know Spud from somewhere?

The table was set for four. It seemed they were expecting me.

"This is Jazlyn Kirnbauer." Cluny indicated a girl with dark hair. "Known to all as Jazz."

Jazz wore a stud in her nose. The front of her T-shirt read EMOTION-ALLY UNAVAILABLE. She rose, and reached across the table.

"Flex Du Lac's already left." Jazz's handshake was like a fish between my fingers. "So there are five staying in the house. He's gone to the Casino."

"Casino? I've never been to a casino."

"We're all going after we've eaten. Wanna come?"

"I'm not eighteen yet."

Hoots of laughter. "As if that matters," Cluny and Jazz chorused. "Get fake ID, like us. Spud doesn't need to. He turned eighteen ages ago."

Spud shifted in his chair, and took a toke on his joint.

"Haven't you ever done that?" Cluny smiled.

"What? Fake ID? Never worked at home, I look too young." A nervous giggle pushed out of my throat. "I never got to see those R-rated films!"

Their eyes bored into me like red hot pokers.

"Where do I get fake ID?" (Not that I really wanted to find out. I had no desire to be taken by the police to the next plane out of here.)

"We all got ours in the Latin Quarter, like everybody else," said Jazz.

"Yeah, right." I pulled at the wisps of hair around my face. "What's the nosh-up you talked about? I can't see anything cooking. This kitchen looks as though it's never been used, apart from those gross hairy vegetables."

The sea of gleaming stainless steel surrounding me was at odds with the rundown look of the house, and the cooking smell seemed to filter through the back door.

"Hairy vegetables? You mean those *ignames*? Aren't they amazing?" said Cluny. "They're yams, and they taste delicious. And they're super for the skin."

I gave a feeble smile. If I didn't have something to eat soon, I'd pass out, I told myself.

"Chantal cooks her bougna outside, in the garden, in an earth oven under hot stones. Bougna is awesome. Fabuloso. Just melts in your mouth," said Jazz.

"I-I'm raw vegan," I mumbled. "I don't, like, eat cooked food."

Silence descended like an awkward cone. They gave me the once over, as if I'd rocked in after parking my spaceship in the street outside.

Cluny broke the silence. "I think that's wonderful." She sighed. "Such self control." She sighed again. "*So* good for the figure. I wish I had the willpower."

Jazz nodded. "Me, too."

Spud remained silent.

I began to relax. I was used to people telling me I was a psycho weirdo when it came to food.

"Where do I sleep?" I pushed my arm through my backpack strap, and hoisted my laptop carry bag over my shoulder.

"I'll show you." Cluny finger-combed her hair. "Follow me."

She led me up the staircase, past a door on the landing. Behind the door I could hear talking, and smell cigars.

"Jacques Forestier spends his time in there, when he's around. It's a library. But he doesn't seem to live here, and I've only seen him once."

We climbed another flight of poorly-lit stairs.

"What's Jacques Forestier like?"

"Silver hair, slicked back. He's bent over, kind of stiff, and carries a cane with a *cagou* bird carved on the handle."

"Have you ever spoken to him?" I decided not to share that this man might be my grandfather.

"Nup. Monsieur Forestier gives you this beady-eyed look, as if he's trying to work out why you're here. We all received welcome letters, though."

"I didn't. I got the details from my teacher back home."

"Didn't you?" She chewed her lip. "My dad, a doctor in Darlinghurst, wonders if he suffers from Forestier's disease; that stiff-back syndrome old men get, discovered by another Jacques Forestier in the 1800s."

"Is Jacques Forestier the full quid?"

"Oh, yeah." She thought for a moment. "I imagine so. Why wouldn't he be?"

"I heard someone say something about a tragedy in his life."

"Dunno 'bout that. He had a young second wife who left him. Was that the tragedy?" She eyed my brief shrug. "I heard he set up that ritzy kitchen to stop Chantal from returning to her family in Vallée du Tir, near the nickel smelter."

"And she never uses the kitchen?"

"Not for cooking. Just to whip up coffee and croissants. Or chop up the vegies she buys at the market in Baie de la Moselle." Cluny turned a cast-iron handle. She pushed the door open, and flicked a brass light switch. "This is your room. Pretty basic, isn't it? Oh, there're no locks." She screwed up her ski-slope nose. "I s'pose it's for their protection. You know! Stop any hanky-panky!"

One corner of the neatly folded towel at the end of the bed, bedside a three-drawer table, was turned back. The rug on the hardwood floor stretched towards a cream-painted freestanding cupboard. A ceiling fan clattered overhead.

"Bathroom's down the hall, mega marble but dated and stained." Cluny gave me a dimpled smile. "See ya downstairs for kai." She paused. "Don't mind Spud. He's a bit of a kevin, but pretty harmless."

"What about the joint he was smoking?" My eyes grew huge. "Bit out there!"

"Banned in the house, but he'll have the roach end gone by the time dinner arrives." She hesitated. "Spud doesn't see borders, lines, or boxes people live in. He doesn't believe in borders, like, *ever*." Cluny pulled the door, which had cast-iron ventilation circles embedded in the wood, to behind her.

The stench of mildew took over from her eau de cologne.

Why had Cluny defended Spud? I pushed the hangers provided through the waist tapes of my tube skirts, and slung spare jeans over another hanger. I folded my T-shirts and knickers into loose wire baskets on the floor of the cupboard.

As I stuffed a bag of chop-chop—illegal loose tobacco I'd brought with me, courtesy of my friend Hetty Geiger, in case I hung out for a smoke—into a bedside drawer, I wondered if I should change. But Cluny and Jazz were in jeans. Examining my reflection in the spotted mirror on the inside of the cupboard door, I shoved wisps of stray hair back into my French plait, and smoothed the creases in my clothing. I brushed fluff off my shoulder and set off down the stairs, thinking about the 'young wife' Cluny had mentioned.

On the landing outside the library, I could still smell cigarettes intermingled with cigars, and hear voices. I was puzzled. *Jacques Forestier had corresponded with the others. Why had he not contacted me?*

Chapter 7

A burst of laughter as I re-entered the kitchen.

Cluny swivelled her head. "Hi Genna, I was talking about an excursion we took the kids on yesterday. We went to the New Cal territorial museum in the city, not far from the Latin Quarter. Just fab." Her cornflower eyes shone. "There's this massive *case* … traditional hut … from Lifou on the ground floor. Not to mention the Great Hut with its *flèche faitière*, or roof arrow, in the Kanak garden. Just, like, *amazing*. But they gave this long talk and the kids, mostly Kanak, got bored and began chatterboxing. This nerdy Caldoche woman wearing a *robe de mission* got stuck into them. She was carrying one of those tribal clubs."

"Wow!" said Jazz. "Here's Chantal with the bougna."

Chantal, clad in a missionary dress with tangerine flowers cascading from a square yoke, sashayed through the back door carrying a steaming banana leaf parcel tied with liana roots. Her hair—the biggest 'fro I'd ever seen—was like a crown of gypsophila drops.

"C'est poulet ce soir." Chantal began to peel open the parcel.

"It's chicken," whispered Cluny. "She softens the leaves over the fire before she wraps the food. We had Mahi Mahi last night. Delish!" She formed a bunch with her fingertips, kissed them and rolled her eyes in an expression of delight.

"But," I whispered in reply, "I don't eat cooked food. I'm raw vegan."

"That's *so* out there, we thought you were joshing." She frowned, and turned to Chantal. "*Mademoiselle*'s a vegetarian. Do you have any vegetables you could, like, whip up?"

"*Casse pas la tête!*" Chantal snapped her fingers. "I remove chicken for her."

"No, Genna means raw, *cru*, uncooked."

"*Awa!*" she exclaimed.

"That means she's surprised," said Cluny.

"I worked that one out."

"Why don't you *try* the bougna?" Cluny leaned towards me, and gave me a nudge. "It won't kill you this once." Her lips went into a pleading shape. "For me."

Cluny was doing a good imitation of Namilly, persuading me to eat when I was six years old.

"Well, okay," I began.

"She will. She will. She will."

Cluny clapped her hands, and Jazz gave her a funny look. Cluny Belpomme—so sweet she was like fairy floss—was cute, but she sounded like a desperado. She oohed and aahed as Chantal peeled back the banana leaves.

"Come and have a look." She flapped her arm at the bougna.

Pieces of plump meat simmered in coconut milk, alongside thick chunks of violet-coloured yam, pale taro, slices of golden pumpkin and long slivers of banana. Steam rose into the air as Chantal dished out the dinner.

I had to admit it smelled delicious.

The *igname* was sweet in my mouth, scented, like perfume. "This is excellent," I mumbled, pointing to the yam on my plate. "Could you eat it, like, um, uncooked?"

"Get real. It'd taste like wood," Cluny giggled, adding, "I imagine."

My mobile phone began to do a samba in my pocket. I wiggled it out, went to the Inbox. *1 message received* from Stefan:

bill einstein still sik 2nite wassup with u?

I punched out a reply guaranteed to make him jealous:

sorree that sux r off to casino 2nite new cal rox

"That's amazing." Cluny peered over my shoulder, chewing the last of her bougna. "You barely even looked when you typed out the message. I get digititis if I text too fast. Numb thumb! You must've been sending SMS *forever* to be so fast."

"Not really. My boyfriend, Stefan Becker, gave me this mobile as a pressie when I left to come here."

"It's cute." She ran a coconut-milky forefinger over the floral surface of the phone. "He must be very thoughtful."

I decided to confess it was also Stefan's response to the guilts he suffered after kissing Elizabeth Stubbs on Christmas Eve. "It's also a sort of *remorse gift*."

"Remorse gift?" Cluny looked pensive. I could see she had no concept of a world where gifts were used as compensation for knocking off cashier chicks, or snogging school friends. "You mean your boyfriend can do whatever he *likes*?" She pointed to his image on the screen wallpaper.

"As if." I stuck out my jaw. "It's just, like, a family custom he's grown up with." I flicked my plait forward, over my shoulder. "I think it's rather nice." I fiddled with the bristly bit. "For example, if he said he owed me a sunken garden, I'd know he'd been seriously unfaithful. Or, even if I was unfaithful and I said *I* owed him a sunken garden, he'd know what *I* meant."

"That's weird, and it could lead to, I dunno, payout for bad habits."

The door of the upstairs library slammed shut. I could hear footsteps. Someone was descending the stairs.

"Sounds like Jacques Forestier," Cluny said, "emerging from that gloomy room he spends his time in."

"Too sprightly," said Jazz. "Must be the guy who arranges the *stages*, the work experience."

"You mean Monsieur Manet? He was supposed to meet me at the airport."

"*Meet* you?" Spud spluttered through a mouthful of his second helping of bougna (the munchies, I imagined). "We all took the bus to Nouméa from Tontouta, then another to Val Plaisance. No one met *us*."

Had I received special treatment? And, if so, why?

"Well, he didn't *really* meet me *either.* This weird, yet kinda cool guy, called Roch—spelled R-O-C-H, but pronounced ROCK—picked me up in his rickety heap."

"*Geneviève*? Can I speak with you?"

I started. The French examiner from that shame job day in Ravella Community Hall was standing in the doorway.

Chapter 8

The blush flew up my neck and invaded my face as I remembered having used the wrong word for 'to kiss', for having thought *frileuse* was something to do with the cold sore on my upper lip.

Monsieur Manet wore neither a shiny grey suit, nor a flapping floral number. He was dressed in beige trousers and a conservative business shirt, striped and rolled up at the sleeves. His forearms were tanned.

I had a Velcro feeling on the soles of my feet. My legs became stiff as a ruler as I walked towards him.

"*Bonjour, monsieur*," I said, too afraid to utter more than that in French.

The lines at the side of his mouth creased in amusement (was he thinking of that day in Ravella?) as he answered, "*Bonjour, mademoiselle.*"

He put out his hand and we shook. His handshake was firm.

"Roch Colline 'as put you down all right?"

"Um, yeah. He dropped me off here, at the house. It was very kind of him."

"He was not too"—and he assessed me with narrowed blue eyes—"'ow you say, *relaxed*?"

What did Monsieur Manet mean by 'relaxed'?

"I tell 'im to be on 'is best behaviour."

Having only heard Monsieur Manet use the words 'cold' and ''e ferked 'is wife' in English, I was surprised to find he was not so hot in my language, either. Better than his brother, Marcel. But not perfect.

"Rocky was cool."

"He is a kava farmer, a bit poor and I very much like to help him. But sometimes he likes kavalactones too much."

"Kavalactones? You mean he's a junkie?" I frowned.

Spud sniggered.

Behind me, Chantal soaped up water in the sink, and began rattling dirty dishes. I could feel Cluny and Jazz skewering my back with their gaze.

Pascal Manet threw back his head and gave a hooting laugh. Had I said the wrong thing about Rocky?

"*Non.* I don't think so. He just sample 'is product and get problems from this."

"Well, he did scratch a bit."

But the French examiner was not interested. "Your room is sufficiently comfortable?"

My room was verging on the pits, but—"It's excellent!" I said.

"I will see you early on Monday morning, before classes. We pray for our weather to improve."

He turned on his heels and strode to the front door. He hesitated, as if thinking. "Do not try it," he said over his shoulder.

"Try what?"

"Kava. Many nakamals do not have flowing water. They wash up in bowls and it is not hygienic. We do not want you to get sick in your stomach."

He let himself out.

Spud unwound himself from his chair, pushed past me and hurried up the staircase.

"Are you coming to the Casino?" Cluny touched my shoulder. "We can all jam up together in a tight group. You'll get in easily without fake ID if we surround you."

Was it the 'sick in your stomach' advice from Monsieur Manet? I could feel the bougna jerking around in my gut. A wave of nausea rippled through me. Uh-oh, I needed to throw up. And I hadn't even been out of this kitchen, let alone inside a nakamal.

"What about the cyclone?" I managed to say.

"What cyclone? The weather's bad, but not that bad."

"They're talking about a cyclone, on the radio, at the tollbooth on the autoroute. Everywhere." I groaned, clutching myself.

"Well, no use stressing about something that might or might not happen." Cluny sounded cheerful. "I imagine they get loads of cyclone warnings in this place."

"What's wrong, Genna?" Jazz looked concerned. "You've gone pea green."

"The luigi?" I gasped. "I think I'm about to seriously spew. Where's the nearest toilet?"

"Down from your room, at the end of the corridor," they chorused.

Skidding on the rug as I went, I scrambled up the stairs.

With a bit of luck I'd make it.

Chapter 9

Hanging over the toilet, I trembled. Yam and taro, banana and bright pumpkin swirled around in the bowl. *Blast! I should never have eaten that cooked food*, I told myself. *I should've stuck to my raw vegan diet.*

I could hear voices outside the bathroom, low whispers. *"You shouldn't do that."* Louder whispers. *"It's not right."* More whispers. Silence. A hissing argument. I was unable to make out the words.

Running water from a humungous brass tap, I splashed the coolness over my face. Straightening, I noticed a peculiar set of sit-down scales towards the far wall. The seat was in shiny brown leather, beside a brass bar with a weight on one end and a hook at the other. A small dish hung there to take the counterweights, all black and shiny against the central pole. I reminded myself to try this antediluvian weighing machine later.

I smoothed down my Mambo T-shirt, grabbed the handle of the door and hauled it open. The welcoming committee stood there waiting.

"Are you better now?" Cluny looked upset.

"I've got something you might like," said Spud. "Open wide."

I did as he requested.

A small object flew through the air, lodging at the back of my throat. I swallowed, and felt a *thing* descending my gullet. The *thing* ground its way towards my stomach.

"That'll make you feel better." Spud's smile was slimy.

I gulped. "What was *that*? Disprin? I don't usually take painkillers unless it's really necessary."

"You've just dropped the love drug." He palmed a pill from his pocket. "Pharmaceutical grade. None of that crushed herbal garbage."

I saw the imprinted heart, and knew he'd given me ecstasy.

"I don't do drugs, and I've never even been to a rave party."

"Then what's that stash of dope doing in your room?"

My jaw went slack. Spud had been snooping among my things. He had discovered the chop-chop.

"It's not a stash of grass." My face went shaky. "It's chop-chop."

"What the hell's chop-chop?"

"Chop-chop is cheap loose tobacco, that's all."

"And what does this 'cheap loose tobacco' do for you?"

"Chop-chop is good for your health. If you discount the bleach, the sticky straw used for padding."

"Sounds disgusting," he said.

"Give her back her stuff!" Cluny sounded aggro.

Spud handed over the cliplock bag. "I still think it's shit."

I rammed the chop-chop into the back pocket of my jeans.

"C'mon!" Cluny grabbed my arm. "You won't be able to sleep. So at least *try* the Casino." She batted her eyelids. "For me!"

"I don't have enough dough to go gambling." Ants were on the march in my gut, crawling around in my intestine.

Spud pulled a green card from his pocket and handed it to me. "You can use this." CINQ CENT FRANCS was stamped across it.

"But how will we get there? It's raining."

He waved a FREE SHUTTLE ticket. "I rang, and they offered me a taxi instead of the shuttle. It should be here soon."

I'd run out of excuses.

The blood was rushing, rushing, rushing up my neck. I was on fire. My heart was surging in my chest, rising up, about to burst through my skull. My mouth was dry. I ran my tongue over my lips. Left, right. Left, right. Left, right.

I was flying. The world felt great. And all those creepy doubts I'd had since arriving in New Caledonia were gone. Cluny Belpomme, now wearing her trendy maxi jacket, was my closest friend ever. My other buddy, Jazlyn Kirnbauer, was ace too. Sleek and elegant. Even Spud

Underwood was great. Spud had cunning. Spud had class. Spud was a man of the world. He was far more sophisticated than my boyfriend, Stefan.

These were my new best friends. And I loved them, *loved* them, LOVED them.

"Of course I'll go!" I shouted. "Try to stop me!"

"Well, slip on a jacket. I'm wearing my Indigo hipsters with my Diesel jacket 'cos there's always a cool breeze at night here, the reason they call it the Land of Eternal Spring." Cluny wound a strand of hair around her finger. "Something about those trade winds," she added.

Chapter 10

Chantal waved goodbye from the front door. *"Tata,"* she called as we piled into the taxi.

"Tata? That doesn't sound very French," I said.

"No, but lots of people say it," said Jazz. "It must be a hangover from the American occupation during the war."

The rain was no longer falling; the stars had taken over. They were spinning and whirling, embracing me in their glittery arms.

I tapped Spud, seated in the front of the cab, on the shoulder as we prepared to hit the town. "Tell me how you play roulette. I never have before."

"There's a central spinning wheel," he explained, "with thirty-seven pockets around it. Eighteen of the pockets are black, eighteen red and one green. The wheel is spun in one direction, a small ball rolled in the other. The ball eventually lands in one of the pockets. If that's the number you've placed your chips on, you could make money, big time."

"You can also," said Jazz, "bet on colour, or odds and evens if you like."

"How much do you get?" This was fun.

"It depends on how many are involved in the game."

"Wowee!" I said. "In theory, you could make squillions."

"Yeah. Flex Du Lac's been doing it," Spud giggled, "for a while now. Just off the plane and he's already gambling. Dunno about making squillions, though."

I hadn't met this Flex person yet, but he sounded kinda cool.

"Is Flex a big gambler?" I seemed unable to stop rabbiting on, asking dorky questions. Was it the ecstasy? It was as if Cluny and I had morphed into a single being. Everything was wonderful, apart from this terrible thirst.

"Flex forks out a lot of moolah." Spud added, "On the other hand, you *could* fritter the evening away by putting your money on black and red at the same time." His laughter turned into a wheeze. *"But you wouldn't make a profit,"* he coughed.

"You'd have a good time, though," said Jazz.

"Amazing!" I shouted.

"Fabbo!" cried Cluny.

"Sooo bad!" crooned Jazz.

Spud's beard trembled with joy. I wondered if he still had the munchies.

"Unbelievable," we chorused as we sailed along Promenade Roger Laroque. Lights reflected on the water from the boats moored at the marinas. Now the rain had stopped, the night was sparkling.

"Oh man, oh man!" Cluny was jumping with joy as she eyed the glimmering clubs and restaurants I'd seen when driving past with Rocky. Only now they seemed glitzier. "Have you ever seen anything so sick?" she screamed.

"Incroyable!" I shouted in French.

"Simply excellent," said Jazz.

By the time we neared the Casino my throat was as dry as the Simpson Desert. I ran my tongue over my lips. Back over them again. And again.

The stars raced across the sky, and my heart raced with them. I'd never used ecstasy before. Would I fall to the ground, begin frothing at the mouth, keel over from cardiac arrest? I'd heard about people dropping dead from dropping e.

"Regardez le coal tar!" Our driver pointed to the surface of the road. Steam wisped into the air, swirled and danced with the breeze.

On our arrival Spud handed the driver the Free Shuttle pass with the word *Bienvenue* printed on the top as payment. We bundled out of the taxi and pushed our way along a path lined with palm trees, beside a brightly-lit hotel.

"Isn't this spech?" Cluny's eyes gleamed.

"Tight group, tight group. Stay in a tight group." Jazz sounded like a sergeant major. "We have to make sure Genna gets in. Tight grooo-oop!"

My body was pumping. I hadn't had so much fun since I nicked a hairclip on a dare from the Zabaglione Woollen Shop. Floating with the others, I was being swept along on a tidal wave of their affection. Together we formed a matrix of spontaneous humanity, a oneness.

A moon-faced man in the entrance gestured left. *"Casino à gauche."* Then he signalled a flight of stairs. *"Réception de l'hotel en haut."*

"He thinks we want to book in at the hotel," whispered Cluny.

"As if!" I said.

Spud explained in immaculate French that we were here to enjoy ourselves at the Casino. We were ready to gamble the night away with our vouchers.

"Excellent!" said the moon-faced man.

I could hear the clanking of the poker machines, the rattle of coins in the distance.

"Rien ne va plus," filtered from the gaming room.

Little shivers ran up and down my spine. I was about to become a high roller, make my fortune by using the green card Spud had given me.

And then I saw a greasy eyeball giving me the once over, examining everything from my French plait down to my sneakers. Did my footwear bother the manager? Or was it the duds? A sinking feeling came over me as I knew the answer. The real trouble? *I looked like a kid.*

I was transported back to the evening when a group of us trowelled on the make-up. Some fluffed up their curls. Others removed oversized nerd glasses. And I tizzed up by dragging on a pair of fishnet pantyhose. Everyone gained entry into the bar of the Grand Hotel—*except yours truly*. The bouncer shoved me out the door, and I caught the bus back to Ravella.

My heart sank further.

This was no different. It was the same old deal: MOUNTAIN RANGES. I had no mountain ranges, probably never would have mountain ranges. I had been the last in my class to purchase booby traps, and it was the bane of my existence. Moon-faced man never even asked for Cluny's, or Jazz's, fake ID. He just looked at their chests.

"'Ow old?" he said.

"I'm eighteen." I tried not to look roasted as I lied.

"Passeport?" He held out his hand.

I wriggled my passport from the pocket of my denim jacket and gave it to him, praying he wouldn't contact the fuzz.

He flicked through the pages, and then indicated the door. "You are beneath correct age. You cannot enter Casino. It is forbidden of you."

"I'm *almost* eighteen," I begged. "Please. I won't gamble. I'll only watch."

His finger looked a mile long as it stretched towards the exit.

"My friend's very responsible." Cluny fluttered her baby blues.

"Dunno about the rest of you, haggling over getting Genna inside." Spud snorted. "But I'm off to make my fortune."

He rolled up his sleeve. Like a bolt of lightning, I saw the snake tattoo on his forearm. I went cold. Hank, or his friend—I could never remember which—had worn a snake tattoo on the day I was jumped in the ti-tree bushes in Ravella.

The power of the eccy flooded back, and I shrugged off the feeling. It was a coincidence. Lots of people had tattoos. You didn't have to be a bogan to have a snake tattoo. Spud was nice. Spud was my friend. Spud was nothing like those lowlife losers. Spud was a good guy.

"I don't even know where I'm staying, like, where Jacques Forestier's house is," I said. "How do I get back?"

"You could walk. It's not far." Cluny raised an eyebrow at Jazz. "Anyone got anything to write on?"

Jazz pulled a scrap of paper and a pencil stub from her pocket.

Cluny wrote *1, rue de la Guillotine, Val Plaisance* in a neat hand. "It'll be a super stroll back to the house now the rain's stopped. Just follow Promenade Roger Laroque in the direction of Ouen Toro, and chuck a left at the other Laroque road. Rue Gabriel Laroque. You can't miss it."

"Thanks."

She snatched the piece of paper back from me. "We won't be home late, despite any big ideas that Spud might have. You've got a bludge day, but *we've* got classes in the morning." She sketched a quick map as she talked.

"But tomorrow's Saturday."

"Derr, Genna. School's open on Saturday in France. And New Cal is part of France, *in case* you forgot. But we get Wednesday arvo off." She smiled. "Lovely." Her face briefly clouded. "The worst thing is that seven o'clock start. I can barely croak at that hour of the morning, let alone lead an English conversation group."

Jazz nodded. "It's a drag."

I'll be able to snoop around the house while they're away, I said to myself, and then out loud, "I'm not looking forward to starting *that* early in the day."

"*Plus*, we finish at five. It's really off." Jazz sounded depressed.

By now, Spud had disappeared into the Casino.

"That snake tattoo Spud's wearing?" I hissed. "Have you seen it?"

"Yeah, isn't it *amazing*?" said Cluny. "I don't usually like tatts, but that one's classy. Just the best. Snakes are as popular as the groovy Maori ones these days." She gave a bell-like laugh. "See ya." She blew me a kiss, followed by a little wave.

"Gimme me back that voucher." Jazz held out her hand for the bill-shaped card. "It'll go to waste. We might as well use it."

Arm-in-arm Cluny and Jazz went off together. The moon-faced man walked me from the establishment, through the exit and out into the street.

I stuffed my passport in my jacket pocket. I was on my own now.

Chapter 11

My friends had abandoned me, yet I still felt on top of the world. I felt in the moment. All I needed was someone to talk to.

I looked around to get my bearings. The rain had stopped. The threat of the cyclone was apparently over. A breeze blew, but my denim jacket was enough to keep me warm. I dodged through the cars, heading for the beach side of the promenade. I felt great. I could wander back home past the bays, chat to anyone interested in yacking.

Should I chuck a right, go in a southerly direction? Or head left, towards the north? Pulling out Cluny's map, I tossed it high in the air. Forgetting the map—now skittering and swooping along the footpath—I decided to go for a swim, fully clothed. I undid my joggers, tied the laces together and hung them around my neck. I balled my socks into my jacket pocket, and made my way across the grainy sand to the water. I dipped in my toe. *Fabuloso*! Rolling up my jeans, I waded further out, thinking I could swim home with my joggers acting as flotation devices.

Then I remembered Rocky's words about sewage flowing from the racecourse into Anse Vata. I sniffed. The smell seemed no different from the beach back home.

Two guys were horsing around, pretending to play polo with a luminous ball. Should I warn them? But they might be locals. In class we'd never discussed the waste problems of this country, apart from a brief talk about the nickel pollution. Rocky might simply have been pulling my leg.

I thought of tropical nasties, also lurking in this water. Poisonous fish? I'd be dead in no time. My toe stubbed against a rock. *Was that a stone fish?* Scrambling from the shallows, I fled back to the safety of Promenade Roger Laroque.

Back on the footpath I set off in a southerly direction, uphill. I skipped, jumped over lines in the footpath and banged my fists on the bonnets of cars. Alarms screeched. I found myself having an out-of-body experience, watching myself have a good time. I was ultra-alert, with not a hint of jet lag from my trip. Simply thirsty.

A surge and cough. I heard a car following me. Was someone gutter-crawling, trawling for tarts? I broke into a run. The car sped up when I sped up, slowed when I slowed down. I no longer felt so upbeat. *Was the eccy tablet wearing off?*

"*Mademoiselle*," the driver called out in a Creole accent, "*putééé, t'es jôôôliiieee*. You come wis me. I will show you good time."

Who *was* this guy, telling me I was pretty? How dare he! Was he trying to pick me up? I turned to head for the beach again. That inky water was safer.

"Just joking! How do you like my Kanak accent?" The voice was different now, the words tinged with an Aussie twang.

I turned to see a grin on the caffeine face of Rocky Colline—the okay bloke who'd picked me up from the airport.

"G'day, Rocky!" I scooted to his car; at last I had someone to talk to. "What're you doing here? Buried your cat, or belled it, or whatever since I saw you last?" Waves of affection washed through me, warm and fuzzy feelings. I was floating. *Hey, ground, what's it like down there?*

"Bury my cat? Cute kid like you shouldn't be wasted."

"*Cute kid?*" I was indignant. "I'm more mature than you think, and I never touch alcohol, only champers on Christmas Eve. Oh, and I tried some of your friend Marcel's Jack Daniel's which, to tell the truth, was preeetty fiery."

"I don't mean grog." The passenger door creaked open. "What have you taken? You'd better get in."

I slid in beside him.

Rocky's eyebrows knotted into one long eyebrow. *"Merde, Geneviève. Qu'est-ce que tu fais? T'es seule, les pieds nus. Ça ne va pas du tout."* He glared at me. *"T'es toxicomane ou quoi?"*

"Aren't you speaking English to me anymore?"

Rocky scowled.

"My name's not Geneviève! And I'm on my own because I was kicked out of the Casino." I dropped my bottom lip. "Sooo … I took my shoes off to paddle in the water. And no way am I a drug addict!" I took a deep breath and, like a true dobber, told him what Spud had done.

"You should have had the sense to keep your mouth closed," Rocky muttered as we swung around a zillion curves on our way to Jacques Forestier's house at 1, rue de la Guillotine.

Rocky was right. But I refused to give him the satisfaction of agreeing.

"Was everyone stoned, or just you?" Despite his cool appearance, Rocky was beginning to sound like a boring adult.

"Well, Spud was smoking a joint when I first arrived, after you dropped me off, but Cluny and Jazz seemed sober. Though I wonder about the relationship between Spud and Cluny … there's something funny going on there. At first glance, Jazz and Cluny are the ones who are close." I leaned across, eased the beanie off Rocky's head and ran my fingers through his curls. *"She,* Cluny I mean, defended Spud's actions. So I wondered … whoops!"

The car swerved, shot between the gap in the median strip and chugged off in another direction.

"Where're you taking me?"

"To a place where you can sober off from your Special K, or whatever it is you are on."

"Oooh, nooo, nothing as bad as that. It was just the eccy. I've never dropped it before. Win might've, but I'm not sure. She's got some weird friends, like Hank … did I tell you about Hank? … and this other dude, bogan really. They were both bogans, in fact, and they tried to rape me in the ti-tree bushes. I still feel dirty when I even think about it. They called me a skank and a virgin slut, but how can you be a virgin and a slut. It doesn't make sense. But, hey, did anyone tell you you've got the *coolest* hair?"

Puttering along the RT1, we soon left the city behind. I continued chatting, never having felt so alive. I had no idea where we were going, and I couldn't have given a rat's rear end about a thing.

I felt great, *great*, GREAT. Bring on the eccy!

The road was free of cars, but I barely noticed. And soon we were choofing up a hill in the middle of nowhere. Not a soul in sight. The sky black. And, for all I knew, Rocky was planning to abduct me.

I heard a scratching. Felt something furry. Something soft against my neck.

"Omigod, it's a rat!" I screeched.

Chapter 12

"Go back to sleep, Belle." Rocky joggled the car to a halt beside an open terraced space. He hauled on the handbrake, picked the cat up by the scruff and slung her onto the back seat where she curled into a vibrating ball of fur.

My heart stopped thumping.

"I thought she was a rat," I giggled, still on a high from having swallowed Spud's little white pill.

Rocky gave a brief laugh.

"Where are we?"

"Nakamal du Ciel, and it's one of the nicer watering holes, with views over Baie de la Moselle." He pulled up his sleeve, gave a quick scratch, and pulled it down again. "Best of all, the owner buys our piper methysticum. We supply him with our quality product, from the roots of the old trees, after K-Mel grinds them up. Our kava is good." He smiled. "Better for you than a *topette*."

"Topette?"

"You won't find the local word for a bottle of beer in your Larousse dictionary. But Number One is the brand to drink in *Le Caillou*, as we call New Caledonia."

"Cool, but I don't drink beer. Too bitter, and, anyway, I'm not eighteen for a couple of weeks." I ran my tongue over my lips. "But I am kind of thirsty."

"In mediaeval England, beer was served with breakfast." Rocky saw me stare as he climbed from the car. "I read a lot!"

The ground was still slimy from the rain. The lights of Baie de la Moselle whirled around like fireflies in the distance. A breeze flittered over my skin, and it felt as though electrodes had been connected to my body. *Was it the eccy?*

"Tibou must be preparing to leave." Rocky indicated the heavy links of the low-slung security chain.

No Dogs, No Drugs were the first words I saw on the sign hanging near the chain. Smaller instructions were beside it—*Parler à voix basse; Surveillez vos enfants; Alcool interdit*—telling me I should speak softly, watch my children and not bring alcohol onto the premises.

"What about your cat?" I hugged my jacket to me. "Is Belle allowed in?"

"Belle stays in the car. All animals are forbidden." Rocky pulled at his beanie.

Another sign read: *Ouvert du lundi au samedi, à partir de 16 heures*—a long week for a nakamal proprietor, with only Sunday free and forced to open at four in the afternoon.

An ocean of white gravel confronted me as I stepped over the security chain. The quartz was dotted with sawn-off tree stumps for seats. Four thatched-roof *farés*, supported by carved poles, stretched up a terraced slope. The concrete steps leading to the *farés* were wide and edged with slim logs. Material woven from pandanus leaves hung from the side of each thatched roof to ward off the wind. Open fires smouldered.

In a kitchen near the entrance, a Kanak with a bristly moustache and a bullet head—shaved, with a skinny plait erupting from the back—ran a rag over flat surfaces.

"Roch. Salut, ça va?" He emerged from his kitchen.

"Oui, ça va. Et toi?"

Rocky turned to me: "This is Tibou. Tibou, meet my friend, Genna."

We all shook hands. (I found myself becoming used to the flesh pressing, this unfamiliar formality.)

"Tibou is a *broussard*, from the bush. As I am."

"Deux shells?" Tibou went back into his work area.

Rocky nodded. He pulled two hundred francs from inside his windbreaker.

"Non, ça va." Tibou refused the money.

"Those seats are wet." Rocky pointed to the sawn-off tree trunks. "Let's sit under cover."

We lowered ourselves onto a long wooden bench in the first *faré*. The woven fabric, smelling like wood shavings, flapped behind us. The curtain gave out a sweet scent.

"The effect of the eccy's almost worn off." I was iffy about trying kava. "So I don't think I'll need that, um, drink."

"Tibou is preparing your kava right now, squeezing it through a palm fibre cloth to remove the lumps. He'll be hurt if you don't have one shell … or *biloo*, as we call it."

Ten minutes later, Tibou gave us our shells. Still hyped from swallowing Spud's pill, I took a scared sip from the dried-out coconut half. The taste was like dirt, like drinking something dredged from the bottom of a river. My tongue had no feeling. This was weirder than dropping e.

"Tongue numb?" Rocky gave me a gentle smile.

Nodding, I gazed at the liquid, now turning milky beige, afraid to speak in case my tongue jumped out of my mouth and burrowed into the gravel.

"It's ideal if you cannot feel your tongue. It means the product is psychoactive, a good brew, nature's stress buster."

The relaxing effect spread quickly through my body. I became warm and loose. My face felt as though it had been massaged. My muscles were supple. My mind was at ease. I felt content to sit in the nakamal forever with my new friend, in the quietness, sipping kava from our bowls and checking out the glowing embers of the fire. I didn't see anything goobie, like faces or monsters, in the flames. Just good old wood burning.

"You seem concerned by our introduced rats," Rocky murmured. "I am, too. They're a real problem, particularly for the birds that nest on the ground, like the cagou. Rats menace the ecosystem, by eating the fruits of the trees, hence the sheet girdling I mentioned earlier. And they can't be poisoned because of the fauna. So we put out traps."

Rocky had the same vague look on his face as Jack Bradfield, when I'd listened to Jack rave about his butterflies in the ti-tree scrub at Ravella. "Rats like peanut butter, you know, white chocolate." He gave a secret, closed-mouth smile.

Sitting beside him I felt as if I were with another nutter, obsessed with Mother Nature. Except the butterflies tricked into laying eggs on parsley had morphed into rats lured into traps with the promise of goodies, like white chocolate and peanut butter.

"Control of the rats in the Ni-Kouakoué reserve is urgently needed, to improve the survival of the Owlet-nightjar … if that bird's not extinct already." Rocky lapsed into silence.

This was my chance to find out about the bird Marcel mentioned in one of his letters. "Tell me, what is a Notou bird?"

"A Notou is a giant pigeon, with lush black feathers, large red eyes and protected. Some bastards kill and eat them."

And, I thought, *one of those bastards is your old mate, Marcel Manet.*

"I ate bougna for dinner, but I don't think it was a Notou bird." I chose not to confess I'd grommited the delicious meal into the toilet.

"Was it *roussette*?"

"*Roussette*, what's that?"

"Bats, big fat ones. I used to catch 'em as a kid, using a *bibiche* … a sort of stone, a slingshot. They're big and hairy, delicious to eat." He bunched the tips of his fingers and made a kissing motion.

"Bats?" Surely I hadn't eaten a bat?

Calm took over. I felt serene, unable to stop smiling.

"Cluny Belpomme, my new friend, told me there was chicken in the bougna. She never mentioned *roussette*." A grin was fixed to my dial, as if stuck by superglue. This was a different kind of happiness from the one I'd experienced after dropping e. I was no longer jumping, just relaxed.

"I can see the effect of the remarkable piper methysticum plant is beginning to work on you. It happens quickly, in just a few minutes, and it's written all over your face. Slugging down the aqueous drink is the hard part, for everyone. But it delivers a concentration of kavalactones, the ideal herbal extract."

I was at peace, yet strangely alert. Everything seemed so uncomplicated now, but—"That kava taste is a bit of a marketing negative." I made a face. "Although, I am used to a regime, raw vegan, munching uncooked rice …" My voice trailed away of its own accord, detached from my body.

"It's all to do with the mixing." Rocky contemplated his cup of kava. "Starting with the digging out of the plants, you remove the soil from the roots, and wash them. All parts, apart from the leaves are dried next. The stems are peeled, cut into pieces and sun-dried. The roots are left for drying, and bundled. The dried roots are then pounded in the iron mortar with an iron pestle. K-Mel used to prefer hard coral for the crushing, but he switched to iron."

"More modern, I suppose?"

"Kava should never be taken with alcohol, it can be dangerous." Rocky gave me a sidelong glance. "My mum used to give kava to Douce, my baby sister, to relieve her bronchitis." He sounded mellower than previously, when talking about his mother.

"My mum talked about giving me the 'local drink' before we fled to Australia during the Events." *Had Namilly given me kava?* I wondered. But I needed to know more about Rocky. "How did your olds meet, as your mother's Australian, your father Melanesian? It can't have been easy."

"They met behind the barricades in May '68." He cleared his throat.

"Barricades?"

"The student revolution led by Daniel Cohn-Bendit … known as *Danny Le Rouge* ... was the revolution that inspired the Events on *Le Caillou* during the '80s." Rocky's expression was thoughtful.

I remembered learning about May '68 in my French class, but not the details. Not wishing to appear dumb, I nodded wisely.

We sat there talking in fits and starts.

Rocky picked at his yellowed thumbnail with the nail of his middle finger. "Kava was, and still is in some places, for men only. Virgins used to chew up the roots before spitting the pieces into the carved presentation bowl for the men to drink."

"How disgusting!"

"Some people claim hepatoxicity … liver damage … from kava use, but I refuse to believe that. There are too many positives. For example, it calms the nerves without numbing the brain. It's anti-convulsive, analgesic, a sedative and a muscle-relaxant."

Feeling warmer, I took off my jacket, folded it and placed it on my knee. "Sounds like the perfect drink."

He gave a laid-back smile.

I wanted to find out more about Marcel Manet, the man who tracked me down in Ravella. "Tell me about Marcel."

"Another time." Rocky rose. "I should get you back home, or I'll be in trouble with Pascal."

Tibou was busy winding a thick chain around the refrigerator. He turned a key in a chunky lock to secure the fridge as we strolled towards the entrance.

"Tibou's kava is valuable." Rocky pointed at the fridge. "So he needs to lock it up, or someone will steal it and sell it." He halted. "You go on ahead, Genna. I'll join you in a minute."

Rocky and Tibou began to talk. Tibou pulled out some cash and gave the money to Rocky, who slid the roll into an inside pocket.

Transaction completed, they joined me at the nakamal entrance.

"Au revoir." I shook hands with Tibou.

Folding my jacket over my arm, I lifted my foot to step across the security chain when I sensed movement behind me, a scrunching of pebbles. I felt a shove against the back of my jeans, and lurched.

"What is zis?" Tibou thundered in English.

I turned.

His onyx eyes bored into mine. "Can you not read ze sign—*No Dogs, No DRUGS?"*

Chapter 13

Through rapid French, I heard the word *poken* and knew they were talking about me. *What was going on?* I should never have come to the nakamal with Rocky. I should've jogged on home, spurred on by the power of the eccy.

"It seems you are not as innocent as you appear." Rocky held up the cliplock bag Tibou had snatched from my pocket.

"Oh, that!" The calm was taking over once more, my body turning to jello. "It's no big deal. It's only chop-chop."

"What's chop-chop? Hash? *Is it grass?*" Rocky sounded fizzed off. "If I'd known you had drugs …"

"It's just rolling tobacco, cheap loose stuff sold by Mrs B in Ravella."

Raindrops began to spit into the gravel, began to drum around me. Stray wisps of hair from my French plait glued themselves to my cheeks as I watched him rip open the packet.

He sniffed. "Phew, this stinks of mould." He sniffed again. "*Javel?* Bleach, also?" He gave me back the plastic bag. "That's revolting. I wouldn't give it to my *chien bleu*, my Australian cattle dog, who deserves it because he does *pipi* on our veranda. And you certainly couldn't give it as a *coutume* wedding gift, better to stick to money or a piece of fabric wrapped in a *paréo*—a *manou* as we call it."

Tobacco as a wedding gift?

"Chop-chop is good for you!" I was becoming drenched, and cranky. The rain was pounding down in great cords of water; in the distance, the lights of Baie de la Moselle had almost disappeared.

"We'd better be off." Rocky ran ahead to his car.

We bundled ourselves into the vehicle. Tibou continued to stand in the wet, with a look of doubt on his face.

Rocky wound down the window. "This might be Liliane. Maybe she's made up her mind to come, *mon pote*," he shouted to his business associate.

"You mean this is the cyclone?" I pointed to the drumming rain.

Rocky gave Tibou a wave. "Not yet." He jerked the window up again. "She'll rip through the place. Not tonight, but soon. There'll be enough warning for you to hide under the bed, or bunker down in the bath, whichever is most convenient." He cleared the fog off the inside of the windscreen with the sleeve of his windbreaker.

From the depths of the back seat, I heard the cat yawn.

"I must get Belle home, before a rat tears our cagou to pieces."

"Can the cagou bird fly?"

"No, the cagou is a flightless bird, able to glide for a short way when in danger. Obviously, not when in a cage. And mine has a chick."

"Wouldn't your bird be better off free?"

Rocky shook his head. "The reason their numbers plummeted on Grande Terre, the main island, was due to the dogs, pigs, cats like Belle, and rats introduced by the colonisers. Cagou numbers are back up to about six hundred now, due to the work of the renowned ranger at Parc Territorial de la Rivière Bleue—Blue River Park. But the situation's still fragile."

"Doesn't Belle harm the cagou bird?"

"She can't get through the wire of the cage." Rocky tapped his thumb on the steering wheel. "Belle doesn't like to eat the giant snails the cagou enjoys. But rats eat the cagous and she kills the rats before they can get to the cagou. See!" He grinned. "It all makes sense if you think about it."

With the rain muffling the rattle of the motor, the car flew down the hill as we headed in the direction of Noumea. The Mount Koghi peaks loomed majestically behind us.

"I'll take you past Oriel Lycée, if you like," he said, "so you can see the place where you'll be working on Monday."

"I'd like that."

We swirled around curves again. An airport flashed past in a blur. I could just make out the propeller of a single-engine aircraft through the streaming glass.

"Magenta is the local airport. From there you can fly to the Northern Province, or to the Loyalty Islands to mix it with the pink-skinned tourists."

"Maybe I'll go one day, when I have some spare time and, more importantly, enough money."

My mobile phone did a shimmy in my pocket. I pulled it out. *1 message received* from Stefan. I checked my Swatch. Almost midnight.

bill einstein still sik

A bad feeling came over me. Why was Stefan still helping Win so late in the evening? And then I realised we were an hour ahead of the East Coast of Australia, but the situation was strange, nonetheless. Stefan and Win had always hated one another. Stefan thought Win an airhead, and Win always bundled Stefan into a basket labelled: *people never to be touched*. I shoved the doubts to the back of my mind. At least he wasn't with Elizabeth.

"You are far away." Rocky nodded to the left. "This is Oriel Lycée, a new school with most of the buildings only recently completed."

Peering through the rain at the place where I'd be starting my work experience on Monday morning, I saw a domed metal roof over a pink and cream building. A spacious quadrangle was surrounded by classrooms, two storeyed and with matching balustrades.

"It's nice." I was still bothered by Stefan's SMS.

The engine hiccupped and fluttered as it idled.

"Well, inspection's over." Rocky pushed the gear stick with its baggy leather base into first gear. "You seem preoccupied. I'll get you home."

We struggled up a hill, around more bends, down again, up again until we reached 1, rue de la Guillotine.

"Still want to come tomorrow night?" Rocky lifted an eyebrow. "Would you like to meet my independence colleagues?"

The feeling of contentment flooded back. "That'd be grouse!"

I decided to take a photo of Rocky to show my friends in Ravella, and maybe make Stefan jealous.

I raised the mobile phone. "Smile! Say *fromage!*" I was about to press *Capture* when I saw the alien look in his eyes.

Rocky covered the lens with his fingers. I hastily slid the phone back in my pocket, extracted my Dracula front door key and scrambled from the car.

He leaned across. "All right for six, then? No, make it five. Kava should be taken early in the evening." He ran his tongue over his lips. "I shouldn't tell you this, but you'll have trouble sleeping for a few hours." He gave a slow, shiny smile. "But at least you'll be calmer than you would've been after taking the ecstasy."

Steam seemed to rise from his beanie as he put the car in gear.

Contrary to the French examiner's 'sick in your stomach' warning I felt fine. And I'd seen no running water in Tibou's establishment. Perhaps kava really was the perfect raw vegan drink.

Pierrot the Peugeot chugged off.

Belle's eyes stared at me from the rear window of the vehicle as I scampered to the front door. Why had Rocky refused to let me take his photo? Only criminals shielded their faces from a camera lens. And why did he never take his beanie off?

Brandishing my key I prayed for it to turn quickly. The key was as difficult to turn as it had been previously.

Chapter 14

"Merde, merde, merde!" I yelled. Had Sandrine had this much trouble getting in the house after a date? I jiggled and twisted. Water from the broken guttering oozed down the back of my neck.

My limbs felt heavy from the kava. Making a fist with difficulty, I banged on the door. No answer. Dodging a cycad palm, I cupped my hands in an effort to see through the shutters. No light shone inside.

I returned to the front door, lifted my foot and gave it a hefty kick. The door flew open. The house was pitch-dark and silent, and my Swatch, luminous in the gloom, read nineteen past midnight. *Were the others asleep?* Had they turned out the lights, not realising I was not yet home?

Pulling the key from the lock, I felt around until I found a light switch. Flicked. Nothing happened. Oh heck, the power was out. I groped my way towards the stairs. Colliding with the door that led into the room with the imitation fireplace, I stood still and tried to get my bearings. Despite having drunk kava, my heart was doing jungle drums. I needed a torch. Could I use the screen of my mobile phone to light my way? I wondered.

Wriggling the phone out, I pressed the On button. The hectic blue light glowed. I held the phone out before me, flat and horizontal, stumbling up the staircase to my room.

Halting for a moment on the landing beside the library, I pushed my ear against the door. Silence from the other side, and no smell of cigars. I soon worked out that Jacques Forestier had left. A wave of disappointment whooshed over me. I was hoping to bump into him sometime, see if he was as decrepit as Cluny had described.

Trudging up the steps, I followed the light of my mobile phone to the third floor where my bedroom was situated, second on the left-hand side along the corridor. Leaden-limbed, I crept past Spud's room, first on the right above the kitchen.

I could hear people talking. Low whispers. A laugh. The voices trailed off, and springs began to squeak. Was Spud Underwood having it off with one of my new friends? My skin crawled. Was Spud carrying on with Cluny? Cluny had defended Spud earlier in the evening. But I'd never seen them hold hands, never seen them look at one another in *that* way. And she had said he was 'a bit of a kevin, but pretty harmless'—hardly a romantic endorsement. Then again, maybe she was into the yarndi, joining him in a joint?

But I could detect no sweet smell, and Cluny didn't look the type to get whacked.

Was it Jazz? But Jazz was so bossy I found it difficult to imagine her sucking on swamp, or having sex, or doing anything mildly out there.

The noise level increased. I moved on.

Fumbling for my bedroom doorknob, I managed to grasp the cast-iron handle. As I let myself in, the light from my mobile phone faded. Groping and feeling for my bed, I tripped on the edge of the rug. As I lurched against the pillow, something soft and silky brushed my skin. *Was a spider on my pillow, waiting to bite me?*

Snatching my hand back, I picked the pillow up with my thumb and forefinger. Shook. Stamped. Jumped around the room. Soon I could feel sliminess beneath my joggers and knew I'd killed the gooby.

Panting and hot, yet calm and clear-sighted, I unlaced my Reeboks and set off, barefoot, to the loo. A lingering garden smell assaulted my nostrils as I left. *The death smell of a scary tropical spider?*

Feeling my way down the passage (still pitch-black), I discovered a knob and turned. The marble underfoot was cool and I knew I'd found the bathroom. The wall was cool, too. As I leaned against it, the lights surged back on. I headed for the luigi.

My gaze latched onto the antediluvian bathroom scales. I washed my hands and went to inspect them. Easing myself onto the polished leather seat, I examined the circular weights. Placed a weight on the hanging dish. Took the weight off again. Replaced it with another weight. On, off. Off, on. Until I achieved a semblance of a balance.

Gasp, *gasp*, GASP. Eighty-four kilos? No way! I weighed little more than forty-eight kilos, wringing wet—and that was after a vegie pig-out.

A knock on the bathroom door.

Still under the influence of kava, I smiled serenely. Whoever it was could wait.

A second, firmer knock.

The door squeaked open. Spud poked his head through the slit. His hair was a hay field. He wore a mustard towelling wrap.

"Can I use the dunny?" He nodded in the direction of the throne.

I gave him my new tranquil smile.

"No longer hyped from dropping e?" Spud's beard was scraggy. "Or did the eccy not work?"

"Yeah, the eccy worked, but, given that I couldn't give a rat's that you took advantage of me, I'll let you into a secret." I swung my feet, kicking the polished wood base of the scales. "I had this incredible drink called kava!"

"And you're flooded with sangfroid?" Spud let out an exasperated sigh. "Kava tastes foul, gives no buzz whatsoever, and I don't even have to mention the chundering from those crappy shells."

"I never spewed."

Rain was thrumming on the roof. The sound had a comforting consistency.

"*And* there are side effects." Spud was on a roll. His hairy toes wiggled as he talked.

"Such as?" I slid off the weighing machine.

"There's loss of appetite, which leads to weight loss." His eyes raked my thin frame. "And I haven't even added puffy face, scaly rash, yellowing of the nails and hair, pulmonary hypertension." He hesitated, as if he'd spent years researching the negatives of kava consumption. "And blood in the urine."

"I never noticed anything like that with me!"

"Well you wouldn't, would you, after taking it for the first time?" His voice was heavy with contempt.

Then I recalled Rocky's scratching, his yellow-tinged gums, and his fingernails. Even the colour of his curls. Had drinking kava caused all those things?

Trailing a nooky smell, Spud made for the can.

"Well Miss Privileged, would you please p.o.q.?" The inky head of a snake tattoo poked from the sleeve of his bathrobe. "Or do you wanna stay and watch?"

The heady freshness of the outside downpour filtered along the corridor as I closed the door behind me.

I heard Spud call out: "Oh, and some people hallucinate." A pause. "But the symptoms quickly disappear as soon as you stop."

I sauntered back to my bedroom, sure I wasn't hallucinating. Knowing this was the best reality I'd felt in a long time. I ground to a halt in the gloom. *Why had Spud called me Miss Privileged?* Had the others been talking about me? Was it because I'd been picked up from the airport? Or was it something else?

I turned back to speak to Spud, to ask him about it. Then decided he'd just think I was harassing him.

The polished boards against the soles of my feet felt refreshing as I ambled along, taking my time, ultra-calm from my kava chill pill.

Until I saw a light shining beneath the crack of my door.

Was someone in my bedroom?

Chapter 15

Heart paddling fast, I inched the door ajar. I ran my eyes over the room. A red mess was spread across the floor—like blood. A scream worked its way up my throat. I pushed it back. My room was verging on the pits when I left. Now it was the total pits, an abattoir. Was someone playing a practical joke on me? A prank aimed at a rookie work-experience participant?

My vision bored in on the red smears, more like crimson slime from where I stood. Was that really blood? Or was it a warning—fake blood? *Had Spud done this?* Had he invaded my personal space for a second time that evening? The room had been dark when I left. The light was now on, the rug in a twist. My fresh towel was unfolded, dangling over the edge of the bed. What sort of game was Spud playing? Or had the mysterious Flex du Lac done this?

Had anything been stolen? I wondered. My laptop was on the bed-side table where I'd left it. My mobile phone was in my pocket. These were the only things I had of value. None of it made sense.

Was I *really* hallucinating? Spud had told me I might hallucinate. But I hadn't grossed out on kava, only drunk one shell. Clinging to the door, I wondered whether to go in, or rock on back to the bathroom, see Spud, confront him and force him to own up. But he might think I was a dweeb to be bothered by a bit of blood.

The penny dropped like a lump of lead in my noggin. The power had been out before I went to the loo. I had flicked the switch to check, leaving the switch in the On position. Electricity problem solved. *But not the blood problem.*

Recalling my stamping on the spider, I began to wonder if spider blood was red.

Time to inspect more closely. I crept towards the pulp. Boy, had I made a mess! The area was like fresh road kill, and that garden tang still tickled my nostrils. Crouching down, I saw bits of fluffy yellow scattered among the red slime—like pollen. Sheesh. These were no spider remains. I'd mangled a flower with my joggers. A red flower. A hibiscus? But why? *What was a hibiscus doing on my pillow?*

Pushing myself upright, I wondered who had put it there? Spud? Unlikely. Cluny? Cluny was sweet, but why? Was she a lemon, a lezzo? But she'd made no effort to come on to me. Jazz? She and Cluny had held hands entering the Casino, but not in an intense way. Had I been the subject of some floral jape? *Was* it Flex du Lac? But why would he do a thing like that? He'd never met me. I crossed Flex off my list.

Then I wondered if the flower had blown through my window. Unlikely, as the room was on the third floor. I pushed back the flimsy curtain with the faded pink bows printed on it. The shutters were closed. Rain squeezed down one side of the narrow blades.

My mind was churning as I pulled tissues from my backpack to clean up the goo. I threw the soiled tissues into the basketwork bin, straightened the rug and began to undress. My legs still felt heavy, but the alert effect brought on by the kava seemed to have worn off. I planned on getting a good night's sleep.

Placing the bag of chop-chop back in my bedside drawer, I dragged an old T-shirt over my head. I wriggled myself under the pilled synthetic blanket, and tried to get comfortable. The drumming of the rain sent me into a trance-like state.

Unable to sleep, I lay there thinking. The answer to the riddle of the hibiscus came to me in a flash. *Spud* had put the flower on my pillow. His way of saying he was sorry for having nicked my chop-chop, for forcing me to drop e against my will.

Soothed by the knowledge, I rolled over and tried to get some shut-eye.

The ceiling fan whizzed overhead. I dozed for a while, but in no time I was awake and jumping. I gazed at the whirling ceiling fan. Round and round and round. Round and round and … pale light leached through the ventilation circles in the door. My lids became heavy.

My eyelids flew open again. Energy surged through my body like wild electricity. *Was the eccy taking over from the kava in some sort of internal struggle?* Again, I was hanging out for someone to talk to. I resisted the urge to get out of bed.

I heard giggling in the passage, boards creaking. Someone was descending the stairs, just along from my room.

The rain eased off. The wind picked up. A tree tapped against my window. Tap. Tap. I began to get that grainy feeling. The world was fracturing into pieces. Down, down, down.

A hibiscus was chasing me, flapping its petals. The faded bows on the flimsy curtains swirled and whispered: How dare you destroy me!

"Geneviève, la demoiselle est là-dedans," said the hibiscus.

The flower fell about laughing, flapped its wings and flew away.

"Chut!" hissed its frangipani companion.

"Awa!"

Floating, I was back at Ravella beach. I was swimming. The wind whipped up. Waves battered the shore. Water splashed and surged.

My bedroom door squeaked open. I lurched awake.

Chapter 16

The wind slammed my bedroom door shut. Feverishly, I unzipped my Cartoon Network carry bag. I grasped for my laptop and held it up like a shield. No one entered. The front door closed below. Muffled voices echoed up the stairwell.

I glanced at my Swatch. 5.30 am. Was Chantal returning from the early market at Baie de la Moselle? My heart slowed. I replaced my laptop in its carry bag.

Never having been a school boarder, these people noises bothered me. The rain ploughed down, and I sank back. With no classes that morning, there was no need for me to get up. But I was wide-awake. So I lay there listening to the clattering in the kitchen. Interesting smells began to seep beneath my door.

Hanging out to talk to my new friends, I swung my legs over the side of the bed and dragged on my jeans. Sliding my feet into an old pair of thongs, I set off, dying to find out if anyone had made their fortune gambling at the Casino.

Recalling the sounds from Spud's bedroom, I almost turned back. How could I look Cluny or Jazz in the eye knowing they might've gone all the way with Spud Underwood last night? Or had I imagined it? Had the squeaking springs simply indicated two friends having an innocent conversation? I crept down the stairs. Reaching the kitchen door, I hesitated. I heard someone yawn. A sigh. Spasmodic talking. Immediately I knew what to say. I would thank Spud for the hibiscus he'd left on my pillow—which I'd unwittingly destroyed.

"*Salut*, high rollers!" I rocked on into the sea of stainless steel and spotlights. "Thanks for the hibiscus, Spud."

Determined not to think about his home run life—Spud was no hunk—and determined not to think about who'd been doing what with him, I extended my paw for his handshake. Three pairs of eyes stared at me. Apart from Chantal (now clad in a sombre missionary dress), who was busy cutting up a rockmelon, you could've sliced the silence with a knife.

"You don't give skin at this hour of the morning," said Spud.

Mortified, I tucked my mitts into my pockets and gazed at a basket of croissants.

Chantal yawned.

"What hibiscus?" Spud's eyes were like road maps.

Not admitting I'd destroyed it, I said, "Oh, someone left a hibiscus on my pillow. I thought it might've been you, as an, um, apology for nicking my packet of chop-chop."

"Nope." He bit into a brioche. "Nice try, but I don't know anything about a hibiscus."

Jazz shrugged.

Cluny turned to me. "We're not high rollers, Genna. Apart from Flex du Lac, none of us made money at the Casino." She lowered her voice into concerned mode. "Did you get home all right? Your door was shut, the light out, so you must've had a good night's sleep. Or did the e keep you awake?"

"I couldn't stop jumping. So I went to a nakamal."

"You're kidding! A bit dodgy after eccy!" Cluny's eyes were round. "On your own?"

"Rocky drove by. You know, the cool guy I told you about who picked me up from the airport. He took me to Nakamal du Ciel." I fiddled with my hands. "He's a Kanak. No, I'm wrong. He says he's a *metis*, and we're going to another nakamal tonight."

Chantal flashed me a brief look. She placed a dish filled with tropical fruit in the centre of the table, next to a pile of massive coffee bowls.

"Where *is* Flex du Lac?" I slurped on a piece of pineapple. "I still haven't met him."

"Flex is not on this morning," said Jazz, "so he's doing something else. He arrived in New Cal not long before you did, but he's like a whirlwind. He's off to the reef to surf, despite the *tricots rayés*."

"But the weather's so bad," I said. "Anyway, what are *tricots rayés*?"

"From your expression," Cluny chipped in, "I can see you're alarmed at the thought of poisonous snakes. But the surf is best in bad weather, and it's not often up, considering this place is surrounded by the biggest lagoon in the world."

Cluny was in one of her explaining moods, even though it was not yet six o'clock in the morning.

"Water snakes are everywhere." She spun her eyes in an agonised way. "One bite and you're gone. Thank heavens they're timid and have a small mouth, because it's a painful, painful death." She tore a croissant in half, and spread butter into a sweet-smelling gap in the pastry. "Not at all like a normal snake bite, when you go out on a sort of high." Her lips shone as she began to chew the croissant.

"What are you doing today, Spud?" Jazz picked at a *pain au chocolat*.

"Well, before this rain, I planned to take a group down to Nouville, go over the convict ruins."

"But most of the buildings of the penal colony were destroyed," said Jazz, "through the shame. I even heard of people ripping pages from the convict register when it was released to the public, to protect the family reputation."

"The bakery and the other buildings are enough to give some ambience for a discussion about Louise Michel, even though she was imprisoned at the Baie des Dames in Ducos," said Spud. "*Louise La Rouge*, or Louise the Red, was the Paris communard, transported here, who worked with the Kanaks." He eyed me. "She taught at a time when only males were allowed to be educated, and helped the Kanaks in the uprising of 1878." He uncoiled himself from his chair, and wandered to the window. "But the weather's stuffed that idea up. Looks like we'll have to go to the *Bibliothèque Bernheim*, or the museum in the old bank."

"What about *Le Centre Tjibaou*?" said Cluny. "You can wander around in there. There's plenty of space in that awesome row of arcs, in those abstract huts, and so much to see. Like that wonderful exhibition of the life and times of Jean-Marie Tjibaou, the Kanak activist who was assassinated."

"But it's near a swamp," shivered Jazz, "and there're stacks of mossies there. The dengue mossie bites you during the daytime. I can't even stand to think about it."

"Think I'll keep 'em in the classroom." Spud stroked his beard. "But I wish the rain'd stop. There's a reggae festival on at Kuendu Beach this evening." He made to leave. "We were going, but I s'pose it'll be cancelled now." Hoisting folders from a side table into his arms, he disappeared towards the front door. His umbrella clicked open.

Jazz stood. She smoothed back her hair, and followed Spud.

Cluny finished the last of her coffee.

"Who's the 'we' Spud was referring to?" I shuffled in my chair.

Cluny made negative signs with her fingers.

Chantal was rattling dishes in the sink. I decided to brave it, and ask my new friend if she'd done it with Spud—an okay bloke, but no studmuffin—last night.

"Did you and Spud have it off, back here, after the Casino? If it wasn't you, who was it?"

Cluny's eyes went spazball. Her mouth formed a hasty 'shush' shape.

Chapter 17

"Spud is *sooo* intelligent." Cluny's voice was a mixture of enthusiasm and anxiety. "He speaks the most incredible French. He's from the Mornington Peninsula, and he won a scholarship, did his schooling at Grange College in Melbourne."

Ravella was also situated on the Mornington Peninsula. Was that the reason Spud's face seemed familiar? I put the thought to the back of my mind.

"He comes to the territory every chance he gets, so he's almost a permanent English assistant. He even did a *stage* at the prestigious Lycée Jules Garnier."

"Strange name for a high school." I was distracted by Cluny telling me Spud lived not far from Ravella. "Anything to do with the cosmetic company?"

"D'oh, dummy! Jules Garnier was this amazing engineer and explorer, the instigator of nickel mining in New Cal."

Then Cluny did an odd thing. She grabbed my hand, dug her nails so hard into my flesh that I began to regret having brought up the subject of her and Spud. This chick had issues. Why was she so tense at the mention of his name? And did she think Spud was a spunk?

Chantal wore her hair in two fluffy bunches on her shoulders. Yawning, she opened a stainless steel cupboard, and extracted a basket filled with brushes and cleaning fluids. She set off, missionary dress swaying. Yawning again, she climbed the stairs.

Locking eyeballs with Cluny, I hissed, "What's going on?"

"It's her!"

"Whaddya mean? Who's 'her'?"

"Spud is in love with Chantal. It's the reason he comes to New Cal so often."

"No way!" Though it explained why Spud wasn't bothered about Chantal seeing him toke on a joint in the kitchen, and all that stuff about him not believing in lines and boxes and borders. "Does Jacques Forestier know?"

"Don't imagine, or he'd chuck a mental."

I recalled Marcel Manet's letter regarding Jacques Forestier and his attitude towards Sandrine's Kanak partner. "Yeah, I know he's very racist."

"How do you know?"

Still not ready to tell Cluny that Jacques Forestier might be my grandfather, I said, "Just guessed." I pushed strands of uncombed hair away from my face. "You know, the size of the house sort of, like, says he'd be, um, ultra conservative."

Cluny gave me a funny look.

I wanted to know more about Flex. "Is Flex du Lac Australian, too?"

"Flex is from FNQ, Far North Queensland, near Mission Beach."

"His name sounds French."

"His great-grandfather, a Kanaka, came from these parts. He was blackbirded." Cluny saw my confused expression. "You know, kidnapped, taken into slavery and put to work in the sugarcane fields of Queensland."

"How awful! Doesn't he have problems coming back to New Cal?"

Cluny pursed her lips.

"Just kidding."

"Flex is a fabbo guy." She glanced at her narrow, tasteful watch. "Well, must go, or I'll be late."

"*Your* surname?" I was still hanging out for a chat. "Belpomme, does that mean your parents are French?"

"My dad's family was French, way back, but not me."

"Not you?"

"I'm adopted."

My jaw dropped. "Have you ever tried to find your mum?"

"No need. Dell Belpomme's my mum. She's the one who was desperate for a daughter after four sons, who fed me in the middle of the night, changed my nappy, looked after me when I was sick, and rubbed Vicks on my chest." Her eyes bored into mine. "When I got older, she worried about me when I came home late. Still cares. Always will care." Cluny sounded angry.

"Even if you do drugs? Does she still care then?"

"Like you, I don't do drugs, despite what you may have thought." Her eyes remained steady. "Except when I tried the chewable aspirin thing, and my dad caught me. I was *so* ashamed."

"How did your mum react then?"

"She was very supportive."

"Have you discovered your birth mother's whereabouts?"

"Why would I want to find my birth mother? I know the sort of person *she* was. My natural mum was a patient of my dad's and I can find her any time, but I choose not to." Cluny sounded *really* angry now. "Put it this way, she wouldn't have a *clue* about the identity of my natural father."

"Isn't it important to know about your origins?"

"My dad has all the information he needs for medical purposes." A pause. "I don't need to use the Post Adoptive Resource Centre. It's all there in a sealed envelope, *if* I wish to open it. I can, but I never *will* open it. My olds are too special."

I was glad Cluny felt so grounded about her place in the world. I was about to blurt out everything, fill her in about my own search. But her next comment stopped me.

"Like, never forget! Your mum is the person who brought you up!"

She waved a pretty finger at me, swooped up papers from the side table and marched to the front door. A swish, as she shrugged on her rain gear.

I sat there feeling guilty. Big time. Cluny's words rolled around in my head: *your mum is the person who brought you up.*

I remembered Namilly shafting her spade into the soil before I left. "Sewage," she'd said—and all those things which had sounded spazzo at the time. Should I take a leaf out of Cluny's book, forget about searching for information on my past as I had planned? Just be thankful Namilly was there when I was growing up?

I decided not to poke around 1, rue de la Guillotine, decided instead to prepare for my Monday morning class at Oriel Lycée by sorting out the flashcards in my carry bag.

Chapter 18

Chantal was busy polishing light switches in the hallway when I reached the top of the stairs. Which seemed odd. Okay, the switches were made of brass. But I'd never seen anyone polish light switches before. And, due to the darkness caused by the tropical downpour, the hall lights were blazing.

Closing my bedroom door, I decided to take a shower before preparing for Monday's classes. I was still feeling yucky from the trip, and the eccy, and Rocky's less-than-salubrious car.

First, I decided to touch base with Stefan. (We had agreed not to phone one another as I'd have to pay for incoming calls as well as outgoing calls, under the international roaming system.) I typed in my cost effective SMS:

wassup with u?

1 message received flashed back. I pressed *Show. Opening message* wiggled its blue line. His words were the same:

bill einstein still sik

Speculating that it really must be THE END for Win's horse, I pulled open the cupboard door to grab some clean clothing. My eyes latched onto a faded kiddy transfer. Examining the transfer closely, I was able to make out the image of Idéfix, Obélix's dog in the Astérix comic books. Apparently I wasn't the only fan of Astérix. Or had this room been a nursery? *My nursery?*

Extracting a blue G-string—to go under a matching day-glo tube skirt—from the pile in the knickers basket, I wrapped the towel around me, picked up my sponge bag and set off down the passage.

Chantal was no longer there.

Placing my things on the bathroom scales and loosening my French plait, I noticed chipped enamel on the inside of the bath. A container of crystals labelled *La Soude Caustique* sat on the floor nearby. Left there by Chantal? I turned on the taps, gushing water into the bath.

I eased the shower knob into position. The pipes shuddered as water spurted through the pinprick holes overhead. The bath was deep and old-fashioned. I clambered in, standing in my own rainstorm. It felt great to soak the dirt from my pores, while I coated my body with soap lather. I'd never had a shower where bathwater lapped across the arch of my foot—a sort of double-cleansing.

As I shampooed my hair, I could feel the water rise up to my ankles. What an amazing shower! The water kept rising and I kept soaping. Before I knew it, I was calf-deep in bathwater. Should I have used those crystals sitting on the bathroom floor? I wondered. Slung them down the drain first?

Soon the bath was seriously full, and beginning to look like Ravella Memorial Pool. I turned off the taps, swung my legs over the edge and watched as the water continued to rise. Was this phenomenon caused by the rain, some sort of storm water problem? Or was this a normal occurrence? Panicking, I looked for a bucket—or any receptacle for transferring water into the hand basin, to free it, to allow it to chug off down the S-bend.

I could see nothing.

Panting with anxiety, I rubbed myself dry and dragged on my G-string. Should I go for help? I asked myself. Although, what about …? I eyed the leather seat on the antique scales. Was it detachable? With a heave I managed to twist the seat off, and found it was hollow.

Using my makeshift bucket, I began to bail. I carried water from the bath, tipped it down the basin and saw it flow away nicely. I was chuffed by my ingenuity. While bailing, I noticed the seat dripping about the edges. I kept on. The bathwater was still rising, and I was now struggling to keep up. I noticed the water in the hand basin was rising, also. Uh-oh, the basin was blocked.

Wrapping my towel around me, I fled to find help.

"Chantal?" I shouted. With my wet hair flying, I dashed down the hallway. Chantal was nowhere to be seen.

As I scampered back into the bathroom there was an almighty roar, a humungous gurgle, a stupendous slurp. With a whoosh and a splash the soapy water vanished down the plughole. Stickier than I'd been before my shower, I stood there sweating. I placed the scales seat right way up on its metal frame.

Saggy with relief, I set off for my bedroom to get dressed and go over my flashcards for Monday's classes. As I passed Spud's bedroom, I heard snoring and pushed open the door.

Chantal lay curled up on Spud's bed. Out to it.

Chapter 19

Wondering if Chantal would be sacked if she was caught in Spud's bed, I hauled my Bridget B studded T-shirt over my head and wriggled into a pair of rodeo hipster jeans. (I planned to wear the day-glo tube skirt that went with my G-string to the nakamal that night.)

Sitting cross-legged on the floor, I spread my flashcards around me. With my hair drying under the clanking waft of the ceiling fan, I considered my cards. Which would be most appropriate for my first class at Oriel Lycée?

Stacks of topics were earmarked for discussion. *'Kangaroo cull'*, my favourite, was bound to get them stirred up. I liked *'Aquaculture'*, too—having read they farmed prawns in New Caledonia, even exporting them to Australia. I thumbed through *'Greenhouse effect'*, *'Mining on coral reefs'*, *'Land degradation'* and *'Over-fishing in the Pacific'*. Over-fishing was important; half the world's total tuna catch was taken out of the Pacific Ocean each year. *'Rodeos'* was good, as well —perfect for talking about cross-cultural ties, which could lead on to arguing about the merits of RM Williams boots and Ford pick-up trucks.

Inscribing the matching words in French on the back of the flashcards, I began to write *'Le massacre des kangourous'* on the reverse side of the *'Kangaroo cull'* card. The pen was dry—odd in this weather. I pressed down hard. Ink spurted out. Uh-oh. A humungous blot had leaked onto the centre of the card. I turned the card over. Rats! The blot was seeping through, blurring the word 'cull'. I had to replace the card, find a lightweight one that wouldn't flop as I held it up. Even good quality paper would do.

Where to go? The rain was thundering, rocketing down outside, making a terrible din. It was not the weather for exploring. And were there shops in Val Plaisance? I hadn't seen any the previous evening; only clubs and restaurants on the Baie des Citrons and Anse Vata tourist strips. Scratching my head, I worked out that I'd really only become acquainted with a casino and a nakamal since arriving here. And neither was likely to have what I needed. Chantal? She was passed out on Spud's bed.

The answer came to me: *Jacques Forestier's library*. Spare paper was bound to be lying around in a library. *Would I dare to trespass?* Jelly-kneed, I decided to go there.

Stomach churning in apprehension, I pushed my hair into a ponytail and set off down the stairs to the landing on the first floor. No light shone beneath the crack of the door into the library. A positive sign. I wouldn't be forced to confront Jacques Forestier. (He sounded scary.) I could fossick on my own, and see if I could find anything else of interest while I looked for a sheet of paper, or card.

Inching the door open, I reeled back from the smell of stale cigars, overlaid with the pong of French cigarettes. But the clean smell of polished leather was more welcoming. I crept inside. The room had a dank feel. I flicked on the switch. A door at the far end of the mahogany-panelled room was closed. *Where did that lead? Was another room connected to the library?*

Groaning shelves of tomes towered above me, like a weight of learned thought. Had Jacques Forestier read all these books? Or were they purchased simply for their value? My eyes scanned the spines of leather-bound *Bibliothèque de la Pléiad* editions by Gallimard. I saw Émile Zola's *Les Rougon-Macquart*. Laclos' *Œvres complètes*—I'd seen the film *Les Liaisons Dangereuses* recently on the telly. Fourteen volumes of *À la recherche du temps perdu* sat neatly arranged, from *Du côté de chez Swann* to *Le temps retrouvé*. Then *Tomes 1 à 111 (complet)* Paris Gallimard, 1947.

These books were worth a bomb.

Combray was there, too, in a cloth-covered hardback. The only volume I'd read of Proust, and that had been a struggle. I pulled the book out carefully. Sandrine Forestier was written on the flyleaf in blue ink. My heart paddled at seeing the woman I believed to be my birth mother's name. My fingers fumbled. Stiff-jointed, I slotted the book back into place.

A heap of thumbed paperbacks lay on a leather divan—torn, dirty and well-read. The titles mostly concerned dogs and the *élevage* of deer. Mud smears soiled the cover of one. A strange stain. *Was that dried blood*? A shiver went through me. I forced myself to keep looking.

The outside shutters were closed, making the room gloomy. Under the window was an oak partner's desk on an Aubusson rug, in foliage colours. The handles of the desk were in the shape of lion masks, carved in the same wood. A computer sat on the rectangular leather-lined, fleur-de-lis embossed top. A baronial chair was pushed back, to one side, as if someone had left in a rush. A chaise longue, also in leather, with a matching gentleman's chair, gave off an odour of fresh wax. It was obvious that Chantal did more than cook bougna, polish switches and hit on Spud.

I pulled out the bottom drawer on the left-hand side of the desk. A mound of folders containing legal papers confronted me. I flicked open the middle drawer. More folders. The top drawer? Only bills, mostly concerning farm products.

So far, there was nothing of interest. Nor had I found spare paper for me to use as a flashcard, not even a business envelope that I could write on. Next, I pulled at the centre drawer directly beneath the desktop. Stuck. I gave it a heave. The drawer refused to budge. Locked, perhaps? Grasping a plastic cylinder of paperclips, I fished one out and straightened it. Poked the paperclip in the keyhole and jiggled. Pulled on the handle again. The drawer was definitely locked, and locked drawers always made me hang out to discover their contents.

A silver letter opener sat beside the paperclip cylinder, slim and pointy like a dagger. I poked the letter opener into the keyhole. Turned it back and forth. Up and down. About to do the back and forth thing once more, I heard a click. Gripping the lion mask, I eased the drawer open. A framed photo lay face up inside the drawer. This was the same couple I'd seen on the walnut table in the house on Ti Point. Yves-Laurent and

Sandrine smiled at me. I gulped as I looked, feeling my throat go rigid. Were they really my birth parents? Marcel's words flooded back: "You is ze one." *But was I?* If so, why did Sandrine not want to see me? "Never again," her partner had told me.

Gulping back tears, I looked around. No other photos were on the desk, or perched on the shelves beside the books. Not one baby photo. This scene was weird, and I regretting having snuck into Jacques Forestier's library. It brought back unwanted feelings, the 'is she, isn't she' thoughts that kept me awake at night. I should take a leaf out of Cluny's book, I told myself. My mum was Namilly. I should accept it and move on. Get a life. Go home to Ravella, as soon as I'd finished my work-experience programme.

I was preparing to close the drawer when another legal document slid from beneath the photo. (Jacques Forestier's life seemed to be dominated by legal documents.)

I attempted to ease the drawer back in but it wobbled, and then stuck. Had the humidity caused that? I lifted the drawer into position, pushed again. Still stuck. Uh-oh, a locked drawer found open in Jacques Forestier's library would mean we'd all be lined up that night and questioned—probably by Pascal Manet. I shoved as hard as I could, but the framed photo slid further, until … *I found myself gazing at my mum's handwriting.*

Namilly Perrier's firm, rounded signature was almost as familiar as my own. (I had forged it often over the years.)

Shivering with tension, I edged the document out. The word *PROCURATION* flashed like a neon sign. I was holding a Power of Attorney written in French. I tried to make sense of the words, which appeared to involve the child, Geneviève Bas Salaire de Lyon. The safety and wellbeing of the infant had been handed over to the *nounou*'s care for the duration of hostilities in *le Département d'Outre-Mer de Nouvelle-Calédonie.*

And the *nounou*'s name: NAMILLY PERRIER.

My eyes raced back and forth over the words: *agir par procuration.* Sandrine Bas Salaire de Lyon's signature was there, too. This was no Consent to Adoption Order. It seemed Sandrine had signed away any responsibility for the welfare of her daughter. Blown away thinking about it, I managed to joggle the drawer back into place. My fingers were sweating. My head was sweating. My whole body was sweating. A knob rattled, as if someone was having trouble opening the door. *The door at the end of the room!*

A walking stick poked through the gap.

A twisted hand grasped a carved cagou bird. Heavy breathing.

Skidding from the library, I hurled the door onto the landing shut behind me. My legs seemed to be running up and down on the spot. I got traction. I leapt up the stairs two at a time, heading for my bedroom, hoping Jacques Forestier hadn't seen me.

Chapter 20

Gasping, I fell into my room, knowing I'd stumbled across evidence that Sandrine was my birth mother. All the proof I needed was there in the Procuration document. Forget about the DNA tests. The whole tacky affair was written down, sitting in a locked drawer in Jacques Forestier's library.

I felt like blubbing. A hiccup rose in my throat. *If she didn't want me, I didn't want her.* Soon I was weeping. I curled up on the bed in the foetal position, and sobbed and sobbed until my bedroom was almost as damp on the inside as the outside of the house.

My nose became blocked. I climbed off the bed and grabbed a tissue from my backpack. As I began to blow, the mobile phone burped. *1 message received.* I sighed. Hopefully Stefan had more interesting news than the same old stuff about Bill Einstein. I pressed *Show*.

Bienvenue dans la vie de Nouméa. Marcel

Sniffing, I boggled at this message. How did Marcel Manet know my mobile number? It was recently acquired, and I barely remembered the number myself. In Ravella, he had told me he guessed my email address. But telephone numbers?

Curled up on the bed again, I tried to work out how to reply. Should I tell him I'd just discovered Sandrine signed my life away? I decided not to, figuring he probably knew of the Procuration's existence.

My mind was scrambled like knotted string. I lay there until my lids became heavy and the rain pattered, and spat, and chattered and, finally, began to drum full bore again. I heard no thunder, only this ongoing avalanche of water. The noise was soothing. Comforting. A sort of certainty…

☆

A voice echoing in the passage jerked me awake.

"The seat of those fantabulous antique scales is dripping from the *inside*, a soapy extrusion. But dry on top. How very *X-Files!* Do you think the house is haunted?" said Cluny.

My new friends had returned from their work experience programmes, and discovered the mess I'd created.

"You could slip." Jazz's voice was disapproving.

They stood in the passage talking.

"That Philosophy teacher is a fully sick bro in those chinos." Cluny paused, and continued, "I'm so desperately in need of a facial in this climate. Back home, I go with my mum at least once a month."

My eyelids felt like superglue from the crying, but they bulged as I tried to imagine visiting a beauty parlour with Namilly. Their voices lowered to a hoarse whisper. I heard my name mentioned.

"Genna could do with a few streaks to take away that severe look." Cluny cleared her throat. "She's out-of-sight cute, though, a serious dudette if she fixed up her hair."

My insides squirmed with embarrassment.

"Yeah. Genna could be wicked," said Jazz. "And that reminds me, I wonder if Chantal has an iron. I could straighten your hair for this evening."

"I'm not too sure it works with an ordinary iron." Cluny seemed doubtful. "What about the edges? You could burn my face."

"Oh, I wouldn't do the bits around your face." Jazz sounded shocked. "Just the long bits, which I'd place over a towel. Wanna give it a try?"

"It could look kinda weird." Cluny's voice faded as she descended the stairs with Jazz. "Did I tell you Timothy's gonna have a baby? Stunning. I'll be this crazy aunty." Her laugh trilled upwards.

My Swatch read 4.45 pm. Rocky was due to pick me up.

I had fifteen minutes in which to get dressed.

Chapter 21

Cluny called out, "Oh, wow, you look good!" as I closed the front door behind me. I was nervous about going anywhere without my passport. I patted the pocket of my jacket to make sure it was still there.

No sign of Rocky. I pulled out my mobile phone to acknowledge Marcel's text message. After the constant pounding, the rain had stopped, but there was no sun. Only stillness. A silence, as if the birds had flown elsewhere.

The broken pipe over the front door slurped, and then made a grating noise. Without warning, it vomited water over my arm, drenching my mobile. My special floral phone slipped from my grasp and landed in the centre of a potted cycad palm. I pulled it out, pricking my finger on the spiky leaves in the process.

I sucked my forefinger, gave the phone a shake with my left hand and pressed the On button. The screen lit up in a weird way, with a sort of tinkle. I hit *Reply*. Nothing. My mobile, the only connection I had with those I loved in Ravella, was waterlogged. *Would the phone work after it dried out?*

I was wondering about this when I heard Pierrot the Peugeot grunting up the hill. The car turned into the drive and Rocky threw open the passenger door. I ran, hanging onto my day-glo tube skirt. Gathering my legs together in mini-peril mode, I slid in beside him.

Kinky Reggae was playing on the car radio.

"You're looking very trendy, Genna. Well, for a night out in a naka-mal. My independence friends will be impressed." He lifted his hand from the wheel and pointed at my hair. "Your plait looks different, too. It's great. Much less severe."

Not admitting I'd done my hair in a rush, now curly round my face from having been wept on, I said, *"Merci beaucoup!"* and went beetroot.

Rocky, in a different beanie (ragged on the crown this time), wore a trendy jacket and clean jeans. "How are you finding the other *stagi-aires*? Getting on well with 'em?" He looked at me.

"They're just the best." I attempted to sound like Cluny Belpomme with her swish private school voice. "Not a bit stuck up, even though they're from brand-e sorts of schools. I'm not sure about Flex. I haven't met him yet."

"Brand-e schools?" He raised an eyebrow. Bob Marley changed his song.

"Cluny wears Hispanitas Mary Janes and Indigo, and her father's a doctor in Sydney. At first I thought she was a derrbrain, but she's there for me and she's not boring, and I can talk to her and trust her. She's not bossy like Jazz."

The radio announcer interrupted *I Shot the Sheriff.* A voice, agitated, announced: *"Alerte Orange."* Rocky twisted the knob to increase the volume. *"Niveau trois,"* said the weatherman.

"Merde, this weather's starting to look serious. It seems Liliane has decided to pay us a visit, but probably tomorrow."

"Shouldn't we go back so I can, um, hide in the bath or something?" I was terrified at the thought of finding myself in the eye of a cyclone.

Rocky burst out laughing. *"Non, ça va.* Worry when it becomes *Alerte Rouge, niveau quatre.* You'd never do anything in this place if you bothered about cyclones. Have a drink of kava." He pushed up his sleeve, and scratched at his arm. "You won't worry about a thing!"

"Is your rash caused by drinking too much kava?" I blurted, remembering Spud's lecture about side effects.

"There are ants on our poingo bananas. I must've brushed against them. We have bunchy top, one of the perils of my *terroir.*"

"Right." I didn't know whether to believe him. "Bunchy top sounds like a serious disease."

"It is. Bunchy top costs us lots of dollars, meaning we have to rely on the kava. If anything happened to our pepper trees, we would be in big trouble."

The radio announcer sounded excited as we whirled, and chugged, and coughed around streets on our way into the city.

Out of the blue, Rocky said, "What's wrong, Genna?"

"Whaddya mean 'what's wrong'?" Tears began to well again. "There's nothing wrong."

"You've been crying." He took his hand off the wheel and ran his finger above my cheekbone, just beneath my lower lid. "Your mascara's smudged, too."

I was startled that he'd noticed. "Um …"

"You get on well with the others at 1, rue de la Guillotine, so what is it? Boyfriend problems? Family problems?" He gave an impatient sigh. "I know what it's like. I bawled for weeks when my *maman* left. Papa was beside himself. It was hell for a while."

"Yes, but did your father sign a piece of paper saying your mother had the legal right to take your sister. Not only that, but to keep her?"

Rocky stared. "Separation doesn't work like that. Well, not usually."

"No, I guess it doesn't for most people." I decided to ask him about Sandrine.

He changed gears. "Sandrine was a lot older than me. I only ever heard about her, mainly from Pascal, who was crazy about her. He used to hang around the Forestier place after the soldier she married passed away from dengue." He smiled. "Pascal was many years younger than Sandrine. She would have thought him a kid. Since I lived in the Brousse, I never got to meet her. I don't think she would've been interested in a simple kava farmer, no matter what age."

The French examiner used to be keen on Sandrine? It seemed everyone had been crazy about Sandrine. I made a mental note to stop obsessing about the woman I now knew to be my biological mother.

"Wait a minute!" Rocky burst out. "I remember. They said Sandrine fled to Australia with her baby and nanny during the Events." He frowned. "I heard she met up with a Kanak over there, a mining company employee."

I changed the subject. "You didn't bring Belle tonight?"

"She'd have been in the way."

The interior of the car was steaming up. Pearls of sweat formed on Rocky's forehead. *So why did he insist on wearing a beanie in this humidity?* I wondered. Wriggling out of my jacket, I tucked it carefully in the corner of the back seat.

Plumes of smoke reared into the sky from the nickel smelter to the north as we entered the city of Noumea. As I fiddled with my mobile phone, pressing buttons to get it started, I felt the car shudder more than usual. A howling gust of wind picked the car up, sending us hurtling towards the side of the road.

Rocky steered into the skid, setting us back on course. The rosary beads swung, and I exhaled.

"Don't worry," said Rocky. "These squalls will stop."

"Are you sure it's safe?" I still felt edgy. "Perhaps you should take me back home where I can find shelter."

"Too late. We're here now." Rocky grumbled the car into the kerb. He pulled on the handbrake and climbed out. "The nakamal is just down there in the Latin Quarter." He indicated a street lined with gloomy shopfronts. "Noah's!"

Linking my little finger with his, he led me along the narrow, sloping footpath. Rainwater rushed in the gutter alongside, threatening to spill over onto my beaded thongs. Despite Rocky being way more sophisticated and hipper than me, this felt like a date. Was I being unfaithful to Stefan?

"Noah's the nakamal king in town," Rocky said over his shoulder, "but he's originally from Vanuatu. And that's the sign they use in that country to show kava is sold in the establishment."

He jerked his head at the pink bulb drooping over the doorway.

Chapter 22

Inside Noah's, to the left of the entrance, was a narrow stainless steel trough; to the right a birdcage housed a sulphur-crested cockatoo. A Major Mitchell parrot perched in a huddle of pink and grey in the corner of the second cage, beneath a spotlight. A bloated boa constrictor lay in a pretzel tangle in a third cage, motionless and stinking.

Rocky walked me through a sea of stools, like giant wicker cotton reels—no sawn-off logs for seats in this establishment—as we headed for a bar carved with tropical birds and sea serpents. The guy behind the bar, clad in a cyclamen missionary dress, appeared to be doing his laundry in a tub of dirty water. Squeezing and rubbing. Rubbing and squeezing.

"Meet Noah," said Rocky. "He's preparing our kava, and, as you probably recall, it *does* taste as bad as it looks."

"Bienvenue," Noah whispered

The nakamal owner's shoulder-length hair glistened with smelly grease. He followed up his greeting with a high-pitched giggle as he recommended torturing the piece of woven fabric. Noah, with hairless arms and gross lips, was like a towering washerwoman. A gap between his teeth sparked a kaleidoscope of colours when he smiled. With a shock, I realised it was a diamond. He lifted a muddy finger from the tub, touched the gem and chuckled, *"Mon diamant heureux!"* Gazing at his happy diamond, I knew that this nakamal was vastly different from Tibou's.

I could see no 'No Dogs, No Drugs' sign.

A row of tiny mother-of-pearl jewellery boxes was ranged on a shelf behind Noah. The ceiling fan went ackety, ackety, zoof. Noah's hair aroma—like the Invasion of the Body Odours—seemed to spread beneath the blades until it took over the hairs in my nostrils. I resisted the urge to pinch the end of my nose.

Rocky must've seen my nasal twitch. "Noah oils his hair with cocoa butter," he whispered, and then added, "and that's his partner, Kyanthia." He pointed to a guy in a gleaming chocolate trench coat. "Don't be deceived by his youthful appearance. I've had a few run-ins with that one, particularly regarding my product."

Kyanthia rustled round the room, exchanging one-liners with customers. It didn't seem as if *he'd* drunk any kava that evening; he looked wired.

Rocky led me to a woven curtain hanging at the rear. "Some of my independence friends are from the north-east coast, and people from that region don't smile a lot. Don't be worried. It doesn't mean they don't like you." He nodded. "Kanaks believe the group is more important than the individual."

A spitting sound erupted. I turned. A guy in a floral shirt, holding his coconut shell in his left hand, was hawking the residue of his kava into the trough inside the entrance. He hastily swallowed from a glass of water in his right hand.

"Berk!" squawked the sulphur-crested cockatoo, and made throw-up noises.

"Some drink kava that way," Rocky murmured, "and it doesn't mean the kava's not good quality, just that the effect is quicker if you gulp it down, following up with water. The taste isn't so bad, then." He pointed at the trough. "It's a sort of spittoon, I s'pose."

Behind the pandanus curtain was a small room with a bench running along each wall. I was confronted by a sea of dreads; I'd never seen so many dreadlocks before. Long fat dreads framed strong black faces. The only woman present wore a cowgirl strapless dress. The men were clad in short-sleeved shirts banded with green, red and gold stripes.

The woman in the strapless dress smiled at me. Her hair was tipped and spiky.

"Josiane?" said Rocky. "Meet Genna."

"Bienvenue!" Josiane switched to English. "Welcome, Genna."

I fiddled with my French plait.

"My friends," Rocky announced in a loud voice, "I'd like to introduce Genna Perrier, here to do work experience at Oriel Lycée."

One of the men grinned. The others gave me an up-and-down-and-once-over look and went on chatting.

The curtain swished shut, and swished back open. Kyanthia made a hook sign with his index finger.

"Viens!" he said, ordering Rocky to go with him.

"Excusez-moi." Rocky glanced at the others. "Sorry," he whispered in my ear, "but this is business." He closed the pandanus curtain behind him.

Josiane, in a cloud of chichi perfume, patted a space on the bench, indicating I should sit beside her. Hugging my day-glo tube skirt to me, I sat down.

The conversation was in intermittent bites of lazy, island French. *Had Yannick Boudaou, a fierce-looking dude, just mentioned planning to destroy the fibre optic cable up the west coast of the island?* Or had I imagined it? My spoken French was a long way from perfect.

"The government gives an eighty per cent subsidy for any new development," Josiane said clearly in French, "which is quite an incentive for attracting new business to Grande Terre. Can we continue to offer that when we break away from France?"

Yannick again: "Two Airbuses come in from New Zealand every week with our fresh vegetables. We could destroy the landing strip."

Yowee, I'd understood that, too. *Was this group planning to hold the residents of New Caledonia hostage?* A shiver shot through me. Was I meant to be hearing this stuff? Would they kill me later, because I'd overheard their plans? Or had I not fully comprehended what they were saying?

The Invasion of the Body Odours pong preceded Noah. He pulled back the pandanus curtain. On the other side of the curtain, I saw Rocky arguing with Kyanthia. Another patron spat the residue of his kava into the steel trough. The cockatoo yelled, *"Berk!"* and made more spew noises.

Noah, holding a carved presentation bowl in one hand and coconut shells in the other, placed the kava in the centre of the table between the benches. He dipped the shell into the muddy liquid, now becoming clear, and passed me my shell before serving the others.

Sipping, I managed to stop gagging from the bitter taste just before my tongue went numb. The feeling of clarity and calm swept over me and, all of a sudden, it was logical to be talking about cutting fibre optic cables and stopping planes carrying the weekly fresh food from New Zealand from landing. We were drinking from the pepper tree.

The rain continued to pelt down outside, but I didn't give a toss. I was relaxed when the wind began to shriek. Holding my shell of kava, the perfect raw vegan drink, I felt secure.

Josiane's voice seemed to come from a great distance. "They're called breasts," she said in English.

"What are?" I was startled, but sanguine.

"The legs of the presentation bowl are called breasts. Aren't they beautiful? And this kava, which must be from one of the old trees, is of excellent quality."

The legs of the bowl *were* elegant, but I was afraid to speak in case my tongue went funny and refused to articulate the words. My mind was crystal clear from having drunk 'excellent quality' kava, and I noticed Yannick Boudaou hanging on every syllable Josiane uttered.

Rocky re-entered the room. Looking thoughtful, he sat down. He remained silent as the others waffled on about AK 47s, and cutting communications, and stopping food from entering, and even preventing the docking of refrigerated container ships all the way from Singapore.

"Vive la Kanaky!" A fist punched the air. Long live the Kanak state!

This scene was wild. Yet, with the power of kava, it seemed normal for them to be talking like this. The kava bowl emptied. Outside the wind shrieked louder, and I felt like I never wanted to move again. I was happy to sit on this bench drinking kava for the rest of my life.

Rocky stood up. *"On y va?"* He pulled at my hand. "Let's go, Genna. I have things to attend to."

One man yawned. Another stretched. A third looked indifferent. Yannick Boudaou continued to gaze at Josiane. They sat there, talking about the frozen—*gelé?*—electoral roll.

Passing the no longer smiling, but still on-the-nose Noah, Rocky indicated the row of mother-of-pearl boxes on the shelf behind the nakamal owner. "He keeps a fingernail in each box, one from each grower who duds him," he hissed.

My jaw went slack at the thought of having one's fingernail removed. *Would that mean having your whole digit chopped off?* The sulphur-crested cockatoo went *"Berk!"* The bird with the pink and grey feathers remained huddled in the corner of its cage.

No sign of Kyanthia.

The stench of the boa constrictor (still dozing) seemed to cling to my clothes as we went into the street. The night was dark, and I stood beneath the glow of the droopy pink bulb, mesmerised by the rain tumbling and bucking.

"You wait here." Rocky picked at the edge of his beanie.

Would he take it off at last?

"I've got problems. Kyanthia claims K-Mel's been diluting our dried kava, says he's been adding flour to increase the bulk. I'm worried Noah will send his hoons to rough up Papa. I must return to the Brousse."

"But Josiane said the kava we drank was 'excellent quality'."

"The kava Noah served us was from the roots of a fifteen-year-old tree. The roots are okay; my old man can't fiddle with those. The powdered stuff's the problem. And he'll get us both killed if he doesn't watch out."

With the clarity of kava I noticed holes in Rocky's beanie, right above the rolled back rim. Fear began to take over my inner calm. *Was Rocky in fact wearing a balaclava? And if so, what was he planning to do?* Honest people didn't wear balaclavas.

As if in a fog, I heard him say, "You wait for the others here, Genna. It's out of the rain, and they shouldn't be too long." His sun-kissed face looked pale. "Josiane will give you a lift back to your accommodation."

He ran off, heading in the direction of his car. As he went he rolled down the brim of his beanie, until his face and neck were covered.

Through the din of the sheeting rain, I heard the smooth, rich sound of windscreen wipers. A Mercedes with tinted windows cruised along the other side of the road. Headlights blinded me as the vehicle did a U-turn.

Chapter 23

Remembering my jacket, still in Rocky's car, I yelled, "Rocky? Wait!" and began to run.

A car door clicked open behind me. The air choked in my throat as someone shoved me between my shoulder blades, landing on my body and pinning me down. My thongs flew off as I hit the pavement. The Latin Quarter lit up. My mind rotated in a whirligig of heat and noise, until the hairs on my arms were electric. I heard a boom from the direction of Rocky's vehicle. Was it the cyclone?

And who was pinning me down?

Kicking out, I tried to get the person off me. My head was burning. My face was stinging. My knees grated. Hank's face flashed before me. Or was it Spud's? I only knew a bogan was grinding me into the ground and I couldn't breathe. The air was filled with rainy soot, the soil was melting and I was wrapped in the five elements—fire, water, earth, air and ether. And the male weight remained on top of me.

Hank's face morphed into Spud's and back again.

Seagulls began to squawk. My mind was back in Ravella, with dirt in my mouth, fighting for my life among the ti-tree bushes.

"Get off me, get off me, get off me," I yelled as I kicked and fought.

Before I could die of shame, the heat faded to cold and silence.

Through a deep mist and a reek of burning, I heard running. Sirens and whistles. The swish of a missionary dress. Noah's soft voice burst into a parrot's cry: *Keee-aarnttt-eee-aah.* The sound echoed through the air as I was bundled into the back seat of a limousine. *"Vite! Vite! Vite!"* a man said softly. The tang of new leather took over from the scorch smell as the vehicle swayed around curves. The wind wailed, and the rain beat down to the *slap, slap, slap* of the windscreen wipers. I clung to the edge of the seat, shivering and unable to see.

My head hurt, and my knees felt sore and scraped as the realisation trundled through my mind: *I was being kidnapped.*

Everything became red and spotty and fragmented as I passed out again.

The dreams began—kava dreams and snapshots. I was hanging upside down, with my nose buried in a starched shirt. I could smell French cigarettes, mixed with a whiff of aftershave. Footsteps echoed on metal steps. Round and round and round. My head spun. Was this a circular staircase? My ears rang with the clang sound. Bump, bump, bump. The slam of a door. More stairs. So many stairs. The wind howled, and I was being imprisoned in a tower. Up, up, up went the steps, and the wind screamed and the house shook and a tree somewhere made slashing noises.

Someone is dabbing my hands with antiseptic, which stings, sticking strips around fingers and knees. Namilly used to do that. "Kiss it better with a Band-Aid strip," she'd say. Only she never used to be so clumsy, and she never smelled of French cigarettes. She must've taken up smoking. Not a good idea with that wheeze of hers. I detect aftershave, too. Is she wearing aftershave because of Alice? Namilly cares about Alice. It's the reason she stank of pee for a while. Only Alice is dead, and Namilly doesn't smell like that anymore. A candle is burning somewhere, and I can't breathe because it's using up oxygen. We only have candles in Ravella when the power is off, and you don't need candles in heaven. But I'll be home soon. Just as soon as I climb out of this white cloud that's shuddering and hemming me in.

Chapter 24

The creak of a cane chair woke me. I heard a rippled snore, followed by galvanized iron cartwheeling along a road. Windows rattled, and dogs barked in the distance as light crept into the room. The light penetrated my eyelids like white-hot arrows, pierced my pupils as if I had no lids. My eyes oozed and stung as I opened them.

Blindly, I peered at the sea of white above me, spread like a soft ceiling that ebbed and flowed, creating shifting clouds over my head. Had I died? Was this heaven? If so, there'd been no release from the pain. My body was sore and aching. My throat was parched, and it hurt to swallow. My legs were leaden and heavy, and it was an effort to stretch. I kept still, trying to work out where I was.

Soon I realised I was in a strange bed, covered with a doona. The tip of my nose was cold from the air-conditioning, and I could feel the familiar whoosh of a ceiling fan. It was a smooth whoosh this time—unlike like the offbeat clank of the fan at 1, rue de la Guillotine. Was I in a hospital somewhere? (But the person in the chair was a man; male nurses were rare, and they didn't usually fall asleep while on duty.) The white clouds overhead? On closer inspection the clouds were mosquito netting.

My right eyebrow felt singed and stubbly. More hair was hanging out of my French plait than in it. The strands smelled of smoke.

My clothing seemed strange. My fingers were awkward as I felt around beneath the covers to check. I appeared to be wearing an over-sized shirt. Where were my own clothes? Where were my tube skirt and studded top? A spurt of fear ran through me. Had I been raped? I didn't think so. That was the only part of my body not hurting. A question thundered through my brain: *Who had undressed me?*

Remembering the incident outside Noah's, I knew for certain I'd been kidnapped. By whom, I had no idea. And I didn't know why. But I knew I'd been snatched.

Peering through gummy lids, I tried to get a good look at the man shape, lolled sideways in a cane chair with his head thrown back. Who was he? And why had I been having weird nightmares about Spud? This person's jaw was clean-shaven.

A newspaper fluttered on the floor beside a burnt-down candle, the pages stirred up by the overhead ceiling fan. Squinting through the net-ting, I saw a screaming headline:

Attentat—deux morts dans le Quartier Latin

There had been a terrorist attack in the Latin Quarter, with two people killed. I recalled a deafening bang, just as I was thrown to the ground by a heavy man. The man in the cane chair? And had Pierrot the Peugeot exploded? A bad feeling ran through me. Had Rocky been one of those killed? And who was the other casualty? A passer-by? Or one of Rocky's independence mates?

My eyes, already sticky, became stickier with held back tears. *I couldn't stand it if Rocky had died*, I told myself. But I had no proof he had been killed. And it was important to control my feelings. If I wasn't careful, I'd develop hiccups and wake the man in the cane chair.

The hiccups sank back as I wondered how long I'd been uncon-scious. A few hours? Or was it days? Had I been drugged—apart from taking kava? If the state of my body was any indication, I'd been out to it a long time. That newspaper had been published since the night at Noah's; which told me that the man in the cane chair had left me on my own while he went out to buy it. Unless he had an accomplice.

I lay there shivering. The heat of the doona fought against the chill of the air-conditioner, and the cool of the ceiling fan. Squinting again

I saw a smaller headline, lower down, on the front page of the paper: *Liliane arrive enfin*

So, the cyclone had come and gone without me noticing. I remembered having shaky dreams. Was that because of Liliane? I'd expected to spend the night huddled in the bathroom at 1, rue de la Guillotine with Cluny, Jazz and Spud—probably Chantal, too. And maybe Flex du Lac. Instead, I was in a bed, swathed by acres of mosquito netting in a strange man's house, when the cyclone hit.

Who was this man?

Although curious, I was not planning to hang around and find out. I made up my mind to shove a pillow beneath my doona and slip from between the covers before the stranger woke. I could hide under the bed until he left the room to go to the loo, or to get himself a cup of coffee. I would climb out the window, and run back to the safety of 1, rue de la Guillotine. My friends would be able to fill me in on that stormy evening.

As I furtively stuffed a pillow under the doona, a Band-Aid flopped off one of my knuckles. While stuffing a second pillow, another Band-Aid flopped off. Soon blood-soaked dressings were scattered all over the place.

Smudges of blood on the doona? Uh-oh.

My captor—who wore bandages on both his hands—grunted and made groaning noises. He shifted, settled again. I gathered his shirt around me and slithered from the bed, making a bump as my feet hit the floor. Grabbing hold of the angle iron I eased myself beneath the valance and onto the boards. Hugged my knees to my chin.

The man yawned. He sniffed, sighed, and pushed himself out of the cane chair. He was barefoot and wore beige trousers. He padded off. I heard him slowly descend the stairs groaning, heard the suck noise of a refrigerator door being opened in the kitchen below.

Crawling from beneath the bed, I knelt on the tails of the white shirt. Another Band-Aid dropped off. Red smudges from the antiseptic, dabbed upon my knee, became transferred to the shirt. I was leaving a disastrous trail. At this rate, my kidnapper would have no trouble finding me.

Hauling myself to my feet, I eyed the dormer window slanted in the ceiling. A huge cross of masking tape stretched across, diagonally from one corner to the other. It would be hard to break the glass with *that* there. I dragged the cane chair, still warm from my kidnapper's body, to a spot beneath the window and placed my foot on the seat. I'd be out of here in a nanosecond, I told myself.

Footsteps again. The man was climbing the stairs. I jumped off my makeshift ladder, and darted back beneath the bed. In an attempt to conceal myself more effectively, I curled into a ball. The man sniffed. Paused. Headed for the bed. The mosquito netting moved back and forth close to my nose. As if my captor was checking to see if I was still asleep beneath the bedding.

Cringing, I wondered what he was planning to do to me. His cheeks made a cracking noise. I was about to be discovered.

A thump on the front door below. The banging went on and on, as if it were urgent.

"Merde!" the man said. His bony feet made for the doorway.

This was my chance to escape. I slid out from under the bed, and crawled onto the cane chair again. Straightening, I lifted my arms. But I was unable to reach the dormer window. Could I use the other two pillows on the bed, to make myself taller? If so, I'd be able to tear off the masking tape, smash the glass and climb out.

Pushing aside the mosquito netting, and scrabbling with the pillows, I heard a familiar voice. *"Salut, ça va?"* Was that Marcel Manet? I heard kissing noises—grown men kissing in the French fashion. A pain shot through my knees as I ran from the bedroom and peeped over the balustrade. I could see Marcel's navy-blue boat shoes. The two men began to talk in hushed voices.

I was about to cry out that I was a prisoner, and could Marcel rescue me, when I heard the word *"frangin"* (slang for 'brother') uttered with emotion. My captor, wearing a striped over-shirt, turned from Marcel. He put his hands over his face.

"C'est pas vrai!" he cried.

He turned back, clamped his arms around Marcel, and they stood there hugging. I gulped back my plea for help. I'd seen enough. Marcel Manet was the man's accomplice.

And my captor was the French examiner, Pascal Manet.

Chapter 25

This was every sane person's worst nightmare: *I was being held captive by the man who'd conducted my Year 12 French oral examination.*

It was as if I was locked in a hideous time warp, still in the poky mayoral robing room of Ravella Community Hall where I'd had my exam, with the man in the shiny grey suit chortling, and saying, "'E ferked 'is wife." And a ginormous fever blister was taking over my face. Only now I had scabby knees and scraped knuckles. And, worse, I was wearing the French examiner's good white shirt—that I'd smeared blood and Mercurochrome all over.

I was ready to die. I could think of nothing else but to hide beneath the bed again. My plans had not changed. I would still escape.

The sound of a stifled sob erupted downstairs, the words *"Ça va, ça va"* said in a comforting tone.

More male kissing. I heard the word '*Roch*'.

It was as if someone had punched me in the gut. I stopped breathing. I knew they were talking about Rocky, killed in that car bomb explosion, details of which were plastered all over the paper. I felt like screaming. Stuffing the tail of the French examiner's shirt in my mouth to prevent me from being heard, I blubbered.

Through my sobs, I heard the sound of a back being slapped, another gentler *"Ça va aller"*.

The front door closed. Silence.

Anger began to grow in me. Monsieur Manet was wrong to say everything would be all right. It would not. Rocky was dead, and I was unable to breathe. I began to hiccup. My chest heaved and contracted.

The fridge in the kitchen below made another sucking noise. The gurgling sound of liquid being poured into a glass was followed by footsteps climbing the stairs. Monsieur Manet paused at the bedroom door. Bony feet moved towards the bed. He leaned down and slid a tumbler of water over the boards in my direction with his bandaged hand. Straightening, he dragged the chair from under the dormer window and back to its former position. Sat down with a sigh.

Grasping the tumbler, I edged it to me and took a guilty sip. Then another sip. The hiccups stopped. I lay there thinking about Rocky, about his amazing sculpted lips and that permanent beanie he wore. I remembered our pinkies linking as we went down the narrow footpath towards Noah's droopy pink globe, with the rainwater swooshing along the gutter so that it felt like strolling beside a waterfall. Now Rocky was gone. Once more, I felt like bawling.

I tried to hold back the feeling but it was too strong. I bawled. I sobbed and sobbed under the bed, not giving a toss if anyone was listening. The cane chair creaked as Monsieur Manet shuffled and moved his body about. He made no attempt to approach. The boards were hard, and I was cramped. Soon the sobs dried up. Mucus blocked my throat. When I tried to swallow, a pain shot through my ears. I was hanging out for kava, aching for the calm and clear-sightedness it would bring. A thought kept running through my mind: *If only I had one shell, I'd be able to think straight, work my way through this.*

Soft rain was falling. *Pompiers* shouted as they cleaned up the mess left by the cyclone. Street-cleaning machines swished. Chainsaws growled. A tree branch fell. The crack made a splintered sound.

Without warning, the French examiner leapt from his chair and sprinted down the stairs making Ouch! noises. *"Aîe! Aîe! Aîe!"* A mobile phone jingled. I heard him speak to someone in a low voice.

Flashing lights from the street machinery reflected high on the wall as I crawled from under the bed. I began to see reason. I had no need to run away now that I knew I was being held captive by the French examiner. After all, I was meant to see him on Monday morning at Oriel Lycée.

I turned my Swatch towards me with shaking fingers. The date? I was due at my work experience, and I was almost an hour late. Where were my clothes? Plastering down bits of hair escaped from my French plait, I staggered from the bedroom and limped down the stairs.

Monsieur Manet still talked on his mobile phone in the kitchen. Beside him was a platter of tropical fruit and a basket of saggy baguettes.

"Salut, bye." He pressed the Off button with his bandaged hand, and looked at me with red-rimmed eyes. He seemed neither glad, nor sad, only distracted.

"I need my clothes," I said. "I have a class this morning. I don't want to be late. This work experience programme is important to me."

He paused for what seemed like three hours.

Finally he said, "Are you *mad, Geneviève?*"

"My name is not Geneviève, it's Genna, and I have a class this morning." My voice shook. "Or don't you remember?" As I thought about Rocky, I began to get teary again.

"There is no class *anywhere* on Grande Terre, not for ze next, many weeks." He waved his hands in the air. "Oriel Lycée 'as no roof! You not *hear* the cyclone, *hear* the wind?"

"No, I passed out during that explosion, that car bombing, whatever it was. Or don't you remember?"

"Of course, I remember." He added, "I am sorry. But I 'ave 'ad very bad news."

This was a bizarre scene. Monsieur Manet was making it like he hadn't heard me bawling under the bed. Didn't he remember having pushed a glass of water across the floorboards? My body began to tremble. Soon I was weeping like a crazy person.

"Your friend"—and he placed his arm awkwardly around my shoulder—"is, I am very sorry, 'as disappeared."

"No, you're wrong." I could never admit to him that I cared about Rocky. "It's Pierrot the Peugeot I'm crying about." I wiped my nose on the tail of his shirt. "I loved that car. That's why I'm upset."

I caught a ghost of a smile as he turned his head away. When he turned back, his face was composed. He smelled of cigarettes and insect repellent.

"We need to talk," he said.

Chapter 26

They say you can hear the tick of a watch from six metres in quiet conditions. Monsieur Manet's timepiece sounded like Big Ben as he walked me to a casual area beyond the kitchen bench, where the air was thick with the feeling of being unused.

Boom! Boom! My heart thumped in step with his watch, so loud I was afraid he'd hear it.

He indicated a black leather sofa. Gathering the now tacky shirt around my thighs, I sat and gazed at my bruised knees wondering what I'd done. I tucked stray bits of hair behind my ears.

Clutching his stomach, he lowered himself onto a wicker chair close by. "You disobey me!" One long finger emerged from a bandage as he pointed.

This was not what I'd expected. "Wha … I *disobeyed* you?" I gasped, running a nervous thumb over my burnt eyebrow. "I don't, like, understand. How did I disobey you?"

"I *tell* you not to drink kava." His red-rimmed eyes were stern. "Most nakamals do not have running water. They swish shells about in same slimy wash-up slops." He fiddled with the bandage on his left hand as he thought. "Nor are there tiled floors, which is bad for hygiene. Our Department of Health and Sanitation has been trying to clean up naka-mals for a long time. Many people become sick and you risk becoming sick. So I tell you zis, and you take no notice." He paused, and continued, "I realise kava is traditional drink of the South Pacific, and a natural tranquilliser, but mixed with alcohol it is very, very bad for you. Piper methysticum can be lethal and you should never touch it!"

Monsieur Manet went on and on, prattling about how bad kava was, about the aborigines in Australia drinking it as a substitute for alcohol, and becoming addicted, and developing scaly rashes and liver complaints. I sat there, wondering why he wasn't talking about Rocky, and thinking it must be like this if you had a dad—being forced to listen to the old man blabber about health and sanitation and the perils of drinking certain beverages. Only I'd never had a dad, not even of the 'step' variety. For a moment, I was glad to have escaped those lectures. Then I wondered: had I missed out on the staple ingredient of most people's lives—*a long-winded old fart, who truly cared about my well-being*?

"Who do you think you are, *my father*? And what about Rocky?"

Ignoring my words, he said, "Because of this, Jacques Forestier is not 'appy with your behaviour. He is afraid you will go with Roch, so he tells me to follow you."

"And what has *Jacques Forestier* got to do with my behaviour? I've never even *met* him, and I'm only staying in his house because I earned a work-experience stint in this country. What gives *him* the right to boss *me* around?" My voice wobbled as I talked.

"Jacques Forestier is your grandfather. You have been told this, told about your ADN compatibility."

"You mean those DNA tests? I never saw them. My relationship with Jacques Forestier hasn't been fully established," I said, not telling him I had seen the Power of Attorney signed by Sandrine. "Anyway, Sandrine Bas Salaire de Lyon denies I'm her daughter."

"Sandrine led my brother on a long goose chase. If you had not left your information scattered all over the Internet, we would never 'ave found you." A pause. "Sandrine Bas Salaire de Lyon is a fool."

I gulped. "How can you be so scornful? Sandrine had been through a lot in her life. She has every right not to want to have anything to do with me." I sniffed. "I would never have come to this country if I thought it would bother her. But I won the invitation to do that work experience off my own bat."

"You don't think all zis happen by chance?" Pascal Manet raised his voice and waved a bandaged hand at me. His meaning became clear as he continued, "You don't think it *rrr-rea-lly* is coincidence that you end up at 1, rue de la Guillotine?"

"Wh-what do you mean?"

He put his head back and roared with laughter. "Your French is *affreux* ... apart from a rather charming accent. You make many mistakes in your examination, you run away before you 'ave finished. And you sink all happen—*oh là!*—by *chance*?"

I gawped, speechless.

His voice went all funny and high-pitched, his face puce with amusement. His stomach seemed to have improved, too. He crossed his legs in an aggressive manner. His ankle rested on his thigh as he arched his back. His words were hurtful, probably some of the most hurtful words ever said to me.

"I *really* learnt those Five Tramps!"

"Five tramps?"

"The mnemonic, V TRAMPS DREAM'N, that tells you when ..."

"The grrreat Frrrrench language is more than a little word game."

I swallowed back the tears, threatening to erupt again.

"Forget about your French. I 'ave saved your life when I follow you."

"I didn't ask you to save my life! I wish you hadn't saved my life!"

"Much crime takes place at Noah's. And Roch's independence friends 'ave not such good intentions. I suppose they were planning to rise up and turn our island into a South Pacific basket case all over again, as 'appened during the Events?"

"According to you, my French is really, really bad. So I wouldn't have a clue what they were talking about." I stared at a stained wood plate rack on the far wall filled with fancy china. This pompous dude could torture me any way he liked but I would never let on that, yes, Rocky's friends had been planning to bring chaos to New Caledonia.

"Roch 'as no right to take you to such a place."

"Then why did you send him to pick me up from the airport?" My voice was hoarse.

"I never imagine you will become friends!" He gave a deep sigh. "*Eh bien*, Roch 'as paid for it." If his eyes hadn't been so red-rimmed,

I might have assumed Monsieur Manet was pleased Rocky had been killed for daring to befriend me.

My mouth was swollen, and my throat began to ache as I thought of my new mate being blown apart in a car bombing.

"You saved my life, but I wish you'd let me die!" I cried.

I began to bawl. I sobbed and blubbered. Monsieur Manet looked upset as well. He handed me a hanky, and I buried my face in it. I was making a fool of myself all over again in front of the French examiner.

My tears dried up as an idea occurred to me. "I don't suppose it was a coincidence that *you* conducted my French oral examination, no coincidence that *you* turned up in Ravella at the same time as Marcel?"

"I will be hhhhhonest." He emphasised the silent 'h'. "I am working for Alliance Française in Paris, Boulevard Raspail. My brother contacts me, asks for me to be transferred to Alliance Française in Melbourne … they provide many examiners in final oral examinations. I make sure I go to Ravella." He picked at his bandage. "As I 'ave been instructed, I find you there. I also find you very amusing."

Gobsmacked by the deceit of these people, I glared at him.

He changed the subject. "You must have hunger. I will leave you and try to find an open *boulangerie* to buy you something very nice, such as *pain au chocolat*, to eat. You will feel better then."

"I only eat raw vegan, and I don't feel hungry." I indicated the kitchen bench. "The fruit on the platter will be fine."

Ignoring my words, he pushed himself up and slipped on a pair of brown boat shoes. He grabbed a bunch of car keys with the Mercedes star dangling from it.

Peeling myself off the sticky leather, I stood, expecting Monsieur Manet to head for the front entrance. Instead, he opened a narrow door off the kitchen. I heard the deadlock click as he closed the door behind him. His footsteps clattered down a circular metal staircase into a garage beneath the house.

The bad egg smell of fuel filtered through the floorboards as the engine began to smoothly throb.

Chapter 27

Hot and sticky and smelling of smoke, I stood there, heart hammering, wondering why I was being held captive. And why had the French examiner brought me to his house, instead of taking me back to 1, rue de la Guillotine?

I decided to snoop around, try to find out more about Monsieur Manet.

The next moment, I came close to my own mortality. They say you're more likely to be a target for mosquitoes if you consume bananas. I ate bananas constantly. Next moment, a mosquito landed on my left wrist. Knowing Sandrine's husband had died of dengue, and terrified of the same thing happening to me, I screamed. The Aedes mosquito did its feeding during the daytime, and this one was hungry.

I grabbed a baguette from the basket in the kitchen and chased the insect around the room. The mosquito was humungous, with a massive black proboscis. I bashed and bashed. Bits of bread flew about in a storm of crust until the deadly creature dropped to the ground.

I eyed the bloody slick on the floor, wondering: *Had it bitten me before I killed it?* Inspecting the gore, I realised the mosquito had already sucked on somebody else. My left wrist felt itchy. I scratched and rubbed until a red lump appeared. Would I develop a fever and rash, bleed from the nose and gums, and die?

Shivers of apprehension coursed through my body.

My heart calmed. It was time to do a quick lap of the house before Monsieur Manet caught me poking among his things. First, I tried the sturdy front door. Locked. The French examiner had deadlocked the main exit as well. This was no accident. *I was under house arrest.*

A bedroom was situated either side of the entrance hall. In the room to the left, behind Monsieur Manet's unmade bed—his sheets were tangled, as if they'd been in a wrestling match—the casement windows were crisscrossed with masking tape. Carefully applied, and with no bubbling. A locked bolt shafted from the frame into the windowsill. I pulled at the corner of the tape. Stuck fast.

The room to the right of the front door, if the musty smell was any indication, was a spare bedroom. The external shutters were folded back, and the crisscrossed tape had been carefully applied there, too.

In the teensy en suite bathroom, tiled in brown with apricot feature flowers, my eyes latched onto an un-taped louvre window—too small for me to squeeze through.

Back in the guest bedroom, I peered through the angle of the tape across the bolted window. The sea, within the crescent-shaped bay, was flat and grey. A lone seagull ruffled the water, wheeled and rose into the sky. To the right, beneath a sandy bluff, the metal roof of a restaurant had been twisted into witches' hats. Plastic chairs lay scattered and broken on the beach. A sorbet van whizzed past along the road, screeching to a halt in a billow of leaf litter outside *La Sorbetière*.

Gazing at the lank water and thinking about the terrible time I'd been having, I heard the spitfire sound of another mosquito. I bolted upstairs to my bedroom, pushed apart the netting and crawled beneath it. I lay there, snivelling and chewing my fingernails. My hair reeked of smoke, my knuckles were sore, my knees were like a grubby kid's, and I was hanging out for a shower. But I had no clean clothes.

Pondering whether Monsieur Manet was planning to keep me here clad only in his business shirt, I heard the staccato clang of footsteps on the spiral staircase below. The door opened with a crash.

"Geneviève, I 'ave brought you something wonderful to eat!" he shouted. "You will love it!"

My captor was back. Refusing to answer to the name Geneviève, I continued to lie there, gouging grit from beneath my fingernails.

"Genna!" Monsieur Manet sounded excited.

As he had used my correct name, I reluctantly clambered from beneath the netting. Near the cane chair, the newspaper was still spread on the floor. The photos of the deceased lifted and swayed beneath the breeze of the ceiling fan. I bent over to inspect Rocky. Without his beanie, golden-red curls tumbled across his Nescafé face. I began to blubber again.

I stopped crying, and wiped my nose on the sleeve of Monsieur Manet's shirt. I knew that person glaring at me from the adjacent photo. I looked more closely. *It was yours truly.*

Why was my photo on the front page of the local newspaper? And why had Monsieur Manet not told me? Forgetting about dying of dengue, I stormed back down the stairs and into the kitchen.

Monsieur Manet looked startled. "What is wrong?" His bandaged hands were full of wriggling shellfish.

"I just read that I'm dead!" I said.

"But you are not dead."

"So how did they get my photo?"

"If you bother to read ze article ..."

"As you said earlier, my French is really, really bad, so I wouldn't have understood."

Monsieur Manet sighed. "As I was saying, it says your passport was found lying near the car, on the road, probably blown out. They are not yet sure how many people were killed in the bombing until they do ADN tests, which are not so quick, you know."

"You didn't *ring* to tell them I'm *alive*?"

"Police are very busy cleaning up after Liliane."

"But, if they got my photo from my miraculously ejecting passport, how did they get Rocky's photo?"

"They get 'is photo from police files, I suppose."

I was stunned. "If Rocky was a crook, known to the police, why did you send him to pick me up from Tontouta airport?"

"Pffff." Pascal did the Marcel Manet shoulder-shrugging thing. "Roch's crimes were of little importance, the occasional *manifestation*, disturbing the peace, maybe even stealing a car when he was an adolescent."

"Monsieur Manet, I need you to clarify something. Did you lock me in this house on purpose?"

"Call me Pascal!" He dumped thrashing crabs onto the kitchen bench. Bits of claws started dropping off all over the place.

"*Mons* … um, P-P-Pascal, I want you to tell me if you locked me inside deliberately when you went out."

"Of course!" He filled a saucepan from the tap and, dumping it on the stove, began to boil water.

"But, why?" I eyed the writhing in horror as he picked up a knife and started to cut open a live crab. Little shivers ran up and down my legs.

"I lock you in to make certain you do not try to leave *Le Caillou*. Jacques Forestier wishes to see you as soon as is practicable."

He wedged out an eye socket and lifted up a frilly half-formed shell to remove the lungs. Blue bits and blood and black goo decorated his bandages as he began to fluff on about crabs.

"I find it amazing that Kanak women catch *crabes mous*, known in English as soft-shell crabs, wis their hands … it is very brave to do this … among the mangroves. You know, it is illegal to catch crabs after females 'ave shed the shell for mating, because it will deplete our stocks. But a friend sells me these lovely ones, and I think you might like them." He smiled.

"I'm not interested in those poor little crabs, but I *am* interested in why I'm here in your house."

"*La Maison des Cerises* is the name of my home, chosen after the communard song. Louise Michel, anarchist and political prisoner, resided 'ere before she led the Kanak uprising in 1878."

"That's very impressive, but I asked why I'm here at, um, *La Maison des Cerises*, and not at 1, rue de la Guillotine."

"You are 'ere because most of the roof is gone at 1, rue de la Guillotine, damaged by fallen niaouli trees … melaleucas as you call them in Australia. The only room left almost unharmed is Jacques Forestier's library, which is fortunate as 'e has many wonderful books."

"What about my friends? What will they think when they see the paper, find out I'm dead?"

"Your friends, billeted out to other dwellings, may not read the paper." He shrugged. "As for Chantal, she has gone home to her family in Vallée du Tir. Jacques Forestier is back at Bouchon in Bourail, which is like Venice at ze moment with floating cars as gondolas. In the meantime, you are to stay here!"

He tossed the last of the gutted crabs into the boiling water, and placed a brick on the lid of the pot. "The crabs are trapped now, fighting to be free and shedding claws. I 'ave removed the aprons and internal organs, especially lungs. Now I must stop them from attempting to escape!" His eyes gleamed. "In twenty minutes, when they are disinfected, orange-red, and yellow fat comes from the side of the shell, *voilà*, you will 'ave *crabe mou* for your breakfast. So soft it's like biting into a most *incroyable* butter!"

"You don't think I'm eating those?" I turned and ran from the kitchen. "That is *so* cruel! Anyway, I'm raw vegan. I don't eat living creatures."

"I 'ave found you a black sapote fruit all the way from Queensland." His voice rose up the stairwell as I scrambled up the steps towards the attic bedroom, where the brave Louise the Red had slept. "Sapote fruit is filled wis beautiful chocolate flavours, rich pulp."

I dived beneath the mosquito netting, as he added, "I also buy you new clothing from a lady friend who owns lingerie shop."

I put the pillow over my head and cried myself to sleep.

Chapter 28

According to my Swatch, I'd been asleep for almost twenty-four hours. On waking, I had an overwhelming urge to be home in Ravella, on the Mornington Peninsula. There, I'd give Namilly Perrier a mega hug and say, "Ma, I was wrong to go there. You were right. As usual."

I wasn't sure I wanted to meet Jacques Forestier—even though he was supposed to be my grandfather. What could he tell me that I didn't already know? I knew he was racist. I knew he'd chased Claude Ponsinet from 1, rue de la Guillotine when he caught him with Sandrine, simply because he was a Kanak, and then promised Claude a non-existent job in Australia. Jacques Forestier was manipulative and evil, a man who paid others to do his dirty work.

I lay beneath the mosquito netting thinking that, even if I did manage to escape from *La Maison des Cerises*, I'd be unable to leave Grande Terre. The planes were grounded, I had no money, and I had no passport. Even my new laptop—probably wrecked—was at 1, rue de la Guillotine. Without my mobile, still in the pocket of my jacket on the back seat of Pierrot the Peugeot, I couldn't even text Stefan. My phone had become waterlogged from the rain, and the charger was back in my bedroom at Jacques Forestier's.

My life was one humungous disaster. I was aching all over, and I felt sick from the weight of those gone to the other side.

The house was silent. I pushed aside the mosquito netting and hauled myself out of bed. Wary of being attacked by another mosquito, I gathered Pascal Manet's shirt around me and crept downstairs. On the kitchen bench, beside a note, sat a Repel roll-on. Before reading the message, I twisted off the cap and examined the ball. Had he left the Repel there for me to use? Or was it his—personal—already rolled-on, mosquito repellent?

I examined the ball for hairs. Not seeing any, I slopped the Repel over my forearms, hands and legs. Next, I read the note—written in a sort of franglais:

I will return this evening. Jus d'orange is in frigo, also raisins secs and walnuts. Still no pâtisserie open, I am sorry. There is long life milk in cupboard and I have left your new clothing on the canapé.

I sighed. Pascal Manet didn't get it. For vegans, dairy foods were out. For raw vegans, pastry and bread were out, too. Anyway, I was uninterested in food. Was this one of the kava side effects Spud had warned me about?

Another note nearby, written as an afterthought, appeared to be an attempt to make me feel better about Rocky.

Dying is a part of living. There are clean towels in small bathroom off second bedroom.

Staring at his words, my nose began to run. I wiped it on the sleeve of his shirt. I planned to climb out the window, hotfoot it to Noah's nakamal and beg for a shell of kava. But first I decided to turn on the TV for updates on the car bombing and its victims.

Pressing the remote, lying beside a heap of *Le Point* and *Paris Match* magazines, *Télé Nouvelle-Calédonie* came on. Women swayed to island music with flowers in their hair. A band ran across the bottom of the screen. Could this be information about the terrorist attack?

Suite à un mouvement de grève nous ne sommes pas en mesure de diffuser les nouvelles locales habituelles.

It seemed the New Caledonian journalists were on strike. Time to inspect the new clothes Pascal had obtained from his lingerie lady friend.

A mass of satin and lace and spaghetti straps was draped across the black leather sofa. The outfits, in screaming pink, were trimmed with black lace. Did the French teacher really expect me to wear those? My mind spun just looking at them.

Holding the lairy silk slip dress against my chest, I realised this frock was made for a dudette with serious mountain ranges. I let it drop. The dress sank into a puddle of fabric, slithering to the floor as though it had a will of its own.

A top in hot-pink satin, with black roses across the boob area, went with a patchwork mini-skirt in a multitude of pinks—from cyclamen to faded rose. With a band of lace below the waistline clustered with pink spangles, this outfit was way too busy for my taste. But the Charles Jourdan creation could be small enough to fit me. I held it up against my body. At last, something to wear.

Next the knickers: La Perla G-strings in see-through stomach-turning lime, ruffles placed strategically. A floppy fabric flower. To pin in my hair? Or on the clothing? I wasn't in the mood for adorning myself with flowers.

On the way to the en suite for my shower, I searched for a machine in which to wash Pascal's shirt. I discovered the main bathroom, renovated—and at odds with the rest of the house -with beige granite and shining mirrors. Beneath Hollywood lights black towels were folded in a pile, beside Kenzo pour Homme products in marine, with a leaf design on the bamboo-shaped bottles.

In the laundry, I found my day-glo tube skirt and studded T-shirt. They were covered in jagged holes and soot stains. Someone had washed them and hung them over a plastic rack to dry. Monsieur Manet? I lifted the mucky shirt over my head, dropped it into the top-loading washer and tipped in some Javel bleach. I twisted the knob and hurried to the en suite.

Shampoo cascaded over my smoky hair, leaving my body frothing with foam. The bubbles gurgled and snapped into the plughole, and soon I was feeling cleaner and less depressed. I rinsed my locks until the strands squeaked. Apart from a few burnt bits above my forehead and my stubbly eyebrow, scabby knees and scraped knuckles, I was almost back to normal. After patting myself dry with a peach-coloured towel, I finger-combed my hair into a semblance of order.

I took a long look at the louvre window over the basin. I recalled a similar window in the Ravella High portable classroom. Way back, 2E History used to climb through the window, before Mr Wagstaff put the key in the lock of the door.

Assessing the louvre panels, I dragged on the ruffled G-string, slipped into the satin top and slid into the spangled slippery skirt. Hoisting up the overlong spaghetti straps, I ambled to the kitchen, thinking that, even if I did manage to squeeze through the window, my money was in my jacket on the back seat of Pierrot the Peugeot. Did Noah run a tab in his nakamal? *Or should I go through my French examiner's pockets?*

Chapter 29

My face resembled a washed out rag and I had no makeup, not even a lipstick. I decided to raid the fridge, see if I could find berries to use as makeshift colour. *Aha, a punnet of raspberries at the back!* I pulled it out and prised open the lid. Most were mouldy—apart from four.

In the midst of squashing two, and patting the juice onto my mouth with my fingertips, I heard the washing machine screech. I dashed into the laundry. In the machine, I found yellow sludge creeping up the sides of the bowl. Examining Pascal's business shirt, floating in the water, I found stains I hadn't seen before.

Uh-oh, I'd wrecked his good shirt.

My brain was all blots and splotches. I was thirsty, and unable to think straight. I needed to feel calm and clear-headed again. Kava was the answer.

A jar of rubber bands sat on the laundry bench. They wriggled and curved behind the glass, as if inviting me to play. With a blinding flash, as if they'd spoken to me, I knew what to do. I would change my hair-style from French plait to dreadlocks, and turn up at Rocky's funeral making a statement of solidarity with his independence friends.

Reaching to pick up the jar, my hand hovered over *two* jars of rubber bands. (I was sure there'd only been one.) The rubber bands were bleeding now, leaving long trails of gore on the inside of the glass. I backed off from the bench, scratched at my palms. Was this the onset of dengue fever? My mouth was dry, my hands were clammy, and I needed a drink made from the piper methysticum plant. My breath was coming in short, sharp gasps. I was antsy. And I needed dosh.

I darted into Pascal's bedroom. Built-in cupboards lined one wall, with a mirror, and a dressing table in the centre. I eased open the cupboard door to the left. Above a bank of drawers hung a row of tasteful over-shirts, some floral. I edged open the top drawer. Lacoste shirts in a wide range of colours were folded in a pile, with the green crocodile logo face upwards.

I heaved open every drawer. Cotton pullovers, business shirts still in their cellophane packaging, boxer shorts, jocks and hankies confronted me. I fidgeted my hands beneath each stack, hunting for moolah.

No sign of any money.

In the cupboard near the window, I found suits, jackets and trousers. This was more like it. This was the place where men kept their cabbage, I told myself. I paused for a nanosecond. What I was doing seemed wrong. The moment of doubt soon passed. Hands quivering, I worked my way through every Louis Féraud and Hugo Boss slinky pocket.

Nothing—apart from a Paris Métro ticket, a franger and a phone number scribbled on a scrap of paper.

Until the last pocket. The shiny grey suit Monsieur Manet had worn on the day of my oral exam in Ravella Community Hall smelled of cigarettes and chalk. Sliding my fingers into the inside Kenzo-labelled pocket of the jacket, I found used tram tickets and a blue Bic pen. And, finally, something greasy and familiar. I snatched the note out. I was holding a 'lobster' in my hand—a plastic, Aussie twenty-dollar bill.

Was there more where that came from?

Clawing my way through a trillion pockets, I halted. I'd never realised men's suits were so complicated before. I'd never known a man who wore a suit to work. In Ravella, all my friends' fathers rocked up at their day jobs in casual duds.

I ploughed on, wading through more and more pockets. I discovered a 'grey nurse'—an old-fashioned, hundred dollar note. I had lucked out. I had money for kava. I folded the notes, and tucked them into my G-string. All I had to do now was negotiate the window of the en suite bathroom.

The louvre window was unlocked. Tugging at the lever I opened the glass slats, and inspected the aluminium strips securing each one. I inserted my fingernail, prising until I was able to bend the metal back. The strips were like cooked Play-Doh, firm but pliable enough for me to be able to jiggle out the glass. I laid each slat carefully on the floor, until I had a space wide enough to get through.

I heard an ominous crack of the porcelain as I drew myself up onto the hand basin. I straightened, and peered outside. A gnarled frangipani tree leaned against the side of the house. I pushed my head through the window, positioned my shoulders sideways and placed one foot on a branch. I lowered myself, dropped to the ground.

Hoisting my spaghetti straps onto my shoulders, I tiptoed through broken twigs, leaves and bits of paper on the lawn. Dodging a fallen melaleuca, I adjusted my G-string.

Barefoot, I hurried along the footpath. Following Promenade Roger Laroque towards Port Plaisance marina, I headed for the Latin Quarter. *Would Noah sell me a shell of that muddy-tasting drink?*

Chapter 30

The Port Plaisance shopping centre was closed, its roof covered with tarpaulins. Looking about me, I saw stacks of tarps on roofs—plastic swathes in a landscape ragged with twisted tin, broken branches, bits of bougainvillea, warped timber and fallen bricks. To my left, the lagoon was glassy, with not a sail in sight. Few pedestrians were about, and even fewer vehicles. Across the road, a man on a ladder gnawed at a tree with a handsaw. A woman in a floral missionary dress swept a balcony with a witches' broom.

Flicking back my damp, un-plaited hair, I hurried on.

Bypassing strewn branches, broken palms and fractured tree ferns, I picked up speed and jogged off down the hill, then up again, past yachts with broken masts in a marina crawling with concerned men. I headed along Route Jules Garnier in the direction of Baie de la Moselle. In no time, I would see the pink bulb drooped over the entrance of Noah's nakamal in the Latin Quarter.

As I approached the Municipal Markets in Baie de la Moselle, I made out a crushed car slewed to one side. The blue roofs of the huts had been damaged by the cyclone. The pull-down doors of the market were in place. The carpark was deserted, but I spied a canvas lean-to, close to the water.

Floating fish guts and watermelon skins bobbed nearby, and a hand-written sign on the lean-to read: Nakamal de Chouchou.

Another nakamal! *Should I try Chouchou's for my kava?*

Dodging puddles of car grease, I made my way across the asphalt, avoiding banana skins, dried-out fish heads and scavenging seagulls. Empty juice containers and floating paper rattled past. I skidded on some papaya, and my big toe collided with a yam. Crunchy quartz bit into my soles as I hobbled into Chouchou's.

With the light behind me, the interior seemed dingy. This place was a cross between Noah's and Tibou's, with a sea of white stones dotted with sawn-off tree stumps. A wooden bench ran along the west wall. A trough sat to the right of the entrance. Past the carved posts supporting the fabric ceiling, I was able to make out a small kitchen and a heap of glasses piled on a wobbled bench. Coconut shells shaped like goblets were propped on a shelf nearby.

I called out, *"Il y a quelqu'un?"*

No one answered.

I repeated the question in English. "Is anybody there?"

The silence was creepy.

A smell, like the Sticky Berry dessert wine Namilly drank in the evenings, crept into my nostrils. Was this nakamal just an ordinary bar? Disappointment flicked through me, and I shivered in the dankness. I was hanging out for that shell.

A beaded curtain—rather than woven pandanus—hung from the ceiling at the rear. No overhead fan moved the air about, but the carved glass jangled from the breeze lifting off the water as it crept beneath the sides of the tarpaulin.

"Il y a quelqu'un?" I shouted again.

No reply.

As I turned to leave, a woman complained behind the beaded curtain. *"Non, chéri!"*

Heck, had I stumbled into a brothel? Had this shack been erected for the pleasure of sailors coming ashore off the boats?

I was about to flee when the glass beads clattered. A guy appeared. He wore dreads bunched into a crocheted Rasta bonnet. His camel knees protruded from a hessian sarong, beneath a flowing floral shirt in missionary dress material. His thongs were flattened plastic bottles, tied on with rope. The palms of his hands were stained bright green.

"Ouais?" He yawned.

"Chéri!" screamed the woman in the distance.

"Je peux vous aider?" His eyes were sludgy as he asked if he could help.

"Uh-uh-uh …" I began. Then in flawless French, as casually as asking for a bag of apples, I told him what I wanted.

"I will not be long," he answered in English.

The greasy dollars I'd nicked from the French examiner's suit pressed against my stomach as I lowered myself onto a sawn-off tree stump to wait. I was so thirsty I could hardly bear listening while he squeezed the cloth over the presentation bowl. The rustling and massaging and slopping of the muddy water reminded me of Rocky, and the nights we'd spent drinking kava together—just us, under the stars. I thought of the funky atmosphere of Noah's, the men in dreadlocks planning to wrest control of their land from France.

Pushing myself off the sawn-off stump, I moved to the wooden bench against the wall and settled back, lulled by the swish and swoosh of Chouchou making my drink.

I must've dozed.

A touch on the shoulder, and I floundered up. Chouchou handed me a long glass of fizzy green fluid, rather than the coconut shell I'd been expecting.

"I asked for kava, not some stupid cocktail."

"Is not some stupid cocktail. Is kava kava, made with *grrreeeen coconut water*. You try. Is good." He nodded. "Twelve hundred franc."

"Twelve hundred francs? That's dear. It's nearly twenty dollars." I poked a finger beneath my waistband, and extracted the 'lobster'.

"Special drink, special price!" Chouchou wrinkled his nose as he inspected my Aussie dosh.

"Ché-é-é-r-r-r-i!" wailed the woman.

Chouchou slouched off, and disappeared behind the beaded curtain.

I sipped. My tongue went numb. I sipped some more. My tongue went number, until I was unable to feel my lips. A zillion elves tickled the roof of my mouth as the green drink fizzed up my nose. This was the most incredible anaesthetic: no bitter taste, no muddiness. A calm, clear feeling swept through me.

My muscles relaxed. I was in control. I slurped the last of the fluid, and slid my fingers around the inside of the glass. I sat there sucking my forefinger. *Should I buy another?* I decided not to. If I used up my one hundred I'd be all cashed out.

Placing the empty glass on the bench, I sauntered into the daylight. The sun had broken through. The sky was clear. The air was sweet. I floated across the carpark, serene as a goddess in my screaming pink slip top with its black lace trim and spangled patchwork skirt. I swam through a perfume of overripe mangoes. No need for me to hitch back home. I was flying on the perfect raw vegan drink.

A German car with tinted windows raced across the bitumen, tyres shrieking as the vehicle did a U-turn.

Chapter 31

The Mercedes screeched to a halt. The passenger door flew open.

"Monte!" The French examiner looked furious. "Get in my car! *Tout de suite!"*

"Hi, Pascal!" I floated towards him. "You said you wouldn't be back 'til this evening. Come to buy yourself a shell of kava kava?"

I slid into the Merc.

"Why you not listen when I tell you how you must be 'ave?" Pascal's eyes were so cold you could've gone skating on them.

"Who do you think you are, my father?" I gave him a gentle smile. (They say it's impossible to hate when you've drunk kava.)

Pascal lurched across the seat. He grabbed a fistful of my hair and pulled it tight against the nape of my neck. *"Regarde!"* Flicking down the visor, he shoved my face at the vanity mirror.

"Ouch, that hurts!" I stared at the alien in the glass, stared at the grotty, uncombed hair, cracked lips and red-rimmed gaze. My eyes looked like two burnt holes in a blanket. One stubbly eyebrow. Spit glistened at the corner of my two-toned mouth. And was I drooling?

"What is on your *lips*? And what 'ave you been *drinking*?" Pascal was tooshy.

"I just had one shell"—and I decided I should be perfectly clear about what I'd drunk—"no, it was a *glass* of kava this time, a tall one in a green colour. The glass wasn't green, I mean. The *kava* was, sort of, coloured green. And it tasted delic-*ious*."

Pascal dragged my hair tighter. My body went rigid.

"Your lips, what is that stain?" From the corner of my eye I could see his knuckles protruding, bound with strips of plaster. Bits of cotton poked from the ends of the dressing as he pushed his hand into my neck.

"Stop it, you're hurting me!"

He swivelled my head around to face him. His mouth was pursed into a squinty line. I tried to stare him out, but my eyes slid away.

"I didn't have a lipstick, so I rubbed squashed raspberries onto them. I know it makes 'em look kinda dry without lip gloss, but I had no choice."

"And green in the middle?" He pointed a plastered finger. "Is that from the drink?"

My bottom lip trembled as I shrugged my shoulders. He let me go. My head jerked back. My eyes rotated, and finally settled.

"Some sort of dye, I imagine." He sighed in exasperation.

"Chouchou said it was, like, green coconut water." My mouth went into free-fall. I forced my lips together, clenching my teeth to stop from bawling again.

He released the handbrake, pressed his foot on the accelerator. The car cruised past the American monument, soared up, turned left and zigzagged down towards Baie de l'Orphelinat without missing a beat.

I sat there, saying nothing.

The heat of the sun shone against the tinted windows, and the air-conditioner kicked in. As we sped along in his super-sleek driving machine, I thought of Rocky, of us chugging up hills, wheezing around inclines, in Pierrot the Peugeot.

Pascal's voice broke the silence. "I am sorry, perhaps I overreact. But I 'ave never 'ad any children"—he paused as if there might be some doubt about this—"of my own."

"I'm not a kid!"

"It is all good and well, but you look like a *gamine*." He added, "I found you some Notou bird for dinner."

About to protest that I was a raw vegan, I decided not to push my luck, saying, "Isn't it illegal to shoot the Notou bird? Rocky told me." Damn. Rocky's name seemed to crop up all the time when I was talking to this guy.

Pascal let out a whistle of air. "My brother likes to shoot Notou bird, in fact 'e shoot this one. And I take it back to *La Maison des Cerises*. A blackout 'appen earlier, and I wish to see if the *frigo* is working. The *frigo* is fine, but I discover you are gone."

Had he noticed I'd been through his things, and nicked his money? I wondered.

I was unaware we had passed *La Maison des Cerises*, until we rounded the Baie des Citrons headland and zoomed along Promenade Roger Laroque in the direction of Anse Vata. At Anse Vata beach all but one of the *faré* roofs had been blown off.

"Les Jeudis de l'Anse Vata!" He gunned the car past the trendy tourist beach and up another hill. "Our Thursday markets will be cancelled for a while."

"Where are you taking me?" I scrabbled at the door handle.

"The car is locked."

My kava calm deserted me for a moment; my heart began to paddle.

"I am taking you to Ouen Toro, a place I used to come and visit when I was feeling bad from time I spend in hospital … Sydney, first, on a medical visa, Gaston Bourret after that … a consequence of my being stabbed during the Events. One can see a most beautiful view, and I think it might make you feel better, as it used to do with me."

We left the car in the pinky dirt of the parking area, and climbed up into a paved circle. Through the skinny feathered trees, the waters of the lagoon were hazy.

"Araucaria, also known as column pines." He indicated the trees.

"Awesome," I said.

"In the distance one can see Le Rocher à la Voile, the rock with a sail. And, closer, Anse Vata beach. Marcel and Roch used to get a ride with the fish supplier from Yaté and come to … 'ow you say, perv? … on ladies sunbathing topless in the monokini beside the jetty. Not Kanak women. They bathe dressed." With a hint of a smile, he waved his hand. "We are on a peninsula and, left, you can see Baie de Sainte Marie, where yachting regattas are held, and many little islands which are very beautiful."

"What are those guns?" I frowned at two cannons.

"An Australian coastguard artillery unit, named Robin Force, spent seven months on Ouen Toro in 1941 to install them and to train our Caledonian fighting men." He pulled a pair of shades from his pocket and placed them on his nose. "One gun is aimed at a narrow pass through the reef at Boulari, where is situated Amédée Lighthouse." He gestured. "The other gun faces towards Dumbéa pass. Neither was needed against Nippon, as American soldiers stopped the Japanese army at Guadalcanal." He pushed back his hair with his fingers until the strands stood up straight. "Long before I was born, of course."

"It's good that New Cal was safe during the war."

"We have mainly Yankees to thank for that. Yankees were stationed here and also build Tontouta airport. My father tells me about it."

"I feel like a tourist, rather than someone who was born here."

His eyes briefly crinkled as he continued, "From Lemon Bay, Baie des Citrons where we are living, through Anse Vata and on to here, one can come to see the sunset. This, as you know, happens quickly in the tropics." He pointed to the orange ball plunging to the horizon. "We call it our walk of happiness and, if you are lucky, you will see a green ray which appears below a yellow sky. But you will not see this green ray if the sky is red, as it is today."

Pascal was making an effort to be nice.

"There is an annual running race to here. It is named *Le Kilo de Ouen Toro*, also *Triathlon de Saint Pierre*." He suddenly changed the subject. "You do not remember anything?"

"Of what? The cyclone?"

"*Non.* I know you are capable of sleeping in winds of more than two hundred kilometres per hour."

"You mean my so-called childhood in New Caledonia?"

He nodded.

"I was three years old when I left. I only have shadowy memories of being shut in, and feeling a sort of rocking and hearing the sound of water. I had dreams for ages about it." I waved a green-stained finger. "Namilly told me I was a Caldoche. I used to ask her if she ever wished she had a real child, and she would say I *was* her real child."

I blinked away tears.

"But I don't remember Sandrine. And Namilly said my birth mother worked for *her*, instead of the other way round." I thought for a bit.

"Marcel found my details in a chat room and turned up in Ravella, did the DNA thing by pinching a piece of my hair. But, oh heck, Sandrine doesn't believe it's true, and maybe she's right. But I saw ..."

"What did you see?"

"Nothing." I decided not to let on that I'd found the Procuration in Jacques Forestier's desk. "Anyway, you know everything and I know zip."

"I will get you home, and I will cook for you our wonderful Notou bird."

He propelled me towards the car. I wondered how I was going to wriggle out of eating Marcel's illegally shot giant pigeon.

Chapter 32

We sat at the wooden table with its high-backed chairs and rush-plaited seats, our plates piled high with Notou bird and rice.

"There is not any salad," he said, "because of our cyclone."

"I don't think I can eat this." I was unable to stop thinking of the magnificent giant pigeon this'd been before Marcel shot it.

"Eat!" Pascal pointed at the food, and at me. Grease shone on his plaster. "You are too thin."

With a sigh, I picked up my knife and fork and made a stab at the food.

"You have 'eard from your little friend?"

"My little friend?"

"Stefan Becker, your friend with the German name."

"You know about Stefan? Who, by the way, is very big and ultra-cute." I was on my favourite subject now. "Stefan collects blue-ringed octopuses, blue ringers he calls them. But I lost my mobile in the car bombing, so I can't contact him."

"I know more about you than you probably realise. Marcel make it 'is business to become friends with Stefan's sister, Skye, and she tell 'im much about you."

"Is there nothing you people do that happens by accident?" I murmured, fiddling with my fork.

He stopped chewing and looked at me.

"Actually Stefan's tied up with a horse at the moment, Bill Einstein, who's got a terrible bowel problem."

Pascal seemed about to do the same crack-up routine as he had during my oral exam. His face went puce, as if 'amused' by what I'd said. But, instead of bursting into laughter, he spat. A pellet hit the plate.

"Il me fait chier, Marcel," he grumbled.

"It's disgusting to have bullets in your food." I paused. "Anyway, where is Marcel?"

"This afternoon my brother set off in his yacht for the Northern Province to go bonefishing. Bonefish travel very fast, maybe fifty kilometres an hour." He chewed and swallowed. "Bones are a challenge for a fisherman. He will forget about Roch."

"He wrestled with a crocodile in Cairns. He'd enjoy fishing." Rocky's death still gnawed at me, too.

"Of course. And Marcel likes an outdoor life." He jabbed his fork into the food.

"Tell me about your being stabbed during the Events."

Pascal leaned on one elbow, his knife in the air. "Everything began at the end of November, 1984, when independence people boycotted our territorial elections. Fifteen days later, ten Kanaks were assassinated." He looked thoughtful. "I forget on what day, but sometime after Noël that year I was testing out my new sleeping bag, a Christmas present, on the floor when *Maman* comes into my room. In those days, we farmed deer in the Brousse."

"Yeah, go on."

His voice was croaky, as if he'd told the story a trillion times.

"She says, 'Quick, the Colline house is on fire, and K-Mel is missing. Roch and Marcel have gone to Nouméa with the Yaté fish supplier, and your father is in Hienghène. Jeanne and the baby need you'." His gaze wandered across my right shoulder. "I would 'ave done anysing for Jeanne"—he pronounced her name *jjunnn*, in the French way, with a sliding J—"who was so beautiful wis her hair covered in tiny braids and beads."

"Rocky told me she was a hippie."

"Non. Roch's mother was more than that. I used to confide in 'er. I would tell her my teenage problems, all my anxieties and she would comfort me." He let out a sigh.

"You must miss her."

"Well, I run up the hill to Colline traditional hut. Black flames are rising into the sky, as my *maman* always said would 'appen. I see K-Mel in the distance with one of his independence friends. They are laughing, but perhaps I imagine it. Perhaps it is the morphine I was given afterwards." He pushed a forkful of the dark meat into his mouth, chewed and spat another slug onto his plate.

"Go on."

"My shoe laces are undone, my hairs not combed. Two soldiers confront me, and not in a good way. They 'ave guns, and I stop to reason with them when they say I cannot pass, and that all the roads of Grande Terre are blocked off. Their hairs are in ..." He made a squiggly shape with his fingers.

"Dreadlocks?"

He nodded, and continued, "They swagger and hum Bob Marley song as they approach me. Get up ..."

"You mean the song *Get up, Stand up?*"

"Of course! You are correct. And zey call me Caldoche, and tell me I must stop, that there 'ave been killings in the north and I am to blame in some way. I *do* stop. But it is not enough for these men." He placed his knife and fork at a ninety-degree angle, and picked up one of the slugs from his plate. "I raise my hands in the air, like you see in an American movie. Still not enough."

He dropped the slug, and nudged it slowly round the edge of his plate. The smell of sweat pushed through his aftershave.

"I am sure they only mean to terrify me, but they enjoy their moment of power, and they go too far." He punched the table with his fist. *"Salauds!"* he shouted.

His knife flew off his plate and hit my glass. The water rocked and slurped.

"It had no sense," he continued, "so I ask, 'Why are you doing this?' and he just repeats that they are blocking all roads with the aim of keeping away tourists and harming economy. But we are a good hour from Nouméa, so why do they bother?"

He picked up a piece of Notou bird with his fingers, stuffed it into his mouth, chewed and spat out another slug. "One opens a packet of Gitanes cigarettes ... oh yes, he was arrogant ... and begins to puff smoke in my face. I wonder if 'e will burn me with 'is cigarette, just because I am a Caldoche. In fact, he then asks if my family have their suitcases packed for the last one hundred years. I do not know what to say."

Pascal drummed his greasy fingers on the table.

"Then he talks about Hienghène, tells me *again* it is my fault zose people were slaughtered. I am very afraid."

"Didn't your mother have a gun?"

"Of course! She needs to scare away men in their pick-up trucks when they come to steal our deer. But she wasn't there. And, by now, I was a half kilometre from my home." He picked up another slug, tossed it from one hand to the other. "You know how they learn it?"

"What?"

"Learn how to rise up." He slowly shook his head. "The Kanak students in Paris, including Jean-Marie Tjibaou, see the riots in May '68 and learn the power of protest, which is not such a bad thing." He leaned forward, and hunched his shoulders. "But I digress. The soldier wis the Gitanes pushes the barrel into my chest. I lose my balance. I fall over. I am lying humiliated in the red dirt on the road, and I don't even dare to look at the Colline *case*, or hut, but I smell smoke. Was everyone in the land prisoner, like me? Were fires like this occurring right across our beautiful country?"

"Did he stab you?"

"*Oui*. And it was quick. The arrogant one puts 'is bayonet into place on the rifle and moves towards me. *'Arrête!'* I scream, sliding my heels in the dirt as I try to get up and run from there. But he jabs me in my gut as I twist."

"Wow!" I exhaled. "I mean I'm sorry."

"I see K-Mel and his friend in the distance. The hut is on fire and they are standing there. Jeanne, holding baby Douce, comes running. Everything begins to go dark in my head. *'Ça va aller,* Pascal,' I hear her say, then, *'J'en peux plus.'* In that moment, when she says she 'as enough, I know she will leave *Le Caillou*"—he ran his fingers down his throat, leaving a greasy slick—"forever!"

He pushed his chair from the table and stood up. "Last thing I remember is Jeanne bending over me. After, I am on a plane and off to Sydney, Australia, with operations and wearing a bag for many weeks, which is not so cool for a teenager, and with only visits by voluntary Caledonian support workers. Life is so fast in Sydney, but for me it was very slow."

"Did you ever see Jeanne Colline again?"

He gave a brief shake of the head. "*Non.* But she 'as told me after the uprisings begin, 'Douce will not survive on *Le Caillou.* Not only is she fair, she is different.' So maybe it was also another reason for her to leave. Anyway, my life is changed. No more free diving off reef, no National Service as Marcel 'as done. I finish my *baccalauréat*, do university in France and end up working for Alliance Française in Paris with other people who do not wish to be soldiers. Only, I *cannot* be a soldier even if I wish very much to be a soldier."

His hands shook as he cleared the plates from the table. He scraped the leftovers into the garbage, not noticing I hadn't eaten any of Marcel's Notou bird.

Quite suddenly, and with certainty, I knew Pascal Manet had not been in love with Sandrine Bas Salaire de Lyon; he had been in love with Rocky's mother. I decided to test him.

"Rocky told me you used to have the hots, um, be keen on Sandrine."

Pascal's laughter crackled like the detergent bubbles in the sink as he moved a brush over the dishes. "Every guy in Nouméa was crazy about Sandrine, no matter what age! I was no different!"

☆

In the living room, he pressed the remote. The television lit up.

"Have you told the police I'm alive yet?"

"Of course. But they are still doing ADN tests. They were 'appy to know you are not a casualty of the *attentat.*" He sounded uninterested, as if wrung out from talking about the Events.

I watched the TV talk show host bound off his stool and kiss one of his male guests. Not a handshake, or formal *bise*—air kisses on either side of the face—this was a big, fat, juicy smooch on each cheek. *Mwaaah. Splack! Mwaaah. Splack!* Gentle, but blokey. I liked the physical closeness of the French people. But, despite the 'wog' comments from the kids at school, I didn't belong in that culture. I just felt Aussie.

"I think I'll go to bed." I hoped the kava had worn off enough for me to sleep. "Could you please get my clothes from 1, rue de la Guillotine?

Your lingerie lady friend's duds are okay, but I want my own things. I want my laptop, too. And my mobile phone."

"You must be patient. I will give you a clean shirt to lie in tonight." He slid his feet into his boat shoes, pushed himself up tiredly and disappeared into his bedroom. I heard him rustle around. A long pause.

I held my breath. Again I wondered: *Had he noticed I'd been rummaging among his things, and made off with his cabbage?*

Looking distracted, he emerged and handed me the unopened packet.

Seeing the label on the shirt through the cellophane, I blurted, "You *really* like Kenzo!" *Uh-oh, would he guess I had been snooping?*

"*Kenzo Pour Homme* is situated in the same boulevard in Paris as Alliance Française. It is convenient." He shrugged and pointed, saying, "Your foot?"

"That was where Namilly …" I hesitated, not wanting to provide him with ammunition to use against my mother. "My scarred toe was, like, a kiddy accident."

"*Non*. I mean, why are you barefoot?"

"My shoes flew off outside Noah's, when you jumped on top of me."

"I will buy you a new pair." He added, "*La femme de ménage* returns from Koné, maybe tomorrow, when she has fulfilled her obligations to her family. The housekeeper is a good woman. Her name is Marie-Françoise."

After hiding my hundred dollars 'grey nurse' in one of the lime green La Perla G-strings, I crawled beneath the mosquito netting. I lay there wondering if his housekeeper would be my watchdog, or my ally.

To the whoosh and click of the ceiling fan I began to drift off, with the boggy dressing smell of his new shirt in my nostrils. Below, I could hear the soft tap of a hammer. Pascal was shoring up the louvres in the en suite bathroom—cutting off my avenue of escape.

Chapter 33

A chainsaw whined in the distance, teeth grinding around its endless chain. A street cleaner shushed past. A shout. The clean-up from the cyclone continued.

Under house arrest until Jacques Forestier said otherwise, and trembling with cabin fever, I sat at the granite bench in Pascal's bathroom. The Hollywood lights blazed. I wore a Chanel lipstick he'd left me (sepia, which made me look as bad as I felt) in a jet case with a gilt band. Pascal still hadn't brought me any shoes. Did he think that if I *did* manage to escape from the house, it would be harder for me to run away barefoot? I hated being incarcerated, hated waiting until the floods were down so the cars no longer floated in Bourail. I hated this itchy urge to get out of here.

I wrenched the lid off the jar and the rubber bands tumbled out, collapsing in a mangled heap, bouncing around as if they couldn't wait for me to join them. I thought about Pascal being stabbed by a sicko wearing dreads, and briefly hesitated. But only briefly. I was determined to do dreads as a statement of solidarity with Rocky.

With my implements spread before me, I had the weirdest sense of communing with him. Like a power propelling me.

Tears blurred my vision. As I sat there, a rubber band flew from my fingers and sashayed across the bench to have a natter with one of its cousins, lounging about near the Kenzo Pour Homme Deodorant Stick. *Was this a kava side effect?*

Just thinking about kava made me hanker for the drink that made your tongue go numb, and your worries fly away, and the hatred seep out of your body. The thought of kava also made me speculate: At Rocky's funeral, would his independence friends be sombre? Would they cry, or simply stand there, stoic? A wave of nausea flittered through me at the thought of Rocky's body being shovelled off the road.

Doing my best to push the image to the back of my mind, I reached for the tube of toothpaste from the bathroom cupboard. I squeezed until the chlorophyll oozed along my forefinger, held my finger to my nose and sniffed. The gel smelled almost as good as the green coconut water. By now, I was *really* hanging out for a glass of the fizzy drink.

Separating a section, I held my hair and twisted as firmly as my shaky hands would allow. I massaged the toothpaste along the length of my hair, from my scalp right down to the bristly bit. Grabbing a metal dog comb I'd discovered in the laundry, I teased as hard as I could until my scalp hurt and my eyes began to tear up from the pain. I twisted once more, and then dipped my finger into a jar of natural honey. Smoothed the honey along the knotted hair. I licked my finger and wound a rubber band around the end.

I separated another section of hair, and went through the process again. Twist. Toothpaste. Tease. Twist. Honey. Finger lick. Rubber band.

In no time my arms were aching, my insides churning. Was it the toothpaste? Or the honey? Or was I suffering from intestinal fur balls? But the minty taste of the gel was refreshing, and the honey tasted good … *No, no, no.* Honey was a living creature by-product.

I ploughed on, wiping (instead of licking) my finger on a black towel, making sure I didn't ingest the honey.

Soon I was sweating from the heat of the exposed bulbs on either side of the mirror, and my eyelids were twitching. But I'd completed my task. My head was now covered in chunky hair-sausages. I moved my head from side to side. Up and down. I resembled Shirley Temple in one of those Classic movies—but with dark eyes and olive skin. Although— yeah!—I definitely appeared assertive. I felt like marching in the streets waving a blue, red, green and yellow Kanaky flag.

I assessed my image. *Who was I kidding?* I was like a floppy rag doll. I pressed on. All I had left to do was apply the beaten eggs and the

Stately Homes of England beeswax—in a rusty tin, also discovered in the laundry—and I'd be finished.

Which came first? The eggs? Or the Stately Homes of England beeswax? My mind was in a muddle. I opted for the eggs. I slopped the goo on the dreads with the aid of Pascal's toothbrush, so that I wouldn't be tempted to lick my fingers and consume dairy food. Next I rubbed the sticky beeswax from the scalp to the tip, careful to wipe them on a towel. As I worked, I wondered: *How did you wash dreads?* Was it a case of the more knotted the better? Did you just scrub the scalp with a toothbrush?

I gazed at my reflection, and a wave of sadness came over me. Rocky would never see me like this; never see me in my freedom fighter dreads. Tears pricked at the back of my lids. My insides hurt. Had Sandrine felt like this when my father died? And why did my hands feel so slippery?

The state of the bathroom distracted me. The bench was grungy with honey and eggs and toothpaste, sweaty wriggling rubber bands and beeswax crumbs; not to mention the doggy comb stuffed with twisted bits of hair. *Yaaaark.* Egg was smeared on Pascal's Kenzo Pour Homme Eau De Toilette, dribbling down the veined leaves etched into the glass. What a mess! Would Marie-Françoise, the housekeeper, turn up today? If she was as sweet as her name implied, she'd be bound to help me tidy up.

Oh, *heck*, was I seeing things? Even more egg was on the narrow bottle of Kenzo Pour Homme Shower gel.

Briefly wondering if my birth dad had worn products like these, I noticed honey on Pascal's Kenzo Air Pour Homme. A sticky blob clung to the opaque glass panel. I lifted the window-shaped bottle, mesmerised by the contents swirling around inside. I gave the bottle a shake, squirted some Kenzo Air fragrance on my skin. Sniffed. The scent was manly, sort of woody with a touch of star-anise spice. Had my biological father smelled like this? My stomach was turning feral. Was it the aftershave? Or from thinking about Rocky's funeral?

Sliding off the stool, I reeled into the kitchen. I hauled open the pantry door, looking for something to settle my queasiness. I pushed aside the basil, oregano, mixed spice, cinnamon and nutmeg. I chucked rolled oats to one side, watched the packet burst, and the contents scatter across the shelf. Bits fluttered to the floor, settling between my toes. I thrust away carob powder, and cayenne pepper, and self-raising flour.

No Alka-Seltzer. Nothing.

Finally, I found a bottle of vanilla essence. *Vanille*, read the label. *That'd do the trick*, I told myself. Vanilla essence was raw vegan. I unscrewed the lid and swigged. Did I feel different? No, probably more nauseous. *Was vanilla alcoholic?* I wondered.

I shoved aside the Italian Olive Oil and vinegar, searching for something to make me feel better. I eyed the bottle of vinegar again. Vinegar was definitely vegan, *definitely* non-alcoholic. Unscrewing the top, I sipped. *Yuck-eeee!* Would the answer to the foul taste be to drink it in one gulp, as one did with kava?

Berk! My body squawked as I gulped the lot down.

The room began to spin.

Slowly, slowly—faster, and faster.

The overhead lights whirled. I was on a merry-go-round. Gut cramps attacked me in waves. The bile rose up. I ran. I hit the en suite, and retched into the toilet. Vinegar and vanilla essence, followed by honey and toothpaste, swirled in the bowl.

I spat away the bitterness and stood there, bent over, swaying and shivering. Clutching myself around the waist, I slumped to the ground.

I didn't hear the front door open.

Chapter 34

I heard a scratching, a scraping, followed by a scrunch. An old house was bound to niggle and groan from the sea breezes, I told myself.

The noises were followed by footsteps. Heavy breathing. Was that the *clicking of a tongue?* I thought I really was hallucinating, this time. Or was I asleep, these noises a dream? Then I heard *"Awa!"*

I floundered up off the floor of the en suite.

The heavy breathing moved away, making for the kitchen.

"Oh, là." A gasp. Thunderous footsteps headed towards Pascal's granite bathroom. A throaty cry. *"Mon Dieu!"* a voice boomed.

Scampering from the en suite, I hid behind the spare bedroom door, hoping whoever it was would go away. Footsteps ascended the stairs. Creak! Groan! The house seemed to shake. This was breathing like I'd never heard before. And it was getting louder.

A goobie sigh. Footsteps descended the stairs, and I peeked out. The most enormous Kanak woman I had ever seen was clinging to the banister, so hard the timber seemed about to snap in her grasp. Was this Marie-Françoise? If so, Pascal's housekeeper was at least twenty feet tall and ten feet wide, with a humungous mole on the bridge of her nose like the sign of the devil. One of her eyes was milky white.

Her good eye latched on to me. *"Voleuse!"* she boomed.

"But I haven't stolen anything!" And then I remembered the money I'd pinched from Pascal's suit. Had she rummaged in my G-string upstairs, found the cabbage?

"Dégagez!" she said, indicating I should leave.

I stood there, gobsmacked and barefoot.

"Prenez la porte!" She stormed to the front door, and hurled it open.

Heck, Marie-Françoise really did want me out of here. Or had the vanilla essence scrambled my brain? I wondered.

"Dehors!" Her finger was arrow-straight and unwavering.

"Cool it! I'm leaving!" I zoomed across the veranda and down the front steps.

Standing at the bottom of the steps, twisting my dreadlocks, I yelled, "Please tell me! Are you Marie-Françoise?"

The front door slammed shut.

"Pascal … I mean, Monsieur Manet … will be so peed off that you chucked me out!" I shouted at the silent house. "I'm meant to stay inside!"

The broken melaleuca tree, still lying on the front lawn, gave off a camphor scent as I stumbled over it.

"Well, now I'm free, I'm off to a nakamal," I muttered to a gull pecking on a burst seed. "I plan to find myself a fabbo, healthy, raw vegan drink."

I crossed the almost deserted road, and jogged off along the footpath beside the beach towards Baie de la Moselle and Chouchou's. Or, if Chouchou had packed up his lean-to and left, I planned to hotfoot it to Noah's nakamal in the Latin Quarter.

Gulls screeched. A maxi-yacht flying the New Zealand flag was in port. A few fishing boats rocked nearby.

I was surprised to find Nakamal de Chouchou was crowded. Perched in the gravel on sawn-off stump seats, sailors sipped kava from their coconut shells. Indians, Tahitians, Wallisians, Vietnamese and Melanesians were there. But no one of European extraction.

Chouchou now wore a sardine can on one foot, a flattened plastic bottle on the other. He lifted a corner of his Rastafarian bonnet, scratched hard as I picked my way across the white pebbles.

"Du kava, s'il vous plaît." Straightaway, I realised my Aussie hundred dollars was back in my bedroom at *La Maison des Cerises*, hidden

in the La Perla G-string. "It's okay, forget about the kava. I don't have enough money." Disappointed, I turned to leave.

"Un shell pour mademoiselle!" shouted a man with saddlebag skin and wearing a straw hat. He pulled a roll of money from his pocket, and peeled off a one hundred franc note.

Settling myself on the bench against the wall, I sipped. My tongue went numb, my lips went numb and I shuddered from the taste. But the familiar calm swept over me. I sat there smiling. All the men smiled back as they watched me finish the remainder of my drink. We all laughed together, and the world was beautiful.

"Un shell pour mademoiselle!" cried an Indian, with his trousers rolled up to the knee.

Smiling graciously, I accepted a second shell and sipped.

They say the strongest muscle in the body is the tongue. By now, my entire body was numb. And my tongue was in the zilch zone. I was unable to move, even if I had wanted to. No matter. I would've been happy to sit in Chouchou's, sipping kava forever on my hard wooden bench.

Next thing I knew, the nakamal proprietor handed me a glass of the fizzy green drink made with coconut water. I ran my tongue around the inside of the tumbler. The taste was to die for! I took a mouthful, swallowed. The nakamal rocked, then rocked some more. I swallowed again. My vision began to darken, rather than turn super-duper clear.

Through a strange and spotty dimness, I could hear laughter. Fingertips ran over my skin, and up my legs, and touched me on the thigh. Someone leaned against me, and began to lick my shoulder. And I couldn't shove his tongue away.

Had my kava been spiked with alcohol? The words trickled about in my mind: *Rocky warned me.*

A woman pushed through the beaded curtain at the back. Her dress clung to her body. She had crazy black hair, and laughed a lot. She threw her arms around Chouchou.

My face felt puffy. I sat there like Raggedy Ruth in my dreadlocks, unable to pummel the sleazes away. The glass containing my fizzy drink rolled sideways. The dregs dribbled to the ground. The pebbles gobbled the liquid up. I had no money, no identity, and I was certain these low-life types were about to throw me on a boat and smuggle me to some faraway place. Only, this time it wouldn't be to a nice little town in Australia. This time, I'd be on a slave ship to Thailand, on my way to be a sex worker.

I was scared, but couldn't make a run for it. In a fog caused by the fizzy drink, I sat there blaming Rocky. It was his fault for introducing me to 'nature's stress buster'. Pascal had warned me that kava could be lethal if mixed with alcohol, and I had taken no notice.

By now, I was certain that grog was in my kava. My brows had grown caterpillar feet. Eyebrow hairs were scuttling across my forehead. Turning cartwheels, and dancing a jig. Someone began to pull my skirt up. The hem rose to my waist. A hand yanked at my knickers. The hand was rough.

A sudden shout. The sound of scurrying.

Silence.

"*On y va, Genna?* Let's go." The voice was Pascal's.

"I c-c-can't, uh, er …"

The words refused to come. My legs felt like overcooked spaghetti as he carried and dragged me to the Benz. Night fell as we zipped up the hill and zigzagged around bays, heading for *La Maison des Cerises*.

The garage door closed. Pascal, clad in a floral shirt, pulled open the rear door and hauled me from the car. He threw me over his shoulder in a fireman's lift. Round and round and round we went up the circular staircase leading into the house. Round and *round*—and ROUND. My arms flopped against his denims. My stomach began to squish and do somersaults.

Barf! I puked all over the back of his good jeans.

"Putééé!" I heard him roar.

Chapter 35

My brain rocked from the shivers. Cold water pounded down over me as I cringed in my undies in a corner of the shower recess. Pascal's floral shirt flapped in my face. My eyes began to close.

He slapped me. Paf! *"Ouvre les yeux!"* he ordered.

"Namilly never hit me e-verrr, e-verrr, e-verrr." My words were slurred.

"Perhaps she should 'ave hit you," he muttered. "You behave like a spoilt *gosse*, a brat who makes a mess in my house." His voice seemed to come from a distance.

Everything began to darken again.

He gave me another slap. *"Debout!* Get up!" He hoisted me to my feet and walked me in circles on the tiled floor of the en suite bathroom. He smelled of vomit. And I vaguely remembered having thrown up over the back of his jeans.

Lights blazed throughout the house. He propelled me, dripping, in the direction of the kitchen—which, through my bleary gaze, had been mopped clean of the mess I'd made.

Up, down. Up, down and around we went.

"I wanna shleeeeep." My voice was like a passing gust of air.

"You may sleep when you are awake."

The housekeeper, wearing a mud-green missionary dress, was sorting through a heap of hairy yams, and humming tunelessly. She gave me a vicious look with her good eye and got on with it.

"It is the time of the yam festival," said Pascal, "so Marie-Françoise is celebrating fruitfulness." His tone was chatty and reasonable as he continued to propel me. "There are more than one hundred and fifty species of *igname* on the main island. She feels well blessed. She will take the yams to Camp-Est prison, where her nephew is incarcerated for setting fire to a telephone box in the Brousse."

The sight of the lumpy yams made me want to throw up again. I pushed back the feeling, gulped and turned my head away as we continued our aimless trudge.

"Alcohol was in the kava you drink. I smell it, and I *tell* you to be careful, and you take no notice. Why?"

"Oooh," I croaked, "I feel *ter*-rible."

"Why do you not obey me? If you had drunk straight kava, you would not be nearly as sick." He hesitated, as we negotiated our way back to the en suite bathroom. "You may still become ill in ze stomach from lack of running water, but not so bad in the head."

"That's handy to know. But it's a bit late to tell me."

"*Merde!* I did warn you!" he yelled, making me jump.

Pascal sounded really peed off. I tried to pull away, but his grip was like concrete.

He brought up the subject of my dreadlocks. "What 'ave you done wis your *hair*? The floods have receded, and Jacques Forestier will not be happy. We are driving to Bouchon, 'is farm in Bourail, for lunch tomorrow."

"Oooh," I groaned. "Ooooh."

My headache was killing me, and I wondered how I would get out of going to Bourail.

"I don't think I'll be, um, well enough." A burp erupted, and I covered my mouth. "What time is … is it?" I asked, hoping he hadn't noticed, and forgetting he'd seen, and heard, and personally felt far worse than that burst from my body.

"Deux heures du matin."

"Two o'clock in the *morning*!" I moaned. "I'll *ne-ver* be able to get up."

"You will! You will get up. I will see to it!"

I scratched at my forearm. Pascal reached into the overhead cupboard. He extracted a bottle of calamine lotion and some cotton wool.

"The kava 'as caused your rash." He dabbed on the pink stuff.

"But I only ever drank kava, like, um, oh … I can't think … four times, apart from today." I could feel myself go beetroot as I remembered the sailors. "And only one shell, um, well, on each occasion before that."

"Your liver is suffering. You must promise me never to drink kava again."

My insides were still rugged, my head was hammering, and I felt disoriented. I was happy to agree to anything Pascal suggested.

"I won't drink kava any more, e-ver. I really, really promise."

He steered me out of the bathroom and back to the kitchen, where Marie-Françoise was still fiddling about with her yams. Her brow was so furrowed that the mole on the bridge of her nose had narrowed to a slit. She didn't look to me as if she was celebrating anything, let alone fertility.

"Can I have an, um, aspirin?" Then, hoping he didn't think I wanted to snort it, I said, "Not, you know, chewable, just the ordinary sort."

"You will take nothing for now, apart from drinking very much water." He handed me a bottle of Evian from the fridge.

Unable to sleep, I ached and tossed and sighed in time with the overhead ceiling fan. A sea breeze wafted through the house, and I could hear the whoosh of cars speeding along Promenade Roger Laroque, ghetto blasters thumping. I blinked as I peered through the mosquito netting, trying to make out the cross on the dormer window in the ceiling. I saw it was gone. In my absence, Marie-Françoise had been busy removing the masking tape from the windowpanes.

The cyclone was over. But not my memories of Rocky.

Downstairs, the front door was open. I could smell French cigarettes. Pascal wasn't asleep, either. He was sitting on the front steps smoking his Gauloises Blondes.

After an hour or so, I heard the front door close. No more cars. No more ghetto blasters. The house was silent. Marie-Françoise had retired to her bedroom beneath the house. But—probably due to the kava—I still couldn't sleep. I missed Rocky. I missed Stefan. And I missed my new friends. *Would I ever see Cluny, Jazz and Spud again?*

I didn't get a wink of shut-eye.

☆

A rap on the bedroom door. Pascal wore a pair of beige trousers and a tasteful Lacoste polo.

"I prefer the floral shirt you were wearing yesterday, much more casual and interesting." I yawned, and pointed through the netting.

He ignored my comment. "You will go this morning to the Bernheim Library on avenue Maréchal Foch, *centre ville*. Marie-Françoise will accompany you and, after that, we will depart from *La Maison des Cerises* at exactly twenty minutes to eleven." Pascal sounded like a tourist guide.

"I didn't sleep at all last night, thanks to you refusing to give me aspirin."

"Of course. That is why you were snoring when I knocked at your door." Not asking how I felt, he added. "I will look for your clothing at 1, rue de la Guillotine. And I will bring your laptop and other things back in time for you to change before we leave for Bourail."

I had one small thing to be glad about. I would have my own clothes to wear.

Chapter 36

St. Joseph's Cathedral towered on the hill as we alighted from the Car Sud bus with the yacht insignia, not far from Place des Cocotiers. With Marie-Françoise puffing behind, I passed through the ornate metal gates and crossed the quiet, shady courtyard, heading for the entrance of the Bernheim Library. The colonial timber balustrade—composed of a series of rectangular shapes and crossbars—gleamed white in the sun. The building was apparently unharmed by the cyclone. A woman nursed a baby under a tree. It looked peaceful.

Marie-Françoise, who said little and seemed to speak no English, made for the east wing to thumb through the newspapers and magazines on offer there. Hoisting up the straps of my hot-pink and black rose top, I left her and headed right, into the main section of the library to find reference books on mining in the territory.

My stomach still wasn't great. The sea of green dots on the cream, tessellated floor made me feel bilious. Pascal had told me to use my time 'wisely'. I had a sneaking suspicion he'd sent me to the library with Marie-Françoise so that she could ensure I didn't do anything disastrous before we set off to Bourail. I had a feeling he didn't trust me.

I was hanging out to see my clothes again. Not to mention my laptop and other bits and pieces I'd left at 1, rue de la Guillotine. I hoped to get back my flashcards, assuming they hadn't been spoiled by water damage.

An impressive staircase, curved and brown, reared up towards a second floor. I remained on the ground floor, wandering among the bookshelves, held together with brackets like a Meccano set. Melanesian students studied quietly, apparently unconcerned that their schools might be roofless.

In a book on nickel, I came across the author's reference to an '*haut fourneau*'. Did that mean 'smelter' in English? I decided to search for a dictionary. I climbed the stairs, turned left and headed for a shelf of chunky tomes. I selected a Larousse.

A student beside me pulled out a Harrap.

"Bonjour!" she said.

"Bonjour!" I replied.

I flicked through the pages. I had almost reached 'f' when I felt a breath on my shoulder. A sudden scream.

"It *is* you! I thought you were *dead* or something." Cluny Belpomme threw her arms around me so hard the dictionary slammed downwards, missing my big toe by a whisker. "Wow! That outfit you're wearing looks *really* expensive. Sex-*eee*! Sick on legs! Where did you get *that*?"

"Some lingerie lady friend of Pascal Manet chose it." I ran my fingers over the spangled multi-pink skirt. "It's Charles Jourdan, but I don't think it's my style."

Cluny gave me a funny look. "And what on earth have you done to your hair? I almost didn't recognise you."

"Dreads! Like 'em?"

"Well," she murmured, "I'm not sure. You look a bit like that American kid, only olive-skinned and older. How did you do them?"

I was explaining about the honey and the toothpaste and the eggs and Stately Homes of England beeswax, when my eyes latched onto the swarthy-looking guy I'd seen wrestling with his diving gear and surfboard when I first arrived in New Caledonia. He wore a red, gold and black Koori band around his neck. He made for Cluny and put his arm around her shoulder.

"You know Flex, don't you?" said Cluny.

"Flex?" I twisted a dreadlock.

"Flex du Lac from 1, rue de la Guillotine." She hooked a finger into his jeans' belt.

"I-I never met Flex." I was surprised to see them so chummy. "What with the cyclone, and all those dates with Rocky, it never happened." I decided to fill her in on Rocky. "Did you read that Rocky died in that car bombing in the Latin Quarter?" I felt myself tear up.

"I know. Shocking!" she said. "Flex! Meet my good friend, Genna Perrier."

"Pleased to meet you." He put out his hand.

As I shook, I wondered why Cluny wasn't more upset about Rocky's death. Was she only interested in impressing Flex?

I decided to hang tough. "I saw you at Tontouta, Flex. You were ahead of me, struggling with your gear."

"Yeah, 'aven't used the board much, but. Them winds were far too strong." Flex gave me a Colgate smile. "Dived off the reef, though."

Cluny stood there looking chuffed and amazed at everything Flex said. "So where've you been billeted, Genna?" She removed her hand from his belt, slid it intimately into his back pocket.

"Um, I'm at Monsieur Manet's."

"Yowee! You're right up there, in the big league. Your French must be excellent."

Pascal's comments about how average my French really was surged into my thoughts. "It's not too bad." I hastily changed the subject. "Where's Jazz?"

"Jazz's gone home to Australia. Jazz was shoot scared … the cyclone, the terrorist attack in the Latin Quarter … so she grabbed the first plane outta here."

"And Spud?"

Cluny hesitated. "Spud's got problems. He moved out of the billet and asked Chantal to take him in with her family, despite Monsieur Manet telling him not to. She wouldn't … take him in. Spud got fizzed off. And now he's touring around New Cal on his lonesome." She licked her lips. "Flex and I went to the Monts Koghis yesterday, and hiked. The ground was slippery from the rain, but it was awesome. Fabbo views from there. You should do it."

"Sounds wicked. I'll try to fit it in."

She held out her wrist. "Look what Flex bought me with his Casino winnings." She ran her forefinger around the beads. "Black pearls … bad luck in Tahiti, but good luck for me. Jasper. Clear quartz. And haematite, which is *very* energising."

She glanced up; her cornflower eyes opened wide.

"Wow! Have a squiz at that woman!" she hissed in my ear. "Have you ever seen anyone so *fierce*?"

I turned. Marie-Françoise was standing at the top of the stairs, tapping her watch.

"Oh, that's Pascal's housekeeper. She's not, well, almost not, as spooky as she looks." I touched Cluny on the arm. "Gotta go. Think your bracelet's cool."

"Great CD section!" She pointed to a nearby door. "Lots of Aussies."

"I'm off to Bourail. See ya."

As I followed Marie-Françoise down the stairs, I heard Cluny say to Flex: "It's been a bit funny with Genna, sort of preferential treatment, but also the same as us. *If* you get my drift! Do you think she's *doing* it with Monsieur Manet?"

"Dunno, babe," he said.

And I regretted not having shared with her that Jacques Forestier was probably—no, after discovering that Procuration, almost certainly—my grandfather.

☆

Pascal stowed my backpack in the boot, in case I wished to stay overnight at Jacques Forestier's. Taking the RT1, we drove past Tontouta airport where a plane dropped its wheels for landing. The sight made me homesick. Right now, I would have been happy to hop on the next plane and leave, instead of going to Bouchon to be inspected like one of my grandfather's animals.

Densely covered mountain peaks wreathed in cloud loomed to the right.

"We are in the Brousse now," said Pascal, as the city of Noumea disappeared behind us.

He smelled of Repel and Kenzo aftershave. He had burn marks on the back of his hands. His knuckles were bare and sore looking, but almost healed. His fingers were pale against the tan of his arms from the bandages and Band-Aids. He saw me look.

"I removed the *sparadrap* and applied kava leaves."

I gasped. "But you told me …"

"Kava is very efficient for the healing of wounds."

Smugness invaded my face.

His next words wiped the smile away. "And also for creating abortions. So, you see, you are playing with something ve-ry dangerous."

Flustered, I pulled at my citrus day-glo tube skirt, dragged it down in the direction of my knees. It was good to be back in my duds again.

Out of the blue, he said, "There is no blood in your urine?"

"Shivers! I don't think so."

Silence for a while. The sealed highway curved back from the coast, away from the marshes. Low palms and tree ferns and broken branches flashed past, followed by mud flats. I saw an occasional glimpse of the sea, a hint of blue lagoon.

"New Cal's like Cairns," I murmured. "I expected to see those cute little French bug cars, not boring Mercs and utes."

"Marcel told me you went to Cairns."

"And what a waste of time *that* was! It's the reason I find it hard to believe any of this. Sandrine said it wasn't true."

"Sandrine is too proud." He added, "You look more suitable in your own clothes."

"Mmmm, I *feel* better too." I glimpsed a mud beach.

He fished in his pocket. "I forgot to give you this." He pulled out my floral mobile phone.

"That's so mygodish! Where did you find it?"

"I searched on the ground in the Latin Quarter and I find your portable near Noah's nakamal. The phone was full of water, so I 'ave it repaired."

"That is soooo sweet of you!" I almost kissed him, but resisted.

Pascal's face creased into a smile, and it was the first time I'd seen him appear genuinely happy.

"The trip is not long to go. We 'ave made good time. We will be in Bourail much more sooner than the two hours it usually takes."

I was hardly listening. My fingers flew over the buttons of my mobile phone as I tapped out my SMS to Stefan—first text since the night of the car bombing. I decided not to tell him what I'd been through. Better to boast.

My heart was fluttering as I brought up his number and pressed *OK*. The blue *Sending Message* line roved back and forth as it hurtled my words to him:

r off to bourail wassup with u?

Fidgeting, I waited for his reply. Pascal glanced at me, but said nothing. The mobile did its familiar shimmy. *1 message received* flashed.

Pressing *Show*, I gazed at Stefan's response:

bill einstein still sik

"What's going on?" I cried. "Stefan's still typing the same old message."

Running my thumbnail over the scratches and chips on the floral cover, a reminder of the night at Noah's, I wondered if the marks were an omen. My boyfriend's image stared at me from the screen wallpaper.

I knew something wasn't right.

Chapter 37

Marsh insects and mosquitoes splattered the windscreen. Pascal reached into the glove box and extracted a Repel roll-on.

"When you get out of the car, it is best you not get dengue."

I slopped on the repellent absentmindedly. We turned off the undulating road and drove across a bridge. Mangroves clustered and drooped into the water.

"La Néa," he said.

I barely noticed. Stefan had sent me the same words last time, and the time before that, the same old bizzo about Bill Einstein. And I didn't understand. No way was Win's horse still sick. What was going on?

"Perhaps you should ring 'im." Pascal was trying to be helpful as I squirmed and puffed on the seat beside him.

"But it's so dear, much dearer than SMS." I twisted my dreadlocks one by one. "And, if he rings me, I have to pay for it. Like, it goes on my bill *both* ways."

"I will pay your portable bill for you. Go on, ring your little friend. It will make me feel better if you are 'appy."

With jiggly fingers, I pushed the buttons and dialled Stefan's number. I pressed the green key. His mobile rang once, twice, three times. He didn't answer. After the fourth ring, the phone gave out a recorded message. There was no point in speaking. Stefan would see my number and know I'd called. I pressed the red key, hit *Lock* and slumped back.

"It's on voice mail."

Pascal tried to distract me. "I sometimes find it difficult in the third millennium to send a *texto*, which you call SMS. I 'ave to fiddle with all those tiny buttons."

"There's predictive text, which is easier. I could teach you," I began, but my heart wasn't in it.

"We 'ave time to spare. I will take you to La Roche Percée. You may have seen the rock on postcards. It is shaped like a face." He indicated the low-lying countryside. "Twenty-five per cent of our country's beef is produced in this area." He gave a teasing smile. "Bourail was created for the rehabilitation of convicts. You must feel very at home."

I chewed the inside of my cheek, wondering: Had Pascal made that crack about convicts, because I'd nicked the dosh from his suit?

"I used to do free diving at this beach, immersion," he continued, easing the car into the parking area. "Ah, ze silence down there is wonderful! I was champion of Grande Terre before my injury. Did you see the film, *Le Grand Bleu*?"

As we climbed from the car, I knew he was trying to make me forget about Stefan. "Yeah, I did."

"I was like Jacques, the hero in this film. I was an expert at relaxation. You learn *apnée* by going down a rope, you know. I was experienced at holding my breath, becoming a dolphin and plunging far down into the water. My spirit and mind were free, and I felt connected to a greater being. I could not bear to resurface."

"But did you love Johanna enough to come back to that surface?"

"Ah, you remember this film? It is extraordinary."

"Did you swim with dolphins?"

We wandered onto the narrow beach. The sand was wet from the cyclone.

"I did, and with grey sharks and hammerheads and all kinds of reef fish. Also barracudas and stingrays."

"Do you get whales here?"

"Whales pass by the territory each year on their way to Antarctic, in September."

"And you've seen them?" I found I was beginning to forget about Stefan.

He nodded. "They are amazing when they breach, magnificent. They pass beneath the boat without even bumping into it. Whales are very gentle."

"Did you free dive with whales, or only with dolphins?"

"Only dolphins, but I would 'ave liked to dive with whales. I would talk and talk about the world of apnoea and few people knew what an incredible experience it was. My mother would say, 'Stop holding your breath and eat your dinner, Pascal!' She never understood."

"But you didn't die, as Enzo did."

He pointed to the water in the distance. "And now, when I 'ave time, I go snorkelling farther around, off Poé beach where the sand is white and the shells very good. You must try it." His eyes shone. "There are turtles at nearby Baie des Tortues, and also here at La Roche Percée. I 'ave come at night with a torch, seen the *grosse tête*, or bigheaded, turtle dig a hole and lay over one hundred eggs in the sand, under that rock." He paused. "But the currents are dangerous. You should be very careful when you swim 'ere."

"Wow! Isn't it unreal? The rock's like a person."

"Et le bonhomme de la roche." He indicated the unusual formation that looked like a man. "Some people surf at this beach. But it does not 'ave great waves like your Bondi Beach in Australia."

The pines on the low cliffs were thin and column-like. "This place reminds me of Ravella, only without the bathing boxes."

The waves broke softly, stirring up the water in the rock pools. The same briny smell made me think of Win and Stefan.

"Win used to ride her horse on the sand, when the tide was out and Bill Einstein was fitter." I felt suddenly homesick.

"And Stefan?"

"Stef catches blue ringers in pools like these. And he puts them in jars and sometimes I think it's cruel."

A woman rode past on a horse, reins loose, her shoulders rounded and relaxed. She looked in our direction. *"Bonjour, Pascal!"* She waved, and adjusted her straw hat.

"Bonjour, Emma. Comment ça va?" he called out.

"Ça va mieux," she replied, continuing on her way.

Emma's long curly hair fanned out behind her. She'd said she was feeling better. Had she been ill? I didn't like to ask.

"Emma di Luca's husband Bruno, a former head stockman, owns a cattle station, small in comparison with the ones in Australia, not far from 'ere." Pascal looked at his watch. "We must be on our way, or we will be late for lunch. They will 'ave finished their game of *pétanque*."

A kite surfer surged into the sky as we left.

Araucaria pines reared skinny and spiky behind a traditional Melanesian hut. The wonky brown bricks and shutters of the Bourail pioneer museum winked in the midday sun as we passed.

Pascal pointed. "This building was constructed in 1870 by the penitentiary administration, and used by the *La Néa* cheese company. There is much inside about the New Zealand presence during the Second World War. You would find it interesting."

"But I'm from Australia, not New Zealand," I said, strung out at the thought of meeting Jacques Forestier.

"But your two countries are close. There is also a New Zealand military cemetery." He waved his hand to the right. "You will find tombs of soldiers buried in combat. Also a memorial for soldiers whose bodies 'ave never been recovered."

We cruised past a multi-purpose stadium and along the main street. "The RT1 becomes la rue Simon Drémon," he explained, "and, left, you can see the *Mairie*, supermarkets, shops."

My stomach lurched with anxiety as we passed shuttered colonial houses with battered palms in their gardens, jostling concrete block apartments. Women in missionary dresses wove baskets at a street stall bulging with fruit and vegetables. The street was short.

A troop carrier went by, with young guys hanging out the back.

"There is a big French military base after Bourail, on the way to Koné, ten kilometres out of town," said Pascal. "Remoteness of mountains is good for training exercises."

Soon we were driving alongside a cornfield, the crop so flattened by the cyclone that it resembled a seaweed mattress. Two men in check shirts tramped about with grim faces, turning drenched leaves to inspect the damage.

Muddy water sprayed up over the bonnet as we bumped our way past the Bouchon sign and up the drive to Jacques Forestier's house.

Blue shutters hung beside the windows, fastened back against the white wall.

The sight of the pointy finials on top of the veranda posts made me stiffen. I was packing death now I was about to confront the man who had scared Sandrine away from Grande Terre.

Chapter 38

As we got out of the car I heard a shout: *"Nous sommes treize!"* Someone had gained thirteen points, and won his game of *pétanque*.

My mind was feverishly transported back to the day when my French teacher brought her box of boules to class. Things got out of hand when she began to rabbit on about the *'pointeur'* (who was good at getting his boules nearest the *cochonnet*) and the *'tireur'* (good at knocking his opponent's balls out of contention). The captain of my team, the *'milieu'*, bored with the explanations, hurled his steel boule, aiming for the *cochonnet*. The boule connected with another player's chest. Clutching his *'baguette'*—for measuring the distance between the boules—my classmate collapsed to the ground and spent the next two months in hospital.

Again, I wished I was back in Ravella.

Pascal steered me around the side of the dwelling. He propelled me towards a gravel strip. Beside the strip, Marcel Manet—aviator glasses wrapped around his forehead—was in the process of giving the shoulder of a woman wearing a pareo an affectionate squeeze. His trousers were splashed with muddy water. His Blanc Bleu shirt was sweat-stained. But Marcel was as speccy as ever, and my heart jiggled with relief at seeing someone I knew.

People stared. I twisted a dreadlock. A baby cried somewhere.

Pascal strode to Marcel. He grabbed his brother by the neck, and they kissed one another—a great big smack on each cheek. *Mwaah! Mwaah!* They stood there hugging and backslapping, and the joy of winning at *pétanque* had flown. I knew each guy was thinking of Rocky. And Marcel's shades never shifted.

The man whose walking stick I'd briefly seen the day I fled from the library at 1, rue de la Guillotine heaved himself off a garden seat. His shoulders were bent over so that his head poked between them like a bird as he made his way to me. His hair was grey, his face the colour of cement.

"Bienvenue parmi nous, Geneviève!" Jacques Forestier held out his hand.

"My name is Genna." His skin felt like baking paper as I shook.

"Of course." He switched to English. "I forgot. She always called you Genna."

"Who called me Genna, Sandrine?"

"Non. The *nounou."* He turned to greet Pascal.

"My mother's a person, not a thing," I muttered beneath my breath. Then I blurted, "Anyway, that *nanny* saved me."

He turned back. *"Who* saved you?" His eyes were as round as a pigeon's.

"Her name is Namilly Perrier, and she saved me."

"Saved you from what? I am alive. Sandrine is alive. We are all alive. She rescued you from nothing." Jacques Forestier's English was almost perfect, and it made his words more hurtful.

"Arrête, Jacques!" Pascal spoke in a low voice.

Dogs barked in the distance.

Marcel approached, smelling of garlic and Gauloises cigarettes. He took me by the shoulder and gave me two *bises* in the French way. Then he gave me a third kiss for good luck.

"What 'ave you *done* wis your *hairs*?" His own hair was as I remembered.

"Dreadlocks!" My face split into an unexpected grin.

"And Madame Evian is well?"

"Wrong brand of mineral water! You never get it right!"

My knees were still quivery from my spat with Jacques—now in an intense discussion with Pascal—and I wondered if I should mention Rocky.

The words came out of their own accord: "I'm sorry about your, um, my friend."

"La vie continue." Marcel's voice was tight. "I will leave you. I must change for lunch."

Had I said the wrong thing? He pushed past an anxious-looking woman, whose gloss lipstick had become runny at the corners of her mouth.

Bottles of Number One beer and Mont-Dore mineral water were clustered on a side table covered with a check cloth beside the house. I eyed the bottles, hankering for a shell of kava to calm me down.

Pascal still talked with Jacques—about my kava problems? Pascal had returned all my possessions, including the water-damaged flash-cards, but not *my chop-chop.* Did he believe the chop-chop in my clip-lock bag was ganja? Were they chewing over the possibility of hash in my luggage? They didn't look in my direction. I heard the word 'Spud'. What had Spud Underwood done? Had Chantal dobbed him in for suck-ing on a joint? Or had they found out about the eccy?

"Je m'appelle Angélique!" The woman with the runny lipstick interrupted my head trip. She held out her hand.

"I'm Genna."

From the expression of terror on her face, I could tell Angélique didn't speak English. This was the moment I'd be forced to make small talk in French. Before I could say anything, she grabbed the arm of a passing red-faced man wearing an Akubra.

"Bonjour, je m'appelle Didier!" He put out his hand. *"Je suis le mari d'Angélique."*

Angélique's husband's touch was warm and rough.

"Enchantée!" I said.

I was gearing up to continue my conversation in French, when Didier edged away. He headed for Pascal and Jacques Forestier.

A baby's cry came from inside the house.

"Darling a besoin de moi." Angélique rushed off, leaving me alone and breathing easier.

Marcel barrelled out the backdoor, now clad in powder blue trousers. His frangipani floral shirt had a matching powder blue background. His boat shoes were new. He headed in my direction.

"I see you not wear ring for toe fingers I offer you at Noël."

"You gave me that toe ring so you could pinch a piece of my hair." I pulled my foot from its citrus beaded thong, pushed it back in again. "It kind of lost its significance when I found out."

For once, Marcel seemed lost for words.

"What's wrong with Angélique?"

"Angélique is worried Darling might 'ave contracted *leptospirose*."

"Is leptospirosis a disease?"

"*Oui. Institut Pasteur* does some test in Nouméa. If you 'ave zis sickness, you take antibiotic and, *voilà*, everysing is all right." Marcel's English was more difficult to understand than Pascal's, but I got the drift. "*Leptospirose* is from rats, and it feel a-much like dengue."

"Then Angélique's baby should be okay?"

He shrugged. "We 'ope."

"Is Darling her real name?"

"*Oui.*" He smiled.

"It's a weird name to christen a kid."

"Ooh, people calls zemselves many sings." He gave another of his famous shrugs. "*À table!*"

He led me up the steps and into the house.

Chapter 39

A row of ceiling fans gently stirred the air of the glassed-in veranda, where a long table covered with a sunny floral cloth was set for eight people. I was startled to see Josiane there, not realising she and Jacques Forestier were friends. Was this some French 'cool' bizzo, a sort of *ménage à whatever*?

Josiane's hair was even spikier than it had been on the night I'd met her at Noah's. With a welcoming smile, she showed guests to their chairs. The glasses sparkled. The cutlery shone. The fabric of her dress was printed with bougainvillea blossoms.

Chantal emerged from the kitchen and placed bowls of salad in the centre of the table. Her hair was tied in a fluffy French plait. I gave her a wave, but she didn't respond. The skin on one of her cheekbones was greenish-mauve. The expression on her face was sullen. She looked as though she had been bashed.

Antlers sprouted from a stag's head looking down over the room. I sat to the right of Jacques Forestier, who eased himself into a chair at the head of the table. Didier, manager of Bouchon, with tousled corn hair and a pale band on his forehead where his hat had been, sat to the left of Jacques. Putting their heads together, they began to natter about cattle and deer and horses, things to do with farming that meant zip to me. I heard them complain about the cyclone coming so soon after Erica, grumble about the damage Liliane had done.

Josiane, seated between Didier and Pascal, leaned across the table and said, "Aren't the plates beautiful, Genna? Villeroy and Boch, French Garden pattern." Vine leaves, lattice, cherries, apples, lemons, black grapes and roses dotted the design. "I chose the china myself," she added.

"The china's very nice." I lifted salad onto my plate, wondering whether to mention the night at Noah's, maybe talk about the car bombing.

Jacques Forestier interrupted my thoughts. "I have an interest in beef production. My new prize bull broke a leg. We are eating the bull for lunch."

I nearly choked on a lettuce leaf at the thought of consuming red meat. Should I tell my grandfather I was a raw vegan? I wondered. I put down my knife and fork, and stared at a stuffed fish with a gawping mouth mounted on the wall, as I pondered how to avoid eating his prize bull.

"Ze fish is impressive, *non*?" Marcel sat on my immediate right. "It is a bonefish I 'ave catched and it weighs *vingt* kilos."

"Twenty kilos? Yowee! How does the fish stay up on the wall?" I tried to concentrate on the bonefish, and stop thinking of the piece of beef about to be placed before me.

Marcel made a stab in his stomach with his fingers, scooped them in a gutting motion and rolled his eyes.

"By the way, thanks for the SMS. How did you get my mobile number?"

"Oooh, I guess." His eyes glued onto my burnt eyebrow, and then slid away.

Yeah, sure you did! I told myself. Just like my email address.

Pascal, diagonally opposite, munched on his salad and talked across the table with Didier's wife.

While stewing over how Marcel had discovered my mobile number, I heard Jacques and Didier discuss the housing market.

"Didier has just bought an apartment in Bondi Junction," Jacques announced to everyone in French. "Sydney real estate is very cheap in comparison to Nouméa," he added in English, for my benefit.

Knowing nothing about property prices, I remained silent and strove to appear up to speed on the subject.

Tiring of realty, I turned to Marcel and pointed to the empty place at the foot of the table, whispering, "Who's that for?"

"Jacques 'as it set for Sandrine."

"Is Sandrine coming to lunch?" I felt toey. "I didn't think she spoke to her father."

"It is always like zat," he murmured. "'E is hoping she will change 'er mind." Then, for Jacques Forestier's benefit: "'Ave you paid Sandrine enough money to persuade her to come 'ome to *Le Caillou*?"

"All the money in the world won't bring my daughter back," said Jacques, "but I have her place laid in case she decides to leave that piece of detritus and return to my house." He patted my hand. "But my granddaughter is with me today."

Chantal cleared the plates. She flip-flopped back into the kitchen, and began to rattle dishes. Bad vibes swirled around her. She wore a wooden cross.

The beef steaks were humungous. I gazed at the slab of gory meat, wondering how I could get out of eating it. I saw Pascal reach for the mustard. He began to spread the yellow paste all over his food. He stopped what he was doing, glanced in my direction and pushed back his chair. He went into the kitchen. I heard raised voices. Were Pascal and Chantal discussing Spud?

"Did you enjoy the hibiscus I gave you?" Jacques was talking to me.

"What hibiscus?"

"The perfectly formed hibiscus I left on your pillow the night you arrived."

"Oh, it was *you* who left that flower?" I hoped no one had discovered the pulpy mess. "It was a stunning"—and I tried to think of a more interesting way to describe it—"colour. Sort of like spilled spider's blood."

Pascal placed a plate filled with tropical fruit and nuts in front of me. He removed the untouched steak, and set it down on a side table. I gave him a grateful smile, and continued fluffing on about Jacques' pulverised flower.

I sucked on a piece of cantaloupe while the conversation flowed around the table. Unsure as to the appropriateness of using '*vous*', or the more informal '*tu*', I said little. When I did speak, I spoke in English.

Pascal dropped our having seen Emma di Luca on the beach into a discussion on leptospirosis. This caused a fiery debate as to whether the disease was caused by rats, or by the urine of deer in the water.

I was crunching on a walnut, when I felt Marcel's garlic breath in my ear. "My brozzer 'ad a long adventure wis Emma."

"I don't want to know about it." I remembered the letters Marcel had sent me about Sandrine and her affair with Claude. "It's none of my business."

Those who had finished eating left their knives and forks apart, to indicate the meal was over. Marcel pointed. "Leave zem as you find zem!" he murmured.

Jacques asked Pascal if his mother was well.

"Axelle va bien," he said.

Having established that Madame Manet's health was good, everyone began to complain about Parisians and how rude they were. This led to comments about how people from Paris didn't respect the slopes when they went skiing at Chamonix—which seemed a strange thing to be talking about in the tropics.

Marcel invaded my ear again. "Pascal was ve-ery much in love wis Emma."

"I don't care!" I hissed. "Your brother's no kid. I'm sure he's been in love with lots of women."

"'Is *petite amie* at ze moment is *tahitienne*. Ve-ery beautiful." Marcel flashed his teeth.

"Does she sell black pearls, or *under*wear?" I snapped.

"Can I interrupt your conversation?" Jacques Forestier leaned across and spoke to me. "After coffee, I will show you my giant rusa stags, Geneviève."

"My name is Genna!"

I sulked until it was time to inspect his deer.

Chapter 40

Negotiating muddy puddles, I clambered into the pick-up. Jacques panted aboard, placing his cagou-handled walking stick between us. Dogs barked behind the house.

"Call me *Papi*."

"Can I continue to call you Jacques?"

He nodded, sighed and breathed garlic fumes all over me. We waited for our driver, Didier.

"Why didn't you just invite me to come, Jacques, instead of luring me here with a phony offer of work experience?"

"Would you have come?"

"Probably not."

"There, you see." He pushed his nicotine-stained fingers together, creating a church. "It was meant to be civilized, a little *stage* to keep you occupied. You were studying French anyway, and I could have gradually got to know you." He smoothed his left hand over his head. "But Liliane changed all that." The blast of his garlic breath made me blink.

Angélique hurried from the house. She handed Darling to Didier— now dressed in jungle gear and boots—and rushed back inside. The baby, with scrunched hair and a thumb jammed in her mouth, wore a nappy and T-shirt. Was Darling coming with us? I crossed my fingers, hoping I wasn't about to catch leptospirosis.

Didier, his Akubra replaced by an army hat, settled Darling behind the wheel and walked off. The baby smelled of ammonia and milk. Was I meant to carry her on my lap?

Holding a glass of wine, Pascal ambled from the house.

A sudden pounding of paws. Frenzied panting. A pack of yapping dogs hurtled around the corner of the house, past a tractor and towards the pick-up. Ugly dogs, mangy pit bull terriers and spotty half-breeds leapt into the back, paws scratching and scrabbling against the tray.

Pascal placed his wineglass on the ground.

Didier jumped behind the wheel. He gathered Darling onto this lap, turned the key in the ignition and revved the engine.

Next thing I knew, Pascal was at the front of the vehicle slamming his palm against the bonnet. He yelled, *"Non, Jacques! Pas de chiens!"*

Didier planted his foot down hard on the accelerator. Mud flew.

"No dogs!" Pascal shouted in English.

He jumped out of the way. The Toyota moved off.

"No dogs, Jacques!"

"Why's Pascal worried about the dogs?" I twisted in my seat to see him lift his arms in the air as he watched us draw away.

"He knows we are going hunting." Crow's feet creased the parchment skin around Jacques Forestier's eyes.

"I don't like guns," I said.

"There are no guns, only binoculars. Today we will be hunting in the English fashion."

"What does that mean?"

"It means the dogs will do the hunting. You will enjoy it."

"B-b-but I thought we were going to look at your deer?"

"We are. And it's only fair that the dogs should have some fun. They've been penned up long enough." His smile was sleazy.

What had Jacques Forestier meant when he said "the dogs will do the hunting"? Would they hound the deer into the ground so that it needed to be shot? I wondered. But Jacques had stated that there were no guns, only binoculars. And Didier had brought Darling with him. Then again, the dogs in the pick-up had bothered Pascal.

Didier wrestled with the wheel.

Darling gurgled and fidgeted and wiped a gooey finger along my arm. She shoved her thumb in her mouth. Her jaw made a click noise.

The cagou-handled cane rubbed against my thigh, and I began to feel queasy. With the windows wound down, and no air-conditioning, I was beginning to sweat. The air flowing in from the outside made no difference to the garlic stench in the cabin.

My dreadlocks began to drip, to itch like crazy.

I scratched, exhausted from Pascal having walked me around all night.

The four-wheel-drive slewed and swayed and skidded. We jolted across the savanna, climbing ever higher up the sloping ground. Still no sign of the stags, and I prayed the deer were hiding in the bushes, knowing we were coming to get them. I felt like spewing, and our quarry remained invisible. Stay away deer. *Hide!* I said to myself, forgetting that the animals would be slaughtered and sold for venison at a later date.

Silence in the cabin, apart from the pop sound of Darling pushing her thumb in and out of her mouth.

Grassy plains flowed past, surrounded by skinny pines and rainforest. Far off, I could see lagoon water, shiny in the sunlight. A wisp of river wound through the scrub below. A butte to the right.

The pick-up rocked. The dogs scuffled and whimpered in the back. Didier slammed his foot on the brake and climbed from the vehicle. Still holding the germy Darling, he lifted his field glasses and gazed into the distance. The baby wriggled and squirmed, trying to push herself away.

"It is the time of the velvet," said Jacques, "and stags taken early will still be in velvet."

"Velvet?" Sweat streamed down my face.

"Velvet is the growing stage of the antlers. Antlers are a deciduous growth and must be removed for the preservation of trees and fences, although most of our land is unfenced." Jacques' words sounded reasonable. "The hunting is done mainly by glassing and stalking, from now through to September, always in the rutting season." A pause. "The best trophies are during the rut. And the hunters who pay the money usually come from Australia."

"Is that how your English got so good?"

"That, and I studied engineering in Queensland when I was a young man." He gave a Gallic shrug. "I failed my final year. As you can see, by the life I now lead, I was not cut out to be an engineer, and am not even adept at plumbering."

The word 'plumbering' was the first mistake I had heard Jacques make when speaking English. *Was he rattled?* I wondered.

Didier bolted back behind the wheel. The vehicle jerked, stopped, and jerked forward again. Constant jerking, until: *"Il est là!"* He eased the Toyota to a standstill, carefully dragging on the handbrake.

The dogs stayed silent.

Jacques pointed.

Craning my neck I saw a massive stag with towering antlers grazing and browsing beneath the jagged leaves of a niaouli. It lifted its head, and then grazed again. Its coat was yellowish brown, darker on the hind-quarters and thighs. The stag was awesome.

Didier placed Darling on my lap. He jumped from the pick-up, yelling: *"Allez les gars!"*

The dogs leapt out. The stag began to roar. It turned to run, leaping through low ferns, still roaring. The dogs lunged at its throat, wrestling the deer to the ground where it choked as they tore. They ripped into it as it struggled. I closed my eyes and tried to wipe away the sight of what I'd seen.

"That is *so* gross!" I screamed. Waves of nausea rushed over me as the dogs tore at the flesh. "That's disgusting!"

Jacques' voice, devoid of emotion, sounded far away. "Dying is a natural occurrence and, as my granddaughter, you will need to get used to this. The dogs are *chiens d'attaque*, bred to fight to the death." He pushed at me. "Why don't you get out, take a look?"

"No way!"

Darling began to cry. Didier reached inside the pick-up and pulled the baby from my lap. I hauled at her clothing.

"Don't take Darling with you, please. What if the dogs tear her apart when they've finished?"

Didier laughed. He continued to stand there watching, with his arm around his daughter. Jacques heaved himself from the vehicle, and joined the farm manager. I wimped out, cringed in the ute. I clenched my teeth and stared at my trembling knees, doing my best not to throw up. Sweat continued to stream off me.

Silence. I looked up. The thrashing limbs were still. The roaring of the stag had ceased. With Darling still in his arms, Didier gave a piercing whistle. The dogs wheeled about and raced to the Toyota. I tensed, expecting them to leap and snatch Darling from Didier's grasp. But, mouths bloody, they sprang into the pick-up.

Jacques told his farm manager to come back later for the antlers.

As he hoisted himself into the cabin, Jacques' breath was raspy. "The stag was a big one, more than twice your weight."

Didier climbed in. He placed Darling on his lap, and turned the key in the ignition. The slithering trip home felt as though it would never end.

Chapter 41

Pascal was waiting by the tractor when I struggled out of the pick-up. His clothing was mud-stained, his face as fierce as the dying stag's had been. He strode across and confronted Jacques Forestier. His French was so fast I hardly understood a thing.

Jacques' reply was clear. "You have a weak stomach, Pascal Manet!" He shoved his cane into Pascal's abdomen.

Pascal lifted his hand as if to punch the old man, but thought better of it. He switched to English. "Why did you *do* that, Jacques? Did you want to push 'er away as you 'ave done with Sandrine?"

Jacques did not reply.

The sky clouded over. Rain began to spit into the mud.

"On y va, Genna!" Pascal grabbed me by the arm and propelled me, shivering, past the *pétanque* court at the side of the house. He bundled me into the Mercedes.

"Isn't there someone I should thank?" My teeth tap-danced as I spoke, pitter-pattering in time with the spitting rain.

"Josiane 'as left for Nouméa with Marcel. There is no one to thank, unless you feel a strange gratitude to your *grand-père*." He smelled of Gauloises cigarettes.

The interior of the car was cold. I was shaking, unable to get the sight of the stag out of my mind, unable to stop my body jerking.

Pascal's hands clenched the wheel. One of his knuckles was bleeding, and I remembered the books in Jacques Forestier's library, stained with a mixture of mud and blood. I'll never eat meat again, I told myself.

Pascal murmured that he couldn't wait to get back to Paris: *"Je serai ravi de rentrer à Paris."* And I felt guilty for having wrecked his homecoming to New Caledonia.

The windscreen wipers flicked smoothly across the glass, and I still couldn't stop shaking. He glanced at me, reached for the air-con dial, and turned it to red. Hot air blasted through the car, and my limbs and teeth stopped twittering. The windscreen began to fog up. He extracted a balled-up hanky, wiped the glass in huge sweeps as if it were a blackboard.

"I feel okay now, so you can turn the cooling back on. I'd hate to be the cause of a crash. That would *really* make your day."

The lights from a passing car raked his face.

"You were there for me. So thanks," and the word burst from my mouth, "Dad!"

"I am not your *papa*, but you may call me Dad if it gives you a little comfort."

"I've never had a dad." I was able to push the image of the deer and the dogs from my mind at last. "It's something I've missed."

The windscreen wipers slapped. The rain ran down the glass, and I filled him in on Alice Winstone's Korsakoff's syndrome, how Namilly cared for her without telling me. How helping Alice was the cause of Kingsley Winstone doing a runner, leaving Win, too, without a father.

"Your Namilly sounds like a well-meaning woman." The car bucked through a dip in the road. Water hissed across the bonnet of the vehicle.

"She is. You know, as with Sandrine, I expected to feel some sort of genetic attraction when I met Jacques Forestier. With Sandrine, I felt confusion and frustration. But with Jacques it was different, a strange anger. I felt berko and confrontational as soon as I saw him."

The rain eased, and Pascal switched off the wipers. He suddenly jammed his foot on the brake. I lurched against the seat belt. A deer stood in the middle of the road.

"The stag's back!" I cried. "It's alive!"

The deer shook its head, galloped into the scrub at the side of the road and disappeared.

"Wild deer are common on our roads at night," he said.

The car moved forward and picked up speed.

"Sometimes I do not understand Jacques. He is very generous with 'is money for the work experience programme." Pause."But 'e is not as rich as you might think. He lost much during the crash of the bourse in 1987. But he lives easy and if you 'ad, as they say in English 'played your cards right', he might have given you a Carte Bleue for you to use, as Sandrine did when she was young. Per'aps not as much."

"I don't want his *money*! That is so *off* to even suggest it. Gross!" I added, "I'll never go back to Bouchon."

"Not even for the Agricultural Fair and Rodeo?"

"I said Bouchon, not Bourail."

We sat there in silence. I mulled over Jacques having poked Pascal in the stomach with his walking stick; I pondered about Josiane and her strange friendship with the freedom fighter, Yannick Boudaou.

Pascal gazed into the distance, as if he were a million miles away.

"Is your stomach okay?" I took a breath. "You know, Jacques poking you with his walking stick."

"My stomach is very well."

I was curious. "Who stabbed you during the Events? Do you know his name?"

"Yannick Boudaou." His response was abrupt.

"Omigod, I'm sorry." I felt myself grow hot. "I suppose you knew he'd be at Noah's the night that I was there?"

"*Calédonie* is small place. Yes, I knew. And Jacques knows Josiane is having a little adventure with Yannick."

"How excellent of him to invite her to lunch!" I gave a sarcastic laugh.

The vibration of my phone on the console distracted me. I pressed *Show.* The same message opened:

bill einstein still sik

In a flash, I knew the answer. "I've worked out what's going on."

"What is going on?"

"Stefan's having it off with Fat Betty. He's just making it like Bill Einstein's sick."

"Fat Betty?"

"Elizabeth Stubbs."

"And Elizabeth Stubbs is fat?" He raised an eyebrow.

"She was fat, and then she went to Weight Watchers, or whatever. And now she's super thin. Even her legs are no longer like tree trunks." I cleared my throat. "You know, I'm not a fattist."

"But you do not like Fat Betty?"

He sounded amused, but I was serious. "I hate her. She's an e-bully who called me a 'wog slag'. Do you realise how much that hurt?" I looked at him. "I'll bet *you* never suffered racist taunts?"

"I did, when I was in Australia during the French nuclear testing in the Pacific." A pause. "And you think she is the reason for the text messages you are receiving?"

"It's obvious."

We passed through the city of Noumea, and began to swoop around brightly-lit bays. I remembered Marcel's text.

"Did you give Marcel my mobile number?"

"I do not know your portable number."

I twisted a dreadlock.

"Do you 'ave to *do* that?" Pascal sounded aggravated.

"As a matter of fact I do. Twisting dreadlocks keeps them in shape."

"Merde!" He reached for his cigarettes.

"Now I've done the right thing and gone to see Jacques Forestier, I would like my passport back, and then I can look around Grande Terre before going home."

I could catch up with Spud, travel around the island, I told myself.

I glanced at Pascal. "And what about my work experience?"

"It won't 'appen now," he said, filling the car with his smoke.

"Why? It's not fair."

"La vie est injuste."

"No, I guess life isn't fair."

"I 'ave been disappointed with you, Genna."

"Disappointed? Why?"

"Do you take drugs?"

"I don't *do* drugs!"

"You should know I discover grass in a drawer in your bedroom."

186

"Oh, that's chop-chop." Relieved, I scratched my dreadlocks. "No way is it *ganja*. You should try it sometime, instead of those cancer sticks."

"So if I 'ave it tested, you are confident it will not be *hhhash*?"

"Of course it's not hash!"

We pulled into the drive. He pressed the remote, and eased the car into the garage.

As we went into the house, he said the nicest thing. "I buy you some soy milk. It's in the refrigerator, chilled and ready for your breakfast."

"Bodacious!" I said.

And he handed me my passport.

Chapter 42

I tucked my passport—which smelled of smoke, and appeared to have been washed—beneath my pillow. Dragging on an old T-shirt, I hauled it over my knees and curled up.

Images of Rocky being blown up, and dogs tearing at stags flickered through my mind. When I did get to sleep, my dreams were all blood-spotted and deformed. I spent the night running from car bombs, and a jillion thrashing deer legs. The images morphed into a zillion writhing human legs (Stefan's and Elizabeth's) just before I woke.

The morning sun sent a rectangle of light through the dormer window, which ruffled over the mosquito netting in the downdraft of the ceiling fan. I ached when I stretched.

I could hear Pascal talking on his mobile phone outside. *"Fantastique!"* he shouted. *"Sensationnel!"* He added: *"Formidable!"* Then: *"C'est incroyable!"* He laughed gleefully.

Thinking he must be speaking to his Tahitian girlfriend, I turned over and attempted to get back to sleep. I was glad he was happy that she'd managed to book a good table at his favourite restaurant that evening—or whatever it was that made him so joyful. He said *"Bonne chance!"* He pressed the Off button and began to whistle tunelessly. He sounded over the moon, but why had he wished his girlfriend good luck?

Ants trailed across my pillow. I flicked them away, pushed aside the netting and climbed out of bed. I dragged on a pair of cut-offs. The noise from the grinding chainsaw blasted through the house as I padded into the kitchen to get myself a glass of soy milk. An open packet of cereal sat on the bench. Sipping the soy milk, I made my way onto the veranda. I almost stubbed my toe on a huge bowl of milky coffee and a half-eaten *pain au chocolat*.

The chainsaw sliced through the branches of the melaleuca tree. Pascal, clad in a floral shirt and shorts, wore earmuffs and worked with a grin on his face. The petrol fumes spoiled the taste of my milk. I was about to go back inside when my gaze lit on the flapping newspaper lying on the porch.

My dreadlocks itched. I scratched as I read the paper.

The chainsaw puttered off. Pascal removed his earmuffs. He began to sing: *"Quand nous chanterons, le temps des cerises."* A pause. *"Et gai rossignol, et merle moqueur ... seront tous en fête!"*

My eyes scanned the text beside the photo of Kyanthia Hadjiparaskeva. Wasn't that the name of Noah's partner? And why was his photo on the front page? I took a sip of soy milk.

Pascal had difficulty holding a tune. He started up again: *"J'aimerai toujours le temps des cerises."*

"Oh, shush," I called out. "Cut the communard song; it reminds me of school and I can't concentrate. I'm trying to read the paper, an article about Kyanthia being killed in the car bombing."

"You are awake!" he shouted. Panting, he loaded a pile of logs into his arms and stacked them against the fence. "It is *formidable, non*?"

"What's amazing?" I scratched at my dreads. "Your girlfriend?"

"My *copine* 'as nothing to do with Roch being alive."

The glass fell from my fingers, bounced and shattered. Soy milk went everywhere.

"Rocky is alive? Why didn't you *tell* me?" My heart flipped beneath my T-shirt.

"I just find out, but you were asleep."

"You could've woken me up!"

He marched up the steps, grinning like an idiot. He looked neat in his shorts, younger. Almost cool. His eyes glittered with emotion.

"Roch is alive. Isn't that *fantastique*?" He put his arms around me and squeezed me hard, and it felt kind of weird to be hugged by a French examiner.

"Who were you talking to on your mobile?"

"Marcel 'as rung me before I even saw the paper. Kyanthia was killed in the *attentat*, probably as 'e was wiring Roch's car. Roch has fled to Australia, and Marcel is taking the next plane to meet him there."

"Wow, I'm so glad." I slithered from his grasp, and collapsed on my tush. "So glad."

Pascal crouched down beside me. He pointed to my head and started to crack up, to fall about laughing.

"What's so funny?"

He giggled and chortled, jabbed his digit at my noggin.

"Well, spit it out."

"Ants!"

"What are ants?"

"You 'ave ants in your hair!"

"Ants in my *dreadlocks*?" I ran my fingers over my scalp, and felt scuttling.

"The honey 'as fermented. And now there are ants, as I find in my toothbrush!"

Oh heck, I said to myself, I used his toothbrush to apply egg to my dreads, thereby transferring the honey, and he got ants, too. I recalled the ants on my pillow.

"Quick!" I screamed. "Do something! Grab the Baygon!"

"No, you will make yourself very sick if you spray on your head. Dive in the water." He indicated the lagoon on the other side of the road.

I scurried through the gate and across Promenade Roger Laroque, dodging tooting cars and trucks, and a burly Kanak with a wife and two kids. I fled across the churned-up sand of Baie des Citrons beach. I flung myself into the water and stroked my way along the bottom, through bits of coral, and rocks that winked alongside darting tropical fish.

Diving and tumbling, jiving and rumbling, I watched my dreads spread out and hang like sea sausages around my head. I stretched my toes and swooped towards a stonefish. I splashed and swam. Rocky was safe in Australia, and I had ants in my dreadlocks. And it felt fantastic! I burst through the water, pumped my fist in the air and dived to the depths again.

"Formidable!" I yelled, gulping in brine, rising up, spitting it out and doing a dazzling tumble turn.

A striped creature wiggled in my direction, zigzagging and cavorting. And I cavorted with it.

"Genna!" I could hear Pascal shouting.

I took no notice, just kept dancing with the stripes.

"Merde!" He pulled at my arm, but I didn't want to go. *"Vite, c'est un serpent!"*

A *tricot rayé*? But my cut-offs were waterlogged and I couldn't have given a Rasta.

Pascal yanked harder. He hauled me, unwilling, up onto the sand. He had removed his floral shirt, and wore only his shorts. The weight of the water dragged the shorts down so they sat on his hips. I couldn't take my eyes off the scar on his abdomen.

Seeing my curiosity, he drew his daks up. The sight of the scar sobered me, and my teeth began to chatter.

"You could 'ave died." He placed his sweaty shirt around my shoulders. "One bite from a *tricot rayé* and you are dead very quickly."

"Thanks, but I don't need to be covered up." I pushed his shirt away.

He placed it back around my shoulders. *"Si.* You do need to be covered up. This is a family beach, and wet T-shirts are not appropriate."

We began to laugh again.

"Well, what do we do now? I was planning to leave, hike around the island."

"We are off to Yaté to tell Roch's father, K-Mel, the good news." He paused. "But first, I 'ave one more thing I must do."

Chapter 43

Pascal was acting strangely, as if he had a secret. I was patting my dreadlocks dry after a hot shower, when he rapped on the door to tell me to meet him at the front gate in twenty minutes. He said he had an errand to run.

After inspecting my head thoroughly for ant residue, I passed Marie-Françoise, muttering and mopping up glass shards and soy milk on the veranda. I made for the shade of the Asian Bell Tree. I pushed a white trumpet-like fallen flower with my thongs, rapt to be meeting K-Mel Colline, excited to be seeing (not to drink, of course) the kava plants whose roots had created so many problems.

As I gazed at the lagoon, and marvelled that Rocky was safe and living in Australia, a grey bug car (Citroën Deux Chevaux) clattered to a halt. *How cute!* I told myself, just the sort of car I'd expected to see everywhere in New Caledonia.

The driver tooted. *Was he trying to pick me up?* I turned my back on the sleaze bag, picked up a fallen flower and pretended to examine it.

"Je peux vous emmener quelque part, mademoiselle?" the perv called out, offering me a lift.

I ignored him.

"Get in the car, Genna!" I recognised Pascal's exasperated tone.

He threw open the passenger door.

"Why are you driving this?" I squealed. "I thought you were a sleaze trying to pick me up."

"I am not a sleaze. But I *am* trying to pick you up," he said, with a broad smile. "Do you like it?" He wore clean jeans and a navy polo.

"This is *ultra*-radical!" I scrambled into the bug car. "Where's the Merc?"

"I left my 'boring' car, as you called it, at Location Louis Limou and rented this for the day."

He wrestled with the knob on the end of the gear stick poking from the dash, did a jerky U-turn, and we juddered off in the direction of Magenta.

"We are taking RT2 to Yaté, eighty kilometres to the east."

I fiddled with my flower, nodding my head towards the back. "What's the basket for? Are we having a picnic?"

"*Non*. It is a bougna basket."

"Bougna?" Thunderclouds threatened my sunny mood. "You know I'm a raw vegan!"

"There is no bougna in there."

"Then what's it for?"

"You will see. When I was a student, I too drove a 2CV … also known as a *deuche, deux pattes, deudeuche, deudoche*." Pascal was in full-on teacher mode. "We are both about to suffer from *hhhaemor-rhoids*," he added.

I giggled and sighed. A feeling of freedom washed over me as we puttered past the domestic airport in the direction of the RT2. We jogged through an unmanned toll booth.

"The Savexpress workers are on strike," he said.

"Well, it's too nice a day to work." Pause. "Will we be able to stop at Parc Territorial de la Rivière Bleue on the way? Rocky told me about it, about the cagou birds they breed there, and the friendly wild ones."

"After cyclone Erica, the park was closed for months. It will be the same today, after Liliane." He glanced at the limp flower in my hand. "My Asian Bell Tree must be confused. It usually flowers at Noël."

"But it *is* Christmas! Rocky's alive!"

"*Oui*, it is a second Christmas, and we 'ave received a magnificent present."

He pushed open the bottom section of the window and, flapping his arm beneath the bar, indicated that we were merging right.

"*Merde*, the Deuche is primitive. When you 'ave to indicate, change gears, and turn the steering wheel all at the same time, it is very difficult." He sighed. "But petrol is cheap. One only 'as to wave a nozzle under the car's nose and it is content." He began to wander down memory lane. "I used to smoke Gitanes cigarettes made wis *papier maïs*, much more reasonable in corn paper. But you 'ad to keep puffing or they would go out. I looked ve-rr-ry cool."

"Did you know Emma di Luca back then, when you drove a Deuche?"

He nodded. "We met at a soirée in the Brousse."

"Why did you break up?"

"She prefers to marry a farmer wis horses, to a teacher. Rodeos are less … 'boring' shall we say?"

Embarrassed at being a sticky beak, I twisted a dreadlock and resumed looking at the landscape. I took in the lush countryside, the grimace-like gashes on the sides of the mountains.

"What are those red slashes?"

"Nickel mining."

Men digging on the side of the road waved, and we waved back. Tempted to jump on my soapbox and rant about the environment, I changed my mind. The day was too special to get into an argument about polluting the reef, and destroying the rainforest.

This trip was different from the one to Bourail; we were travelling east across the island now, instead of north. The Deuche struggled up a zillion hills, flew down again, swayed round bends. We passed the turn-off to Mont-Dore. Pascal worked the gear stick and swore in French. I heard the word *"Putain!"* frequently, as he shoved his arm through the window flap to indicate. But few cars were on the road, and those we saw whooshed past us and quickly disappeared.

At the turn-off signpost to Parc Territorial de la Rivière Bleue, I said: "Are you certain Blue River Park is shut? It's only just over two K from the RT2."

"I am quite sure it is closed," he replied, acknowledging a truckload of Kanak workers who grinned back. "We are halfway to Yaté, so I can show you the Chutes de la Madelaine. The falls are not far from here."

A short while later, we pulled into a parking area near toilet signs.

"We walk from here," he said.

Slushy red dirt oozed between my toes as we made our way to the falls.

"They're small, sort of like a fringe of water." I leaned on the post-and-rail fence beside a map of the reserve. "Pretty."

The sky was cloudy now, the landscape thick with foliage and hills. The water beyond the falls shone, and the air was hot and still. Mossies buzzed. Even though I wore insect repellent, I felt edgy at the thought of being bitten.

I was relieved when Pascal said: "It seems like rain. We must go on, or our little Deuche will struggle in the wet."

Back on the highway, the shimmering water of Yaté dam flashed past.

"Yaté Lake is largest artificial water on Grande Terre." Pascal waved his hand. "And Gigawatt will take place soon, when a flood of runners cross the fortifications of the dam in a very tough marathon."

"I'd like to do that one day." I changed the subject. "What is the basket in the back *really* for? You haven't told me yet."

"You will see."

We clattered towards a humungous power station. Cables surged overhead. Gendarmes wearing kepis and walk shorts chatted beneath the crackle and hum of the electricity. Water as far as the eye could see. Lagoon. River. No matter where I looked, there was water.

We pulled up beside a convenience store. Pascal reached across, picked up the bougna basket and pushed open the car door. A group of Melanesian women in missionary dresses turned and looked. Unlike the men on the road, these women didn't smile. Their faces were surly as he disappeared into the dimness.

In no time Pascal was back.

"Those women don't look friendly," I said.

Shrugging, he placed the basket carefully on the back seat. We set off again, rattling over the bridge that crossed the Yaté River.

"Not far to go now."

"Okay, spit it out. Tell me. What's in the bougna basket?"

"Eggs."

"But I don't eat dairy products."

"Not for you to eat!" He wiggled his eyebrows. "And not for your hairs! This Deuche was designed to carry a basket of eggs over a field without breaking even one. I wish to see if it is true."

Traditional houses fringed the shore. Gardens were bursting with banana plants, palms and tree ferns. My backside was sore. I wriggled in my seat.

"The Colline farm is before Unia." He turned the wheel left, and we headed up an unmade road. "Unia is a nearby tribal village that very much likes its sport."

The Deuche skidded sideways up a slope.

"Madame Boudin." He pointed to a fibro shack. "She looks after our house which 'as been empty for years." Farther up the road he pointed again. "That is where we used to live."

"Wow, your home looks Australian, with its corrugated roof."

"My father bought a building pack from Australia, not uncommon in this country. We even 'ave sash windows."

The Deuche edged up the road. I could see no dwelling, only a fence.

"Here is the Colline *maison.*"

Pascal peered through the windscreen. The posts of the loopy fence were charred, as though there'd recently been a fire. Nothing was left but twisted wood and sodden ashes.

"*Putain!* Fire has destroyed K-Mel's house, for a second time." He pulled on the handbrake. "We are too late," he said.

Chapter 44

A cat slunk past, its stomach to the ground.

"That's Belle," I cried. "Her tail's all frizzed." I stretched to pick her up, but she skirted a puddle and scurried off.

"Belle?" Pascal looked puzzled. "Ah, you are right. One of Roch's friends offered a cat as a gift, for 'is graduation. She is not so young, you know."

Blowflies hummed in a feeding frenzy as we approached the burnt building. Corrugated iron sat at an angle beside an exploded window. On the blackened veranda, tied to a leaning post, lay a cattle dog with its legs in the air. Its wormy eyes gazed upwards. I held my nose to ward off the stench.

"*Le chien bleu de Roch.*" Pascal frowned. "I wonder if K-Mel is dead, too, trapped inside. He was an old bastard, but 'e did not deserve this."

A funky-looking bird, silvery grey, with Grand-Prix-check feathers along the base of its wing, paced in a cage. The bird, whose beak, legs and eyes were scarlet, hissed as we passed. Its crest resembled a dinky disco-cape. Through the wire, on a heap of leaf litter, huddled a bunch of brown feathers. A wide caramel stripe ran down a head and beak, leading to bulging brown eyes.

"Is that awesome bird a cagou?"

Pascal nodded.

"And is that its chick?" I approached the cage. "It looks dead, as well. But it's a different colour."

"They are a different colour when born. The chick is alive. The egg would 'ave hatched long ago. It happens annually, thirty-five days incubation, and feeding for fifteen weeks by both parents. So where is the male? And who is feeding the chick? Roch should not keep a cagou in a cage." Pascal touched his brow. "I will contact the head ranger at Parc Territorial de la Rivière Bleue and ask 'im to take it."

Belle ran past us with a rat in her mouth.

"Is that a black rat?" I pushed back a scream.

"Rattus rattus," Pascal said, as if he'd lost the plot from the shock. Straightaway, I realised he was pronouncing the Latin name for this vermin.

He set off to where the land dipped down. Not wishing to be left behind, I hurried after him through wet, scrubby grass and fallen banana branches into the gully.

Pascal stopped in his tracks. "K-Mel's kava crop is gone, stolen!"

The earth had been churned up by the tracks of a prime mover. Heart-shaped leaves lay scattered among bits of broken roots. Only a small wooden hut, whose door hung drunkenly on one hinge, was left. I saw a gutted pick-up nearby.

"K-Mel's crushing shed." Pascal pointed. "This is where 'e pounds the roots."

"Interesting, but are there any snakes in the undergrowth?" I looked nervously around.

He shook his head. "There is nothing on land for you to be afraid of, only in the water, such as *tricots rayés* ..." His voice trailed off. "But who 'as *done* this?"

I had a moment of inspiration. "Was it Noah? He was peed off at Rocky, and then his partner was killed. So maybe it was him?"

"These are dangerous people." Pascal's lips went small. "I must contact the gendarmes in Yaté, tell them K-Mel 'as probably disappeared." Pause. "Although it is strange they do not already do something."

"Could it be payback?"

"I 'ave no idea." He turned. "I will now check on my house, and we will return to Nouméa."

I picked up a heart-shaped kava leaf, and stuffed it in the pocket of my jeans.

Setting off after Pascal, I heard a dog yap somewhere.

Struggling to keep up with his long legs, I coughed, "I think Rocky's blue heeler"—a pant—"is alive"—a puff—"I can hear it barking."

"It is the cagou bird," he said.

"That's amazing." I gulped in a mouthful of air.

We halted beside some banana plants.

Pascal turned back a leaf. "Bunchy top! You see green streaks, dots, short lines." He gestured. "Leaves on suckers are shorter, more erect, and thinner. That one is lacy, and I see aphids. K-Mel would be forbidden to transport 'is bananas on Grande Terre."

"So what are you going to tell Rocky? If K-Mel is dead, he will never know his son is alive."

Pascal marched off down the road to the Manet house.

He said over his shoulder, "First I will check if there is a casserole, and maybe cook some crêpes to eat before we start on our journey back."

"But …"

Before I could protest about consuming eggs, he added: "There is a little vegetable garden, a *potager*, behind the house, near the kitchen, that Madame Boudin tends. You should find something to eat."

"Is she fat, like her name?"

"Of course, and so is 'er husband."

I was suddenly curious to know if this was the spot where Pascal was stabbed during the Events. "Is this where it happened, on the road, along here?"

His expression was blank.

"The *stabbing*!"

"I prefer not to dwell on it."

We passed through a garden stuffed with tropical plants and bougainvillea flowers, as bright as gumdrops.

"The cyclone 'as damaged the roof." Pascal indicated the curled-back corner of the corrugated iron; a piece of soggy paper was wedged into the gap. "I must ask Madame Boudin's husband to repair it."

"And there's a broken pane." I pointed to one of the sash windows.

"*Merde!* People 'ave been using my place as a squat!" He turned the key and threw open the front door. *"Il y a quelqu'un?"* he shouted.

No one answered.

Overhead, a ceiling fan turned and squeaked, barely moving the air.

"Fan's on," I whispered.

"The fan stays on all the time, to prevent mould from forming."

The house echoed from the emptiness. In the front bedroom, a mucky mattress was spread out on the tiled floor.

"Ah, I am right. There 'ave been squatters." He handed me the key. "You can look in the garden at the rear of the house, for a watermelon, perhaps? I will get the eggs from the car."

"Did any of the eggs break?"

"I forget to look."

He pulled the front door to behind him.

I peered through the kitchen window. The land, covered with palms and niaoulis, stretched into the distance. A mangy dog nosed among broken banana plants. Near the back door, I spied a neat little vegie garden, beside it a pile of yams freshly dug from the ground. *By Madame Boudin?* I wondered.

I went to turn the key in the back door, but the door was unlocked. Outside, I could see a bougna basket, like Pascal's, on its side. I heard a rustle, heavy breathing. I smelled stale sweat. Someone was out there.

I wasn't hanging around.

I dashed back inside, shut and locked the door.

Chapter 45

I cringed against the front door, stressing and unable to move. I heard a thrashing through tropical plants. *Was the creepy squatter coming to get me?*

"Ouvre la porte, Genna!" yelled Pascal.

I fumbled the door open. "What took you so long?"

"The eggs are gone."

"I think I know where they are. There's a bougna basket outside, and heavy breathing, and a smell of sweat …"

Pascal snatched the key from me. He was off, out the back door, before I had finished speaking. I heard shouting, the sound of someone being dragged upstairs, a whining complaint in French. *Had Pascal caught the intruder?*

Next thing I knew, he was towing an old man inside by the ear. The squatter was a light-skinned Melanesian, wiry, with steel-wool hair. He wore dirty underwear, held up by a piece of rope. One eye was purple and half-closed. The forefinger of his right hand was bound with a strip of bloody rag. His smile was nervous.

"Genna, meet K-Mel Colline!" said Pascal.

"Enchantée." I wondered if I should shake hands. Eyeing the bloody rag, I decided not to.

"Que fais-tu dans ma maison?" Pascal bellowed at K-Mel.

"He's in your house because he's injured," I said in English. "And you sound like one of those three bears."

Pascal gave me a schoolteacher look—you know, the one that says you're about to be kept in after class to write lines—and continued grilling the old man about the eggs.

"Shouldn't you be telling him Rocky's alive?"

Pascal let go of K-Mel's ear.

K-Mel glanced in my direction. "Was your *maman* behind ze *barricades* in *mai, soixante-huit*?" he asked, in broken English.

"Namilly never mentioned being behind the barricades in May '68," I said, thinking this conversation bizarre. "And my birth mother would've only been a kid. So no, I don't think so."

K-Mel began to rant and rave about his son never being there to help, and how he'd lost his inheritance with all the kava plants having been stolen. And where was he, anyway? It was as if K-Mel had never seen the paper, never known about Rocky's car going up in flames.

"What happened to your finger?" Pascal demanded in French.

"Noah's men removed my fingernail with a knife," K-Mel explained. "They stole my kava plants, and set fire to my house."

Now that I knew those mother-of-pearl jewellery boxes on the shelf in Noah's nakamal had truly contained fingernails, I felt ill.

"Jeanne was a *saint* to stay with you as long as she did!" yelled Pascal.

He stomped to a nearby cupboard and fossicked around. He thrust yellowed gauze, an old packet of *sparadrap* and a bottle marked *Alcool* at me.

"What?" I'd never been good at nursie things.

"You clean 'is finger up while I ring Marcel, outside for a better reception. I don't want K-Mel dying of blood poisoning in my house, and making an even worse stink."

"I *can't*!" I backed off.

"Why not?"

"He's had his *finger*nail removed!"

Pascal looked at my scarred big toe. "You 'ave half a toenail, so you must know how to dress it."

"But a doctor fixed that! And I was only a little tacker."

Pascal let out a heavy sigh. He grabbed K-Mel's right hand, ripped off the dirty rag and pushed him to the kitchen sink.

"This is more than you did for me during the Events!" He tipped the alcohol over K-Mel's finger.

K-Mel Colline howled. He began to jump around the kitchen. His undies slipped towards his hips. He hollered, and swore, and wept tears of pain.

Then he spat at Pascal. I'd never seen such hatred between two people.

"I'll run you a bath." Pascal strode into the bathroom. A hiccup and phut was followed by a staccato gush, as water passed through a tap not recently used. He pushed K-Mel inside, shutting him in.

"See that 'e washes himself." Pascal gave a curt nod.

He made to leave, and then yelled through the bathroom door in French, "Where does Jeanne live in Australia?"

No reply.

"It's some place like, um, I think it's called Kooracoondoo," I said.

Pascal raised an eyebrow.

"Rocky had a postcard in his car. It was from Queensland, and I'm pretty sure it's, yeah, Kooracoondoo."

"I will check with Marcel." He paused. "You may find some old clothing for 'im to wear in my parents' room. K-Mel 'as plenty of money, you know. He keeps it in that filthy mattress." He indicated the front bedroom with his chin. "*Hhhonest* people use banks!" He slammed the front door shut behind him.

Inside the bedroom cupboard, faded newspapers had been spread. A 1984 headline—*Les Élections de la Violence*—seemed to jump out at me. Beneath was a photo of an *indépendantiste* bashing a ballot box with what appeared to be a club. *Was the photo of K-Mel?* I wondered.

I felt my flesh creep, and decided to get on with the task of finding him something to wear. Bits and pieces of women's clothing hung in the cupboard, left behind in the chaos of moving. But K-Mel didn't look the cross-dresser type to me.

Beside a pile of old towels on a shelf, I saw a roomy floral Capri pants number at the end of the rack. Unable to make up my mind about the Capri pants, I decided to check out K-Mel's mattress. I gave the scungy bed a poke to see if it rustled with money. The mattress was lumpy, and the ticking was sewn at one end, roughly, with twine, as though K-Mel opened the mattress every now and then to cram moolah inside.

Straightening, I saw a framed photo on the floor. A hippie chick with golden hair smiled at me, her skinny braids beaded and bouncing around her face beneath a crack in the glass. She had serious grey eyes. Her teeth were white and even. Behind her, palm trees swayed. Was this Rocky's mum?

The photo helped me make up my mind. If Jeanne Colline's hair-style was any indication, K-Mel would be happy to be retro and cool in Madame Manet's groovy '70s threads.

I knocked, pushed the bathroom door ajar and dropped the pants and a ragged towel through the crack. K-Mel made furious splashing noises. *Was he standing by the bath, only pretending to wash?*

Sliding to the floor, I leaned my back against the wall,

Finally, he emerged in his whoa mama flower power slacks, grinned and did a little twirl.

"You look as funky as a cagou bird!" I said.

He hip-hopped his way to a walk-in pantry, emerged clutching the long root of a plant. "You like?"

"That's, um …" I gasped.

"Kava kava!" He waved the root. "Good for pain, good for *blessure*. You try my pip-er methys-ti-cum?"

I pushed myself up from the floor. As if in a dream, I watched K-Mel pull an old jar and a dirty rag from the cupboard beneath the sink. He filled the jar with cloudy water from the tap, put the kava root in his mouth and chewed. He kept spitting the pieces into the rag, until it was full, twisted the cloth with his left hand, and plunged it into the water. He massaged the fabric between his fingers and thumb until the liquid began to turn brown. Lifting the jar to his mouth, he took a sip.

"Very good. Very nice kava kava. You want?" He offered me the jar. I froze.

Next moment, the front door opened with a bang.

Pascal was back. "I 'ave spoken with Marcel. Apart from some serious burns on his hands, Roch is well. He is living with 'is *maman*."

Pascal's face hardened. He marched across and whacked a back-hander against the jar, sending it to the floor where it shattered, scattering glass across the tiles. Muddy liquid snaked between my toes. Blood spurted from K-Mel's forefinger, and he stretched to stop himself from falling.

Pascal used swearwords I'd never heard before. Through his furious French, I understood one phrase—*putain de nakamal!*

"How dare you turn my place into a bloody nakamal!"

Chapter 46

The car was hot, but the silence was icy. Pascal worked the gear stick poking from the dash, his knuckles bleeding from the backhander. And not a word was spoken during our return to Noumea.

The windscreen wipers of the Deuche shuddered and flapped. He kept his eyes on the road ahead until we began to swirl around hills and down into the trendy beach area, whose lights were blurred by the rain.

"Aren't you going to pick up the Merc?" was the first sentence I uttered, followed by, "I wasn't going to drink it, you know."

Pascal didn't answer. He eased the bug car into the garage beneath *La Maison des Cerises*, got out and slammed the car door behind him.

In the kitchen, Marie-Françoise sat weaving a mat. She said nothing, didn't even look at us with her good eye. Just went on poking one leaf under another and pulling the leaf tight, smoothing the zigzag lines of the pattern with her hand.

"I can't believe you don't trust me!" I headed for the stairs and my room. "I wouldn't have drunk any of that kava."

"I 'ave your wallet." Pascal opened the drawer of a small hall table, and handed it to me. "It was found not far from your passport in the Latin Quarter. The police asked me to give it to you."

"Thanks. I'm off to Mount Koghi tomorrow to hike around a bit, and plan to leave a few days later, if that's okay. As there's no work experience, due to the cyclone, I should get home."

"I will organise your ticket."

Closing my bedroom door, I opened my wallet to check that everything was there. Some of my money was missing. I was about to storm back down the stairs and complain, when I re-checked. One hundred and twenty dollars was gone—the exact amount I had stolen from Pascal.

I grew so hot I nearly exploded.

Under the clothes I'd left in a pile on the cane chair, I scrabbled around. The one hundred dollar note I'd nicked was still tucked into the G-string. I slotted the note into my wallet, relieved I was only twenty dollars short from my fizzy-green-coconut-water-and-kava drink experience.

I needed to talk to Namilly. It would be expensive, but I hadn't spoken to her for over a week. I dialled the Ravella number. When Namilly finally answered, she sounded breathless.

"Are you all right, Ma? It's Genna."

She seemed to hesitate. "Where are you staying? You never rang to let me know."

"So much happened. I, um, forgot. A car bomb exploded in the Latin Quarter."

Her breathing was raspy. "And you were not hurt?"

"No, but we thought Rocky, the guy I was with, was dead. But he wasn't, and we've just got back from Yaté …" My voice trailed off.

"You still haven't told me where you're staying."

"I was billeted at Jacques Forestier's. Nobody told you?"

"Why would I be told?" Heavy breathing. "Did he try to buy you off?"

"No, he just took me on this deer hunt, where the dogs ripped into the stag."

"I don't wish to hear any more. It upsets me. He's an evil man."

The words burst out. "I discovered the Power of Attorney … the Procuration."

"What Procuration?"

"You know, where Sandrine signed me over to you, my nanny."

I felt the tears begin to come.

Silence from the other end.

"Are you there?"

"I'm sorry you had to see that." Her wheezing was scary.

I changed the subject. "How's Win?"

"The shop is 'bodacious', as Win"—she paused to catch her breath—"likes to say. We're going flat out, but *we miss you just the same*. Florence Stubbs gave us the bikini she wore in *On The Beach* to sell, which is surprisingly small, but floral and very pretty. And Mrs Bradfield kindly ..." Namilly began to rabbit on about the frocks, bags, shoes and hats the locals had decided to offload, as if relieved not to have to talk about the past.

"You didn't answer my question. Considering her mother's death, how's Win coping, you know, emotionally?"

"You'll have to ask her yourself."

"Win doesn't have the phone connected."

"I'm glad you weren't hurt, dear. But I, I, really must go." Namilly hung up.

I felt flat. There was so much else I hadn't told my mother: the damage done by the cyclone, my dreadlocks, the ants ... She would've laughed about the ants.

Extracting the kava leaf from my jeans' pocket, I smoothed the heart shape out and pressed it beneath my pillow. I linked my little fingers to remind me of Rocky. I was so in the twilight zone, knowing he was alive, that I had trouble getting to sleep. Was I being unfaithful to Stefan by thinking about Rocky? Was holding little fingers with a guy reason enough to tell my boyfriend I owed him a sunken garden?

I thought about K-Mel's kava. *If Pascal hadn't walked in, would I have tasted it?* But Rocky's dad had chewed the root up in his *mouth*, for heaven's sake, covering it with his slag! As if. No way. And yet—I had been tempted.

My mind then moved on to wondering about Namilly's strange attitude on the phone. Why had she been so reluctant to talk about Win?

I lay there, not sleeping.

In the pale light before the dawn, I heard Marie-Françoise in the kitchen below preparing to go to the Municipal Markets. Leaping out of bed, I dragged on my jeans. I could go with her, see what it was like. See if Chouchou's nakamal was still in the carpark. I was nearing the end of my stay, and determined to make the most of it.

Closing the front door behind me, I fell in beside the housekeeper. She wore a square-necked missionary dress, and her footsteps were deliberate. She didn't say anything, just kept walking. She carried baskets woven from coconut leaves. The grips were made of rope. We traipsed up and down hills, heading in the direction of the city of Noumea, without her saying a word—even when I asked her if she was married, had kids of her own.

We crossed the Baie de la Moselle carpark, jammed with the cars and small trucks and pick-ups of the people doing business in the market. The Nakamal de Chouchou lean-to was no longer there. Had the police moved it on?

Chapter 47

The market was filled with Tahitian music and the sound of people haggling. Yams abounded: lilac, white, delicate pink, rose and deep lavender. Big and ugly on the outside, they loomed over the water taro with its thick, striped stalks. I saw taro bourbon at 450 CFP per kilo. Every type of fish you could think of was for sale. And enough tropical fruit to make your mouth water.

A man with crow's feet like canyons delved into a basket similar to Marie-Françoise's, displaying his wild oranges, shrivelled and wrinkly, lining them up with pride.

Children played *cache-cache* behind a stall, from which I bought a ring. The ring was carved from coconut wood, painted with a red hibiscus, and cheap as chips for 300 CFP. As I pushed it onto my right pinkie, a chubby boy ran past. He headed for a neighbouring stall and hid behind it, giggling.

Soon Marie-Françoise's baskets were bulging with pineapple, cantaloupe, mango and green melon. She purchased some *pâtisseries*—croissants, brioches and two baguettes—still hot from the oven.

It was time for us to leave. Lugging one of Marie-Françoise's baskets, I traipsed beside her up and down hills. Highlighted by the early sun, I could see tiny hairs on the surface of her mole. It looked as though a furry spider had landed on the bridge of her nose and decided to set up home there.

Panting, she unexpectedly whispered in English, "Kava not good," and began to scratch at her arm. I could see the tell-tale rash. She pulled down the lower lid of her good eye, and I saw the yellowness.

I said, "I'm sorry, Marie-Françoise, but despite what you think, and despite what you've seen, that part of my life is over. Rocky is alive. I don't need kava."

Not responding, she opened the front door of *La Maison des Cerises* with her key and carried her purchases into the kitchen.

Forgetting that Pascal was unaware I would accompany the housekeeper to the market that morning, I added, "Did Monsieur Manet put you up to this, instruct you to tell me that, as a sort of *warning*?"

Marie-Françoise put her hand out for the second basket. The expression in her not-so-good good eye said: "Gotcha!" She dumped the fruit and *pâtisseries* onto the bench.

"If Monsieur Manet asks me where I am, tell him I'm upstairs packing."

I marched upstairs to my room, stroppy with Marie-Françoise and stroppy with Pascal. I stuffed my gear into the backpack.

Leaving my luggage at the foot of the stairs, I rocked into the kitchen.

Pascal was seated at the table with his nose buried in a newspaper—*Le Monde*—wearing reading glasses I hadn't seen before. He was decked out in a beige suit (Louis Féraud?) with rubber-soled suede shoes and a blue shirt open at the neck. He smelled of Kenzo Air aftershave. One of his knuckles was bound with sticking plaster.

My plane ticket lay beside my plate. I sat down, opened the ticket, checked the day and flight and tucked it in the pocket of my jeans.

Pascal did not look up. He uttered a curt *"Bonjour!"* and went on reading his paper.

I sucked on a piece of pineapple. "Do you realise," I said as I slurped—still tooshy—"that you could've *killed* K-Mel Colline yesterday?" I wiped a dribble of juice off my chin.

"He remains in my house, which is more than 'e deserves," Pascal said softly, his eyes still scanning the page before him.

"I'm off today! I'm leaving!"

Ignoring me, he looked up from his paper, told Marie-Françoise in French not to bother about dinner as he planned to be home late. He had a reception to attend at the Indonesian consulate in Baie de l'Orphelinat. Would he be escorting his Tahitian girlfriend to the event? I wondered.

"I have plans myself," I chipped in, "like touring around New Cal before I leave for Australia." I picked a piece of pineapple fibre from between my teeth. "Which is soon," I added.

Pascal kept reading.

Marie-Françoise poured his milky coffee into a chunky bowl. He placed his hand around the bowl, lifted it and sipped.

"Is it okay if I leave my laptop here, pick it up before I head out to Tontouta on the *bus*"—hint, hint—"to catch the plane?"

His nod was almost imperceptible.

"Well, I'm off!" I pushed my chair back so hard it grated against the floor.

Pascal turned a page of the paper, shook it straight and continued to read.

I fiddled with my pinkie ring, wondering if Pascal would say good-bye in the French way, and give me two air kisses. Or maybe even three, as his brother sometimes did.

The back of his neck looked tense.

I turned to leave.

He pushed himself up. *"Bon courage!"* After shaking hands, and wishing me luck, he sat down again. He re-immersed himself in his paper.

Hurt and bewildered that Pascal was so disinterested in my plans, I grabbed my backpack and let myself out the front door. Were we having a fight? If so, was it because I'd stolen his money? Was he annoyed I'd gone through his possessions? Or was it because he believed I'd been about to swallow K-Mel's kava?

Or had I done something else wrong?

Chapter 48

Slinging my backpack across my shoulders, I caught the bus to Place des Cocotiers. As I alighted, I heard the sound of a didgeridoo. I headed along the square to the *Kiosque à Musique*.

Seated on the ground, in front of the old bandstand, a Koori blew on his 'doo. His hair was tied back in a red, gold and black ribbon. Seeing him made me wonder if Cluny had returned to Australia with Flex du Lac. Were they dating? I wondered. They'd seemed pretty lovey-dovey when I last saw them.

Leaving the haunting music behind, I made for the *Office du Tourisme*.

The queue was long in the tourist office. While waiting for a map of the Southern Province of New Caledonia, I heard shouting and tooting on the opposite side of the road. I moseyed to the window. On the footpath, beside a bookshop, a guy and the driver of *Le Petit Train* were having an argument. I squinted. The guy was Spud Underwood!

Spud took a swing at the driver of the tourist train.

I threw open the door and ran outside.

"What's got into you, Spud?" I yelled. "Chill out! You'll get arrested!"

Spud was clad in a grubby Nike Swifts T-shirt and grimy matching shorts. It was evident he hadn't washed his clothes in ages.

"I thought you were up north, touring around near Koné, looking at nickel mines or something."

Spud tugged on his beard. "Well, well, well. If it isn't Miss Privileged!" He pointed at the driver. "*He* says it's his parking spot, but I got here first."

I checked the sign. "According to this notice, the space is for the tourist train. You gotta move whether you like it or not."

"Wanna lift?" Spud indicated a dusty Renault, almost as decrepit as Pierrot the Peugeot.

"Where did you get the car?"

"Car belongs to Chantal's brother. Germain said I could have it for the rest of the week, and now he's gone and changed his mind." Spud ran a finger over his tattoo. Up close, the snake resembled the deadly *tricot rayé*.

The driver of the tourist train climbed back behind the wheel, scowling.

"Where does Chantal's brother hang out?"

"UNC, he's a Law student at university in Nouville. He's the biggest fruitcake of almost two thousand students." Spud looked hyped, but I could detect no reefer smell.

"Let's go and discuss it with Germain." I slung my gear into the back seat, and jumped in. "He might be willing to change his mind. We could make it like I'm, I dunno, can't say I'm your girlfriend!"

Spud twisted his mouth. "You look different." He turned the key in the ignition.

"Oh, it's my dreads. You haven't seen 'em before." I whirled my head from side to side and back again. "Like 'em?"

Spud did not reply. He smelled of stale sweat—as though he hadn't showered for days. Raised welts, like scratches, crept across the back of his hands.

"I saw Chantal at Bouchon." I wriggled in my seat.

"Bitch!".

"Whoa! Chantal is stunning!"

Spud grunted.

We chugged along the north side of Baie de la Moselle, passing the Captain Cook monument and taking Avenue James Cook. We crossed the causeway to the former island of Nou.

"Water looks good," I said. "I'd love to have a swim."

"Not there you wouldn't!"

"Why wouldn't I?"

"The water's polluted from the nickel smelter." He frowned. "I saw blokes there just the other day in white overalls, carrying blue plastic bags and doing a clean-up."

We passed Camp-Est prison, where Marie-Françoise's nephew was serving time for setting fire to a telephone box in the Brousse.

"Cluny told me you were in love with Chantal," I murmured. "So what went wrong?"

"She got difficult."

"Difficult?"

Spud edged the car into a spot beneath an acacia tree, beside a crumbling brick wall, and climbed out.

"Gonna see Germain."

He jogged across the road to a modern cream building with lofty curved roofs, and apparently undamaged from the cyclone. The building was situated not far from the psychiatric hospital.

I opened the car door to enjoy the breeze. A cool-looking dude in jeans and a floral shirt was pointing out sites of interest in the former penal settlement, to a woman in a wide-brimmed hat. He fiddled with his bead choker, and adjusted his John Lennon tinted glasses. I could hear him waffling on about the administrator's house, the St Thomas chapel, the nurses' building and pharmacy, plus the bakery with its delivery dock.

"One of the oldest buildings in Nouméa," he said.

The woman in the straw hat gestured high in the air at the former Baie des Dames, where the convict women used to be incarcerated.

A group of Kanak students carrying books called out, *"Hep, taxi!"* and roared with laughter as they crossed the road to the lecture theatres.

While discussing an Island Theatre production with the tourist, the guide's eyes suddenly widened. Following his gaze, I saw Spud hurtling across the rough terrain to the car. A chunky Melanesian charged after him.

I slammed the door shut. Spud leapt into the driver's seat. Grabbing the steering wheel, he grated the gears and we jerked away.

Germain whacked the rear of the vehicle with his open hand.

The car shuddered.

"Salaud!" he shouted.

The Renault picked up speed and we headed back across the causeway.

"I dunno what you've done, Spud, but you're in deep *merde* with Chantal's brother!"

"Forget about it. Where d'you wanna go?"

"Well, I was planning to go to the Monts Koghis."

"Mount Koghi it is."

We hit the RT1, heading in the direction of Dumbéa.

"What a piece of luck, bumping into *you*!" I settled back, and tried to make myself comfortable. "I would've had to take the Dumbéa bus, and then hitch at the turn-off leading up the mountain."

Spud pressed his foot hard on the pedal. The car began to tremble. "Bugger these shakes." He pulled at this beard. "This bomb starts to slam dance the minute the gauge hits sixty."

"What's going on between you and Chantal? Have you had an argument?" We shimmied our way along the highway. "She looked pretty down when I saw her."

"Her family's got it in for me, wouldn't let me stay with 'em after the cyclone hit."

"Chantal had an argument with Monsieur Manet in the kitchen at Bouchon. Perhaps they were discussing the issue?"

Spud said nothing. We pushed our way up the hill and past Nakamal du Ciel. A man stood there, looking down. I wondered if it was Tibou, there to set up his nakamal for the evening.

"He's a pompous shithead."

"Who, Pascal?" I looked at Spud in surprise. Then, ignoring the fact that the French examiner was often quite—actually, very—pompous, I said: "Pascal is *not* pompous!"

"So it's 'Pascal' now, is it?" Spud seemed to ooze sweat as he changed gears. His beard was beginning to drip. "How come you two are so chummy?"

I decided not to share with him that Pascal Manet had been controlling almost every move I made in New Caledonia.

The Renault slowed. We turned right and wound our way up a road lined with up-market houses. The air was cooler here, but Spud was sweating more and more every time I looked at him. His body odour was familiar—as if from somewhere else. And I couldn't think where.

By the time the car ground to a halt in the carpark of the inn, I was jittery—and for no good reason. It was Spud's smell, the greasy smell of fear. I rubbed my hands along my arms to shake the feeling off, twisted my pinkie ring as I tried to remember. His Nike Swifts badly needed a wash. *Was that the problem?*

He yanked on the handbrake and we climbed out.

A fresh breeze blew. Far off, the lagoon shone.

"You can see Lac de Yaté on the other side from here if you tramp along one of the hiking trails." Spud's teeth were chattering, and it wasn't cold on the mountain, simply pleasant.

"I can see a board up there outlining those hiking trails." I pointed. "Wanna come and have a look?"

Spud dragged along behind me. I climbed the steps leading from the carpark to a grassed-in area. The trails were outlined according to distance and degree of difficulty.

"Why don't we head right, have a look at the cabins for hire, see what it's like to stay here?"

"I need an ice-cream!" Sounding like a grumpy kid, Spud jerked his head in the direction of the Auberge.

"Nah. Not yet. Anyway, I don't eat ice-cream. Let's start walking."

Spud looked angry. "I'm thirsty, and hungry." His eyelids began to twitch. "I haven't eaten in days."

We stood there arguing—ice-cream, hike; hike, ice-cream—and I didn't understand why. Did Spud have the munchies? Had he been smoking dope? Or was he stressed from dropping eccy?

He changed his mind. "Let's go hiking then." He rushed down the steps from the grassed-in area towards the path heading east, through the rainforest. He pulled at my arm. His palm was clammy.

"What about the cabins?" I gestured to the right. "Let's go that way."

"You wanna walk, we'll walk!" He grabbed me by the elbow, hustled me so that I almost stumbled on a tree root. "*This* way!"

The clay was slippery from the rain. Soon my thongs were sliding all over the place. *Why hadn't I worn joggers?* I asked myself. The path was steep, and the ground was becoming more treacherous. Deeper and deeper into the rainforest we went. The trees touched overhead, creating a canopy. Mosquitoes droned. I had forgotten to slap on insect repellent, and I began to pack death at the thought of catching dengue. Picking up pace to avoid being bitten, I almost lost my balance again.

"How long before we see Lac de Yaté?" I gave my arms another rub. Spud paused.

"Well?"

He came out with a wacky answer. "This time, I've got the upper hand!"

My mind churned. *What had Spud meant by 'upper hand'?*

Chapter 49

Spud smirked. "I'm the one with the advantage now. This time, I've got the joggers. You've got the thongs."

Was it Spud's body odour? Or was it the smell of fear that alerted me?

For no good reason, I was suddenly scared to be alone with Spud. Would he try to jump me? I began to wonder if Spud was the 'other bogan', the one whose name I'd never known; the one who had tried to persuade Hank to rape me in the ti-tree bushes at Ravella. But bogans were uneducated people, I told myself, not guys like Spud who'd won a scholarship to the prestigious Grange College in Melbourne.

"How long have you had your snake tatt, Spud?"

He sniffed. "I had the tatt done here in New Cal. Can't ya see the snake's a *tricot rayé*?" He ran his fingers over the thick cross-stripes. "The snake looks magic with stripes, but slimy brown and ugly when it sheds its skin."

Like you, I thought, saying: "They're awesome in the water. I swam with one, danced with the stripes."

"You're weird." His eyes stared unnaturally. "Verging on sick."

Despite the air being cooler up here, I was starting to turn into a puddle of sweat and nervousness at being with Spud. The edge of one thong caught in a tree root. I began to do the splits.

"Help me, Spud!" I cried.

"Miss Privileged's got a problem?" He looked stoked to see me in trouble.

As I righted myself, my hibiscus pinkie ring slid off.

Spud pounced. He held the ring up. "Come and get it!"

He began to move towards me and, remembering the bruise on Chantal's face at Bouchon, I twisted away and began to run in the opposite direction—deeper and deeper into the rainforest. The path wound around a corner. I darted behind a bunch of tree ferns and crouched down.

By now, I was positive Spud had been one of the bogans who attacked me in the ti-tree bushes. ("This time, I've got the joggers. You've got the thongs.") He probably would've succeeded in raping me if I *had* been wearing thongs.

Muttering, Spud stumbled past and disappeared from view.

I huddled among the tree ferns for what seemed like ten years. I pulled my arms inside my T-shirt, creating a cocoon of cloth around my body. Each time I heard a mossie, I shook my dreads from side to side to ward it off.

The light filtering through the rainforest began to darken. The wind picked up. I pulled my arms from my T-shirt, and made a nest for myself among the leaf litter. A giant snail oozed past, big as my hand, carrying a narrow, banded cone-shaped shell on its back. I snatched my arms away, and tucked them back inside my T-shirt. I suppressed a scream as the escargot began to burrow into the soil beside a rubber tree. A second giant snail sleazed up, and began to burrow.

I was packing.

Easing my mobile phone from my pocket with difficulty, I managed to stay inside my T-shirt cocoon as I typed out the words:

help me am in dire str8ts

Bringing up Stefan's number, I SMSed the message and waited for his reply.

Ten minutes passed, and nothing from Stefan. Not even another text about Bill Einstein.

Pushing my phone into the back pocket of my jeans, I decided that if I stayed in the bushes long enough other tourists might use the same trail, and I'd be rescued.

Spud shuffled past along the track. Then back again. Back and forth he went, searching for me. I cursed myself for not having taken the right-hand turn, gone hiking in the direction of cabins and people.

A grunt. Silence. No more rustling. No more sliding.

Thinking Spud must've gone back to the carpark, I crept through the bushes to the slimy path. My eyes jumped out on stalks. Less than a hundred metres away, Spud sat cross-legged. He was rocking backwards and forwards and—*he had his thumb in his mouth.* Suck, suck, suck came the slurping sound. Uh-oh, Spud had lost it!

Creeping back to my hiding place near the burrowing giant snails, I tried to work out what to do. Was Spud just pretending to be off the air? Would he grab me when I came out of hiding?

By now, I was pushing the panic button.

Unexpectedly I heard a voice, followed by a crashing through the rainforest: "Genna! Spud!" Pascal sounded fizzed off.

Manoeuvring myself up, I made my way through ferns and palms to the edge of the track. Two gendarmes in kepis and shorts flashed torches as they made their way along the path with Pascal. Sliding and stepping with care, they reached Spud. Spud didn't look up. He continued to gaze at the ground, sucking on his thumb like a baby.

The gendarmes spoke in machinegun French with Pascal.

He nodded.

In horror I watched as the *flics* jerked Spud to his feet, and handcuffed him. *Would they handcuff me, as well?* I remained rooted to the spot behind a palm frond, not knowing whether to creep back, and huddle in my nest of leaf litter. Or make a run for it. Or try to act cool and swan on out, as though I'd been busy studying the sex lives of giant snails.

I pretended to act cool.

"Boy! Am I glad to see you!" I attempted to stroll in a casual manner towards Pascal. But my thongs slid out from under me in the mud.

"Am I under arrest, as well?" I gazed up, expecting him to laugh.

Pascal looked serious. "You are all right?"

"Um, yeah, sort of."

"Why are your arms hidden?"

"Mosquitoes." I disentangled my arms from the T-shirt.

Pascal hauled me up. He brushed the dirt off his hands and went over to consult with the gendarmes. He nodded his head again. *Yes, I was about to be arrested.* My heart began to thump, and my insides felt as if ants were on the march in there. I was up schlep creek, and I had no idea what I'd done.

Pascal approached again. "Spud had half a kilo of ecstasy tablets in 'is possession and much cannabis. But the police 'ave decided not to lay charges against you." His eyes were stern. "However, you will remain in my custody until you catch your plane out of *Nouvelle-Calédonie* tomorrow."

"What have *I* done?"

The gendarmes dragged Spud back along the hiking trail, heading for the Auberge carpark.

"You were an accessory to stealing a car."

"Whoa! I never knew that car was stolen. Spud said he borrowed it from Germain, and I had no reason to disbelieve him."

"There is more."

We followed the gendarmes, side-stepping tree roots.

"And the 'more' is why you were aggro with me this morning?"

"I was not angry. I was disappointed."

"I have to admit I, um, did nick money from you."

"Stealing my money means you invade my privacy, and I do not like this." Pause. "But 'aving drugs is more serious. In 'is work experience programme, Jacques Forestier is not content for students to do this."

"What drugs? I don't do drugs! I don't have any drugs!" A piece of leaf litter fell from my dreadlocks.

"Cannabis was found in your possession."

"You mean in that cliplock bag?"

He nodded.

"I *told* you, that stuff's only chop-chop!" I thought of Spud. "Unless Spud spiked it. Or someone else did."

"You do not expect me to believe you!"

A howl echoed over the mountain top. The hairs stood up on the back of my arms.

"What was *that*?"

"Your friend is resisting arrest."

We emerged into the carpark.

A waiter came out of the Auberge, stared and went inside.

"Oh, that's awful. Spud's career has gone down the toilet now."

Tears began to prick beneath my eyelids. I flipped and picked my way towards the police van, hoping to speak to Spud. But the gendarmes slammed the door shut, backed and prepared to do a U-turn.

"I feel sorry for Spud," I said. "But I have this strange feeling he was one of the bogans who jumped me in the ti-tree bushes at Ravella."

"When did 'e do such a thing?" Pascal looked startled. "I did not know you were, ah, attacked."

"Last November, late in the afternoon, after my English exam. And it was *pretty* scary."

"You are wrong. Spud was in *Le Caillou*. He missed a French exam at Melbourne University to be with Chantal. And I do not like zis. White and black do not go together very well in our country."

Pascal was showing his racist side.

"What about Jeanne and K-Mel Colline, Sandrine and Claude?"

"They are exceptions, and neither couple lives here." He paused. "Anyway, K-Mel is a *métis*, a half-caste."

"But Rocky said *he* was a *métis*."

"Roch lies, for political purposes, and is only one quarter Kanak, which explains the colour of his hair."

"I thought Rocky's hair colour was caused by drinking kava."

Pascal shook his head. "'E is naturally a *rouquin*, red-haired, and 'as always been ashamed of it." He chewed his lip. "But back to Spud. You are lucky. He hit Chantal. He might 'ave done the same to you."

"Those bruises at Bouchon?"

"*Oui,*"

The police van still sat there, motor running.

"I can't stand this!" I could hear Spud sobbing. "I'll have to talk to him."

My concerns about Spud had been allayed, now that I knew he hadn't attacked me in the ti-tree bushes. I set off to comfort him.

I heard Pascal call, "Stop, Genna! I make a mistake. Spud was *not* in ze territory last November. He cancels at the last minute. But I do not know if he decides to sit his exams, or …"

I hurtled to the van. My feet kept sliding, and I almost lost my balance. I pounded the rear door with the flat of my hand.

"It was *you*, Spud!" I screamed. "I knew it! You lousy creep! You tried to rape me!" I bashed and bashed, yelling, "I hate you! I hate you! I *hate* you!"

The gendarme climbed out, and asked me to move off. "*Dégagez, mademoiselle!*"

Tears of fury ran down my cheeks as Pascal and the *flic* pulled me away.

"You piece of garbage!" I shrieked. "I hope they lock you up and throw away the key!"

Spud went quiet.

Then I heard him snort. He cackled, "I tricked ya. I tricked ya." He followed up with the words I remembered: "Virgin slut!" And I knew for certain Spud had been the other bogan on that afternoon in Ravella; the bogan whose name I had never known.

My knees shook so hard I could barely stay upright.

The gendarme gave orders to Pascal in furious French. He hopped in the vehicle, revved and drove off down the mountain. With blurred vision, I watched Pascal get my luggage from the Renault. He transferred the luggage into—and I wondered if my mind had become unhinged—the Deuche.

"Where's the Merc?" My teeth chattered. "I was hoping for a comfy ride into town."

Chapter 50

Pascal bundled me into the bug car. "It is a long story and one I do not wish to repeat. Enough to say, I now own this wretched *bagnole.*"

"It's not a jalopy. It's a cute car," I said in a low voice, still shaken at having been alone with Spud.

I sat there, thinking of that afternoon in the ti-tree bushes at Ravella and how afraid I'd been. "Your brother offered me a whisky, after he chased Hank and Spud off. Jack Danicl's, it was. I could do with that whisky right now."

Pascal touched me on the shoulder. "I am sure my brother was the one who needed a whisky, but you were lucky Marcel was there. I now know Spud is a very dangerous person to be around ladies."

"Me? A lady?" I began to brighten. "You told me I looked like a kid."

"You have a wonderful smile. If you find yourself a nice coiffure …"

I started to laugh.

"What is wrong?"

I laughed and laughed until the fear was almost washed away. Although it would never be totally washed away.

Pascal turned the ignition of the Citroën Deux Chevaux, and began to fiddle with the gear stick. The seat was uncomfortable, and my mobile phone was digging into me. I reached around to pull the phone from my pocket. *1 message received* showed on the screen. I'd been so het-up, I hadn't felt the tell-tale shimmy. My heart began to paddle.

I pressed *Show*. The message came up. My heart plummeted all the way to my toes and stayed there. Stefan's meaning was clear:

i o u a sunken garden mate

Staring at nothing, I knew my boyfriend had just confessed to being unfaithful. Our relationship would never be the same again.

Pascal interrupted my thoughts. "You are still worrying about Spud?"

"No, it's Stefan. He just admitted to being unfaithful, and the creep told me"—my voice caught—"by SMS!"

Pascal touched me on the shoulder again, gently this time.

"Because your little friend is unfaithful it does not mean your adventure is over," he reasoned, in typical French fashion. "But I know 'ow you feel."

"No, you don't! You *don't know* how I feel! This is the worst day of my life! I am being deported from the place I was born in. I discovered one of the bogans who jumped me in Ravella was here, right under the same roof!"

"Spud has done work experience before. On this occasion, 'e asks to see my list of *stagiaires* before he decides to come, and I didn't think anything about this. He knew you would be 'ere."

"Oh, heck! He didn't wear a beard then, and it fooled me. I hope he goes away for a long time." I shifted my feet. "And now my boyfriend's doing it with Elizabeth! This really is the worst day of my life."

"Did 'e mention her by name?"

"No, but I *know* she's the rat responsible, the humungous rat who went and got slim!"

Silence for a while. We chugged down the hill, past Nakamal du Ciel. Tibou stood beside his nakamal. He waved to Pascal, who gave a curt wave in return.

"I suppose *he's* the reason you knew where that lowlife, Spud, and I were?" I indicated Tibou with my chin.

"Germain rang Tibou, and Tibou rang me. Tibou is a good man. He runs a very clean and honest nakamal. No animals, no drugs …" Pascal's voice trailed off, as though he decided he'd lectured me enough.

Lights began to shine on Baie de la Moselle.

Pascal changed the subject. "I speak with Bruno di Luca today on my phone, and Emma is still unwell from *leptospirose*."

I remembered the pretty woman riding her horse on La Roche Percée beach. "I'm sorry."

"I warn Emma many, many times about drinking from *canette* without cleaning the top with soap and water. Rats run over them in small shops in the Brousse. But she continues to drink from *canettes*." Pascal imitated pulling a ring from a can of beer and sipping.

I became angry. "Don't you get *sick* of always being right, *sick* of always telling people what to do?" The tears welled up; I gulped them back.

He shrugged. *"Pfft,* I make mistake from time to time. I give you an example. My Mercedes is being driven around Grande Terre by a large Callithumpian family right now. I give wrong instructions to Location Louis Limou. These people come along, need a big car. Louis rents it out … listen to me! … for a *month.*" His eyes glittered. "So I am forced to purchase the Deuche."

An alien smile crept across my face.

"I can just hear them: 'Is eet not gooottt cooor? Woood you like some moooore fooottt.' My car will smell of cheese and sweat when I get it back."

I couldn't help giggling. "Your Callithumpian accent, if that is what it's meant to be, is so bad!"

"But not as bad as my mood."

"The Deuche will cheer you up," I said, as he shoved his hand through the flap to indicate we were pulling up outside *La Maison des Cerises*.

"I am late for my cocktail reception, and I have mud on my shoes. I will quickly change. Marie-Françoise will watch over you this evening. Will you be all right?" Pascal's mobile phone rang. He pulled it from his pocket as he climbed from the car, pressing the button. *"Oui, ma chérie,"* I heard him say. *"J'arrive dans un instant."* A pause. *"Mais ... chérie?"* He pushed the gate open with his foot. *"D'accord. Salut. Bye."* He hung up.

"Your girlfriend is unhappy?"

"Laetitia is PDG, president of a pearl-buying company. She does not appreciate tardiness." He went to go inside, and then held out his hand.

"I will please 'ave your passport until you leave *Nouvelle-Calédonie* tomorrow."

Delving into my backpack, I pulled out my passport.

Pascal rushed off. I was barely in the front door when he appeared again. Laces flapped in a pair of clean shoes. I felt like a gumby kid, watching a parent hurry to get ready while the kid was left to spend the night with the babysitter.

"You've got mud on you daks, Dad." His trouser legs were stained with clay from the hiking trail.

"Merde!" He darted back into his bedroom. Cupboard doors banged, drawers squeaked, and he re-emerged.

Pascal looked kind of spunky. He smelled good, too.

Shrugging on the jacket of a dark green linen suit (probably Kenzo), he gave instructions in rapid French to Marie-Françoise—who leaned on her broom, expressionless—and left.

Watching Pascal go, I felt daggy and uncool. My jeans were scungy from the rainforest. I had a sudden urge to splurge the money I had left on new duds. Something grown-up. Something elegant.

Would Marie-Françoise allow me to go shopping in Anse Vata?

In my best, most polite, French I asked, assuring her I'd be gone for no more than an hour. Surprised, I saw her nod. I nearly hugged the housekeeper, but the sight of the mole on the bridge of her nose made me back off.

She followed me, for a while. Each time I turned to look Marie-Françoise was there, doing her best to blend in with the trees along Baie des Citrons. Buying a sorbet from *La Sorbetière*, I licked, turned again and she was gone. Face it, we both knew Pascal would have the fuzz on me in a flash if I tried to scarper.

In Anse Vata the shops were glitzy and open late as I had hoped. Rich tourists strolled about, complaining that the *Jeudis de l'Anse Vata* markets would be closed for months due to the damage done to the farés by the cyclone.

Trying on heaps of frocks, I forgot about Spud, and the mud, and being with him on that hiking trail. I fell in love with a dusky-pink beaded pareo-style number with funky kitten-heeled sandals to match.

I left my new gear on, telling the smiling salesperson to chuck out my old jeans and T-shirt—forgetting I'd be forced to work for days shelf-stacking at The Store to pay for my extravagance.

Madame offered me a dusky-pink ribbon for my hair. I told her that ribbons didn't go with dreadlocks. She showed me how to secure my dreads at the nape of my neck. Admiring my reflection in the mirror, I thought: *Wow! Eat your heart out, Stefan!*

I left the shop carrying the empty glossy bag with *Fringues du Jour* printed on the front, just because it looked classy.

Back at *La Maison des Cerises*, I trowelled shadow onto my lids—chinchilla to make my eyes look even blacker. I smeared the Chanel lipstick Pascal had bought me on my mouth. (I changed my mind about the colour, deciding I quite liked sepia, and dabbing a bit on my stubbly eyebrow which hadn't quite grown back.)

As I waited for Pascal to come home from his cocktail reception, I draped myself casually over the arm of a cane chair on the veranda of *La Maison des Cerises*. As the hours trundled by, I settled myself into the seat, hoping he'd notice me and see that I, too, could look elegant. When the wind got chilly, I curled in a ball to keep my arms and legs warm, and fell asleep,

Marie-Françoise passing woke me as the sun began to rise. She headed off to the Municipal Markets to buy pawpaw and croissants for breakfast.

Uncurling myself, I moseyed on into the house. I peered into his bedroom to see if Pascal had returned. His discarded beige suit still lay in a tangled heap on his bed where he'd left it; his muddy suede shoes were askew on the floor nearby.

The sun was up. And he wasn't here to see how great I looked.

Chapter 51

Pascal arrived after I'd showered and changed. I wore a tube skirt for the trip and, on my feet, the dusky-pink sandals. I'd retied the ribbon around my dreadlocks.

After placing my backpack and carry bag in the Deuche, beside a basket woven from coconut leaves, I wedged my *Fringues du Jour* glitzy bag (with my new pareo carefully folded inside) on the floor between the seats.

"Was your evening good?" I turned to Pascal, now in a tasteful floral shirt and jeans. "Did you have an incredible time with Laetitia?"

"The reception was very enjoyable." The car coughed to life, and he changed the subject. "I like your shoes."

"And I like your floral shirt." No way was I about to tell Pascal I'd dressed up and behaved like an idiot, hanging out for his approval.

"You are wearing much makeup."

This tit-for-tat conversation was making me twitchy. Surprised, I saw we were chugging along Promenade Roger Laroque in the direction of Ouen Toro, rather than towards Tontouta.

"Aren't we going the wrong way to the airport?"

We began to wind around the curves of Val Plaisance.

My mobile phone vibrated in my hand. I pressed *Show*. A text message appeared:

Hope u were not 2 injured by car bomb. Am thinking of u. I gave Marcel a letter. Roch

I pressed *Save*, feeling my heart bang beneath my T-shirt.

Pascal's words intruded: "Is your message from Stefan?"

I decided not to tell him the SMS was from Rocky. "Just a friend."

"Tiens!" He squirrelled my pinkie ring out of his jeans' pocket. "The police gave me your *bijou*. Apparently they 'ad trouble getting it from Spud."

I jammed the ring on my finger, took it off, and jammed it back on again. I hoped the gendarmes were sticking sharpened bamboo shoots beneath Spud's fingernails right this minute.

"How is he?"

Pascal shook his head, as if to say not well. He worked the knob of the gear lever frantically. An ominous feeling ran through me. Where was Pascal taking me?

"Did Spud have those drugs so that he could sell them?" I tugged at my tube skirt. "None of it makes sense, though. Spud won a scholarship to study at a private school. Why would he want to sell eccy?"

"Spud is poor, and this creates problems for many scholarship students. It is not necessarily wonderful to go to a prestigious college."

"Cluny said Spud doesn't like lines, or boxes, or borders, doesn't even believe in them. Boy, was she right about that!"

"Perhaps."

"I've worked out you're taking me to 1, rue de la Guillotine. I'll be late for my flight."

"I 'ave been asked that you meet someone."

"Better not be Spud!"

"It is not Spud. And we 'ave plenty of time."

"Well, I don't want to be lectured by Jacques Forestier again." I was getting agitated. "He might be my grandfather, but what right has *he* to lecture *me* about my behaviour!"

We rolled into the drive of 1, rue de la Guillotine. Broken branches and twigs filled the garden. A tarpaulin flapped on the roof. Strangely, the cycad palms stood upright in their broken pots.

"Will you please go inside?" Pascal pointed to the open front door, askew on its hinges. "Wait in the library. I think you know where to find it."

Water dripped from the broken guttering.

Pascal stayed in the Deuche as I eased myself out of the car. Inside the house, I climbed the stairs and headed for the landing. I turned the knob, and walked into a stench of mouldy leather and water-damaged books. The smell made me feel pukish. I switched on the ceiling fan. The blades turned and squeaked. The door slowly closed. A car door slammed outside, as if someone else had arrived. I prayed it wasn't Jacques.

People talked downstairs. I heard a woman's voice. I made for Jacques Forestier's desk. My kitten heels caught on the Aubusson rug, and my heart jiggled as I leaned against the lion-mask handle of the drawer. I discerned footsteps, a whiff of perfume.

Hang on! I said to myself. That's Miss Dior, the scent Namilly gives me as a gift every Christmas, without fail.

Was Namilly here to see me? But she never wore perfume.

Whoever it was seemed to hesitate, as if unsure whether to come in. My heart bounced around like a ball, jumping into my throat, plummeting to my stomach. I made for the door, and then rushed back to the safety of the desk.

My face fell like a stone when Sandrine Bas Salaire de Lyon walked in.

The first thing I noticed was her hot-pink dress—so naff, so forever ago. She was pretty, but skinny as a toothpick. Her sandals were scuffed. She was wound like a spring.

"Sandrine!" I stared at my birth mother. "Why are *you* here? I thought you never wanted to see me again."

"I changed my mind." Like her father, she had almost no accent.

We eyed one another, not saying anything. She pushed her bleach-blonde hair back from her brow. Her fingers danced with nervousness.

"I'm sorry but I can't talk to you." She turned to go.

"Hey, wait a minute! You owe me an explanation for dumping me when I was a kid!"

"I don't owe you anything. I do not believe you are my daughter! Your hair is dark, and so are your eyes—*too* dark. I don't believe the DNA tests." She screwed up her mouth, and moved her head from side to side.

"Then why did you come?"

"So I could sleep at night." She made a washing motion with her hands. "And because Pascal Manet is more persuasive than his brother."

"Jacques believes I'm his granddaughter."

"Perhaps Papa needs to believe it?" Pause. "He says you slept in the old nursery. It used to be pretty, with roses on the curtains."

"They're bows!" I said. *What sort of mother wouldn't remember every detail of her daughter's nursery?* I asked myself.

"I spent last night at Bouchon, the first time for almost twenty years. Nothing's changed. The stags roared all night, even though the rutting season has barely begun. I cannot wait to get home to Claude, and to my Amédée Apartments."

I tapped the drawer behind me. "I found the Power of Attorney you signed, in this desk." My mouth felt stuffed with cotton wool. "Why did you *do* that? What sort of mum would sign away the right to care for her kid?"

"After my husband died, I had a breakdown. Only Papa doesn't believe in nervous breakdowns. I was unable to stop crying, unable to get out of bed. The Events were in full swing." She shivered. "When the *nounou* saw I wasn't coping, she offered me a paper to sign away my rights. And I did. You reminded me of Yves-Laurent. It hurt too much to look at you."

"So you hate my hair and my eyes, my skin and everything about me." My voice went wobbly, and I whispered, "Didn't you ever think I might miss my father, too? Grieve for him? Didn't you think I might spend my life hanging out for a dad of my own?"

She shrugged. "Later, when I joined Claude in Australia, I regretted signing the Procuration. Papa began to hound me about money. He was furious at everything I did."

"In the end, Namilly was the only one who really cared about me?"

"The *nounou* doted on you. I knew she would bring you up properly … no normally is the word, yes, in a normal way … and I knew she would do anything for you. That was enough." She made to leave, and then added: "The road to the airport was blocked much of the time during the Events. How did she smuggle you out of *Le Caillou*?"

"She smuggled me out on a ship. Namilly gave me kava … yeah, I'm certain it was kava. She shut me in our hollow sofa. They swung the sofa aboard. The rest was, like, *normal*."

"How ingenious! A carpenter in Magenta used to make sofas for people who needed extra storage. I don't imagine he meant it to be used like that."

"Namilly keeps cans for the needy in it now, but it was, um, just our hollow sofa."

Sandrine hesitated. "One of the owners at Amédée Apartments put his flat up for sale. Claude and I took out a loan, and purchased it." She cleared her throat. "The apartment is one bedroom. If you wish, you may stay there." She added: "Sometime."

Blown away by the lukewarm invitation, I said, "I just might do that."

Sandrine opened the library door. "By the way, I like your dread-locks!" She went to depart, but continued, "I think we should make an effort to know one another. I don't remember much. Depression is a shocking thing." Her eyes shone with unshed tears. "I did look for you, you realise, for a long time, put advertisements in the paper. Only I didn't know where the nanny had gone."

"Marcel told me you used to bail up girls in the street."

"I hope he didn't make me sound too foolish."

I shook my head. "Not really, only when he described your bathers shop in Surfers Paradise where everything was pink and you sold only bikini bottoms, the monokini." I felt my voice go shaky. "And you went broke."

She almost smiled. "I have a taxi waiting." She pulled the door to behind her.

I could hear Sandrine speaking to Pascal. Her voice was high, as though she was arguing. Or was she crying? It was hard to tell.

The taxi door slammed shut. She drove off.

I picked my way back down the stairs, almost tripping, and not knowing how I felt. I only knew one thing: *Namilly gave me Miss Dior every Christmas, because that was the perfume Sandrine wore.*

Chapter 52

"Phew, that was a heavy scene!"

"Was Sandrine very hard on you?" Pascal put his almost-healed hand over mine as we joggled along the RT1. And it still felt kind of weird to be comforted by the man who'd conducted my French oral exam.

"She wasn't too bad, but I got the feeling she never really wanted me, only wanted my father."

"You must forgive 'er. She was very young when she marries Yves-Laurent, who was maybe fifteen, sixteen years above her age … and a soldier in the Events. You were born, and today she is still young, not yet forty."

"I'll *never* forgive her, not after seeing the Procuration."

Pascal looked thoughtful. "I spoke to Noah."

"*You* spoke to Noah?"

"Of course, we are not friends," he hastily added. "But I happen to bump into him, and he says Kyanthia firebombed Roch's car as a warning. He claims 'e knew nothing about it. Noah has escaped going to Camp-Est prison, once again."

He turned the knob of the Deuche's crackly radio. Bob Marley jogged his way through *Exodus*.

"That's appropriate! I'm leaving, and probably never coming back!"

"So you will not be disappointed to miss the making of a giant omelette at Dumbéa."

I made a face.

He laughed. "I must give you this." He pulled my passport from his pocket.

I ran my finger over the gold kangaroo on the cover. "Apart from Spud, who faces charges, when are Flex du Lac and Cluny Belpomme leaving?"

"Cluny is on your flight, although she disembarks in Sydney."

"And Flex?"

"Flex put a notice on the evening news. He has found relatives on the island of Lifou, in the *Province des Îles Loyauté*. He will return home after seeing them."

Jamming came over the airwaves. The bug car jammed its way along the RT1, bopping with the song.

"I may not go back to *l'Hexagone* to live," he said.

"You're not going back to France? Why not?"

"I have an offer to be director of Alliance Française in Melbourne, and am considering taking the position. It is a wonderful cultural centre in a very nice building, the oldest Alliance Française in Australia."

"Sounds good. A studyhead friend of mine won a *Mention Honorable* in the Alliance Française competition. She recited *Chanson d'Automne*, you know, the Paul Verlaine poem …"

"I could see you," he interrupted. "I could come to Ravella, check on Madame Mireille." He paused for a moment. "Perhaps we could drink coffee together." He cleared his throat. "Or maybe enjoy a glass of fruit juice?"

I froze. What sane person would want a French teacher popping in to see them in his shiny grey suit? Even if the suit *was* made by Kenzo? None of my friends would want to speak to me anymore.

I was in such a tizzy thinking about this, that I barely noticed we had pulled into Tontouta carpark. I barely noticed Pascal cry, "Ze eggs!" as I dropped my backpack on Marie-Françoise's basket in my haste to get away. I hardly noticed Pascal give me *four bises*—one kiss on each cheek and *two* for good luck!

But I did notice Marcel appear from the incoming flight. His head was now shaved, and he handed me the letter from Rocky.

The Manet brothers gave each other affectionate smooches. Marcel joshed Pascal about the Deuche, and Pascal called Marcel 'crazy baldhead'. They lit up Gauloises Blondes cigarettes and fell about laughing. *No Woman, No Cry* blared from the car radio.

I fled, clutching Rocky's letter.

Pascal called out, "Genna, I forget to give you your clothes."

"Which clothes?" I briefly wondered if he meant the Charles Jourdan creations donated by his lingerie lady friend, that I'd deliberately left behind.

"I wash the dirt off, from the night of the *attentat*."

"Forget it! The duds are damaged! Chuck 'em out!" I scuttled past the car-hire stalls. "And those eggs don't count," I muttered. "The RT1 is not a field." I scurried into the terminal.

After removing my shoes for the security people, I found a quiet corner and opened Rocky's letter. Inhaling the paper's earthy smell, with a hint of smoke, I read:

Dear Genna, I never realised you were Sandrine's daughter—some of the things you said now make sense. Marcel told me she deserted you during the Events, as my mother abandoned me. (That failed push for independence has a lot to answer for.) We have a lot in common. Is that why I am drawn to you? Are we soul mates?

I put you in grave danger, and do not forgive myself. I had no idea the car bombing would happen. (Obviously!!!) That night, I found myself lying in a doorway like a bundle of old rags—even the gendarmes didn't see me as they ran past with their torches flashing. I made my way like a clochard (tramp) to Magenta local airport, where I found a light aircraft preparing to leave. The pilot was an Aussie, who agreed to take me on board, despite my disreputable appearance and badly burned hands. The cyclone followed us most of the trip. (Pretty hairy, as the locals like to say.) So with God's help, I ended up here, in Kooracoondoo, with the other half of my family!!!

I wish you could meet Douce. A child of the Events, like you, she is beautiful, almost as tall as I. I would have passed her in the street not knowing she was my sister. She is different, though—too difficult to explain on paper.

I am homesick, and cannot return to Le Caillou—too dangerous. Am I reaching too high? I am just a simple kava farmer who wants the best for his country.

I wish I could see you, talk to you. I miss your bright smile, the way you never judged me (a quality you have). Australia is a big place, but please come to my rainforest home, overlooking the city of Cairns. À bientôt—I hope! Love, Rocky

With shaky fingers, I folded the letter and stuffed it down my T-shirt. Moments later, I found Cluny Belpomme hugging me.

"What's that you shoved down your top? Smells strange!" Not waiting for my response, she said, "It's so *great* to see you! Wow! Your dreadlocks look cool tied back like that!" She tugged my hand. "Let's go up to the lounge. We can wait there."

I followed Cluny up the stairs. We flopped down at a table in the open bar area.

"He wants to pop in and see me in Ravella," I said.

"Who wants to pop in and see you in Ravella?"

"Pascal Manet." I twisted my pinkie ring, still thinking of Rocky.

"Monsieur Manet? Well, that's all right."

"He's not popping in to see *you*!"

Cluny didn't seem very interested in the conversation. "How come you're taking your backpack on the plane? And your laptop?"

"They allowed them in the cabin on the flight over." Relaxing, I had time to wonder about my next text to Stefan. "Stefan dumped me, you know. And by SMS!"

Cluny's cornflower eyes expressed horror. "He didn't! Gimme your mobile, I'll change your wallpaper and get rid of his, quite hunky, dial." She grabbed my phone. "Who's the rat that did it?"

"Elizabeth Stubbs! Who else? She's been stalking Stefan all her life."

"Say cheddar!" Cluny pressed *Capture* on my mobile phone as I scowled into the lens. "Now I'll just delete *him*." She pushed buttons. "I'll put *you* there, instead." The phone did a war dance. "Hey, you've got an MMS, a photo!"

"Is it from Stefan?"

"Look, it's his new car!"

"No way." I peered over her shoulder to see a gleaming burgundy station wagon.

"And who is that stunning girl beside him, with the long ice-blonde hair and the cute nose near the sign, um, BEST BURNING FIREWOOD? He's got his arm around her. You can see his hand creeping round her waist."

"That's my best friend, Win. But she says she can't stand to touch Stefan because of his zits!"

"Well, she lies 'cos she's got her arm around him as well! I'd say she *was* your best friend. Past tense!"

I collapsed into my chair, brain squirming. Had Stefan and Win been hooking up in Kingston after her Pilates classes, and his Nature Shop negotiations? I now knew the significance of those text messages about Bill Einstein: *their 'sick' way of putting me off the scent.*

"When does our plane leave?" My body trembled from having been betrayed by the people closest to me.

Cluny stood, and pointed. "*That's* our flight, just in from Sydney."

The last of the tourists straggled across the tarmac and into the terminal. Hundreds of French soldiers began to pour down the steps of the Qantas 747, heads shaved and wearing berets. Lugging duffle bags, they were singing and grinning. They didn't look much older than Stefan.

"Is there an uprising?" I began to panic. Had Rocky's friends begun to implement the plans they talked about at Noah's? He hadn't said anything about it in his letter.

"Nah, it's just the normal military deployment. Didn't you notice the soldiers in Nouméa? There's a big army presence here."

"Only in Bourail," I said, wondering: *Had my birth father, as a soldier, arrived on an innocent-looking commercial flight like that one? Singing?*

The final boarding call for the flight to Brisbane was announced.

"We're next after that," said Cluny.

We sat in silence for a moment.

"Did you hear about Spud being arrested for possession?"

She nodded. "Sad, but predictable."

"Spud's a lowlife creep." I inhaled. "And *I* was forced to leave New Cal because there's a charge against me, sort of. I think."

"Get out of here!" Her eyes grew huge.

"They found grass in my chop-chop, or so Pascal said."

"But you don't?"

"Nup, I definitely don't."

"I have."

"Have you? What was it like?"

"Ah, it's overrated. Afterwards, going home, the traffic went by so *fast*!"

I had so much to think about; my mind seemed to be stuffed with planks.

"What about Flex?" I wagged a finger. "I mean what about *you* and Flex?"

"We flew to the Isle of Pines together yesterday, and checked out the convict ruins then, um, basically hung out. Flex's got a *great* body! Makes me get … you know!… just thinking about it." Cluny gave a long sigh. "But he's gone to Lifou to check out his rellies from way back, in the Island Province." She waved a manicured finger at me. "And now *you* have to find someone else."

"Like who?"

"I dunno. Who is there?"

"Arch Biddle who stacks shelves at The Store doesn't have a girlfriend."

"Can't you drum up someone a bit flasher than a shelf-stacker?"

"There's Rocky, of course, but he's a *bit* old, over twenty." I thought of those incredible sculpted lips, the serious grey eyes, his chicory face, that crazy red-gold hair beneath the beanie.

"The groovy kava grower, who took you to the nakamal? I thought he was dead."

"Nup. They discovered Rocky was alive all along, only injured. He fled to Australia. Now he's living in Far North Queensland, with his mother and sister."

"Hmm, bit too distant for a potential boyfriend." She indicated the bar. "Want a drink? Or a sandwich? Oh, that's right, you're a raw vegan. Perhaps fruit?"

"I'll get it."

"No, *I* will." Her fluffy hair was like a crazy halo.

We stood up together. The soldiers were gone. The Brisbane plane sat on the tarmac. Sandrine walked towards the steps, carrying a small overnight bag.

"That's my birth mother, Sandrine Bas Salaire de Lyon."

"She's good-looking, but I don't like her dress. Where's she going?"

"Home to Queensland, north of Cairns." I recalled my conversation with Sandrine. "There's a place for me to stay at the Amédée Apartments, if I ever wish to go there."

Cluny raised an eyebrow.

"Sandrine manages holiday apartments with her partner, Claude."

"That's nice." She took a breath. "I've got a great idea. Why don't you come and stay with me in Sydney?"

"Like now?"

Her eyes shone. "You wouldn't have to worry about Monsieur Manet popping in. And it'd give you time to think about where you're heading with Stefan." She leaned across. "You could change your ticket. It's easy."

"Nah, there's Namilly, my mum. You said never to forget the person who brought you up is your mum, and you're right. Also I have my French course at South Central Community College."

Another boarding announcement.

"Blast!" said Cluny. "Our flight to Sydney and Melbourne has been put back, due to problems with the Brissie plane."

If it was so easy to change my ticket, should I go north and be with Rocky? I wondered. Maybe take up Sandrine's offer to use the apartment? Even if she was as cold as an ice bucket, I could make her love me, if I really tried.

"Look, I'm off." I fumbled with my things. "I left my dress in the Deuche. I lashed out on a fabbo pareo with beads in a dusky-pink colour, which matches these shoes, and the ribbon in my hair, and the dress is, um, still there, and it took most of my money." I could feel my face flush.

"You better hurry."

"Yep." I hefted my backpack and laptop.

"I know where you're really going, Genna Perrier!" Cluny had a silly grin on her face.

"Where am I really going?"

"You're off to see the groovy kava farmer, off to catch that Queensland flight!"

I didn't know if there was a future with Rocky, or even with Sandrine, but I did know that, whatever happened, I would stand by Namilly. She was my tower of strength, and despite her funny ways, the one who truly cared.

"Wrong. My mum runs a recycle shop. She'd get a lot for a French creation." I headed for the stairs. "Anyway, I have to sort out my relationship with Stefan."

I needed that dress. I planned to wear it one more time. Stefan would see how great I looked, and know he'd blown it.

www.ingramcontent.com/pod-product-compliance
Lightning Source LLC
Chambersburg PA
CBHW060053150626
46556CB00017BA/118